AUDITION

AND OTHER STORIES

Roger Hecht

English Hill Press

Redmond, WA

This is a work of fiction. Any resemblance to actual events, places, or persons living or dead, is entirely coincidental. No "Detroit Philharmonic" exists at the time of publication; it and its hall are entirely constructs of the author's imagination. The story "Audition" appeared in an earlier, serial form in *Positive Feedback*, Vol. 6, '96–'97.

Acknowledgments:

I wish to thank Karen Martin for her proofreading, and Daniel Stofan, Douglas Yeo, Daniel Carno, and Karen for their insights into the audition process and orchestral anecdotes. Their comments were invaluable. So were the sagacious remarks of my trombone teachers Emory Remington, Edward Kleinhammer, and Douglas Yeo, as well as those of players I have known. Thanks also go to Laura Baumann and Eileen Snyder for their help with cover thoughts; Philip Haldeman for his ideas, confidence in me, and his work on my behalf, Ann Haldeman for her tireless and careful proofreading, and their son, David Haldeman for the cover photograph. Most of all, the "Former Mary Smith" aka Mary Hecht who has proofread these stories many times as well as put up with my own frustrations in taking auditions and everything else I do.

Published by English Hill Press
P.O. Box 8521
Kirkland, WA 98034

Cover design by Barbara Silbert; cover photo by David Haldeman; text design by David E. Schultz

First Edition
1 3 5 7 9 8 6 4 2

ISBN13 978-0-9846543-1-4

To the Former Mary Smith

CONTENTS

AUDITION AND OTHER STORIES

AUDITION

Orchestra Player, February 1, 2013

* * * * *

LESSON

About time there was an opening for bass trombone. I hadn't taken a serious audition since bombing in Kansas City last May. For a year-and-a-half, I've been hearing St. Louis was opening up, but nothing's happened. This Detroit job is a pleasant substitute: a solid orchestra with a year-long season. No more working part-time at an insurance agency after my teaching position was cut five months ago. No more freelancing,

11

which means no more hustling, calling contractors, and kissing up to players who might put my name around. No more being an occasional sub in the Boston Symphony, and no more worrying over whether they will get so fascinated with some new guy that they stop calling me. And no more living in a tiny two-bedroom apartment with a trumpet player in the same boat. All I have to do to bring this about is beat out a hundred-plus of the finest bass trombonists in the country.

The process begins with some lessons with veteran Boston Symphony bass trombonist Dave Sims. Each costs two weeks' worth of groceries. It's not that I need to be taught how to play the horn, but orchestra audition committees want to hear how candidates play orchestra parts. That's a different skill from playing etudes and concertos, just as delivering a passage in a one hundred-piece orchestra is different from practicing it alone. It requires insight into what conductors are looking for and what sounds best on stage. These are things you learn from someone who has been there, someone like Dave Sims.

Dave wasted no time at my first lesson. He was generous with his efforts, but I was paying for two hours of his time, and two hours was all I was going to get. Dave's intensity while teaching belied his appearance and manner. If you need an actor to play a stereotypical bass trombone player, you could do no better than Dave Sims. He was a tall beefy guy with very short hair, a ready smile, and a lovingly cultivated beer belly. His slow drawl, plain blue jeans, and flannel shirt made no secret of his rural Oklahoma origins. Not the kind of person you picture playing classical music, but he dispels any misgivings about his gifts the moment he sets the horn on his lips. That huge mellow tone, deft technique, and lyrical line could come only from a great musician.

After opening warm-ups, Dave pulled out the bass trombone part to the chorale from the finale of Brahms's First Symphony. "Remember," he said, "The low C has to be clean and vocal. No swooping. No hammering." I've been told that dozens of times, but Dave knows C's and B's below the bass staff are the bass trombonist's equivalent to operatic tenors' high C's: there is always the tendency to "sit" on them, as if to announce to the world, "Look at me. I made it." He demonstrated by singing the part with a voice almost as deep as the sound of his horn, taking care to smoothly drop the octave from bass clef C to the one below and back up, before caressing the final F.

"Good," he said after I played the passage a couple of times. "Be sure you hang onto the D as long as you can while still getting breath. And make up your mind how you're going to play your C's. Either stay in sixth position, or go valve C to double valve low C. Don't mix them up like you just did. You don't want confused messages from your brain when you're on stage."

"I know," I admitted. "I never can decide which way to go."

"Either one's okay. Just settle on the one you're most comfortable with and stick with it."

"Got it."

"Good. Now let's see." He checked over Detroit's list of required audition passages. "They're asking for the Bach 'Sarabande.' How about that next?"

This was the "Sarabande" from Bach's Fifth Cello Suite, the only non-orchestral work on the list and a favorite on bass trombone auditions because of its repeated dips into the very low register. The trick is not to allow the angular intervals to interfere with the line. You know it wants to go up and down, but it must move forward as well, one note proceeding smoothly to the next. The bass trombonist has the added concern of sounding the low notes firmly without undue emphasis, just as in the Brahms chorale, but it doesn't hurt to give a bit more fullness to low C's that are played on open strings on the cello. Any cellists on the committee might appreciate that insight.

When I finished, Dave suggested breathing before the last note of each of the final four measures, making it a pickup to the next bar. I never liked this idea, preferring to breathe as quickly as possible *after* the note in question. The piece seems measure to measure to me, and to break this pattern at the end feels awkward and inconsistent. Then again, Dave Sims has played this piece successfully in an audition, so his was the best guess as to what the Detroit committee would be looking for. I played the Bach again, his way.

"That's it. Great," he said, obviously pleased. He glanced at me as if to ask if I had any questions. None forthcoming, we returned to the orchestral literature, this time the "Ride of the Walkures" from Wag-

ner's *Die Walküre,* known in trombone circles simply as the "Ride."
With its garrumphing, *Dut da-dat Dah Dah* rocking-chair rhythm, the
"Ride" is one of the hardest excerpts to pull off. I've heard even good
trombone sections mess it up in concerts. The trick is to preserve the
three-to-one ratio in rhythm between the first two notes in the initial
triplet, while placing the third exactly in rhythm. Failure to do so results in a smoother *Dut da-da Dah Dah* pattern that is far less ominous
and powerful than what is written.

"Rhythm's good," was the comment after I played it through once,
"But it has to thrust forward and not plod so heavily. These are gallop-
ing horses those Walkures are riding, not stomping elephants. Remember. Wagner wrote it for four trombones. No one player has to supply
the weight alone. Keep the rhythm crisp and driving, and weight will
take care of itself."

I played it again.

"Better," he said, yet I sensed he wasn't completely satisfied. "I
read something interesting about this passage in Ernest Newman's
book on Wagner's operas. It's something I do instinctively in the orchestra because what's going on around me makes me do it, but the
point's not as obvious when you play by yourself. Normally, you emphasize the first beat of measures, but Newman points out that because the second and third beats of each measure of the Ride are
longer notes than those that make up the first, one is tempted to overemphasize them, especially the second one. *Dut-da-dat DAH Dah, Dut-
da-dat DAH Dah.* That's wrong. It should always be, *DUT-da-dat Dah
Dah, DUT-da-dat Dah Dah.* Like that. Okay? Try it."

I did so.

"Better. The accent is there, but now don't pile drive it. No
WHOMP-da-dat Dah Dah. Just emphasize its position and maybe make
the dotted eighth a tiny bit longer."

Again.

"Much better that time."

But not great. It was so frustrating trying to perfect these things. I
felt my nerves tightening.

"*Hary Janos,*" he called for next. Dave was not one to pound incessantly on any one excerpt in a lesson, which was fine with me. I knew

what I had to do, and I wasn't paying him for practice time.

Coming after the frustrating "Ride," the big bass trombone solo from the *Hary Janos Suite,* with its heavy tread of quarter notes in resonant octaves with the tuba, was a relief. I played it well until I let up on my concentration and plastered the climactic high B against the nice walls of Dave's newly finished basement. I cursed and shook my head in disgust. To do this in front of my teacher two months before an audition! A nice reminder that under pressure things can and do go wrong.

Dave chuckled. "What gets me," he drawled, his blue eyes twinkling in that avuncular way he has, "is you play all the important solo stuff, and everything comes apart on a note the two *tenor* trombones are playing with you and that is in their range, not yours." He went on in a lowered voice, as if passing on a scandalous secret that no one but I was to know: "One concert when I had to play this thing, I had a cold. I played the solo okay, but all the time, I knew that damned B was going to crack; not only that, but just trying for it was going to make my head clatter. I decided to leave it out and let Carl and Ray take care of it." He smiled with muted yet triumphant satisfaction. "No one even noticed. Not even Ray, who sits right next to me. And I never told anyone either. Until now."

I had to laugh. Dave knew just how to dissipate tension. "No one will ever hear it from me," I assured him.

"Appreciate that. Of course, it was twelve-thirteen years ago," he added winking broadly with a sly grin. "The statute of limitations has run out on that crime." The grin suddenly disappeared. "Trouble is, you can't do in an audition what you can in a concert when you're actually working. Not when there are twenty guys who can stand up there, play the solo *and* nail the dinger." His big body shifted uncomfortably. Dave didn't like talking negatively, even if it was for my own good. "Be careful to phrase these," he advised, pointing to the raucous solo glisses at the beginning of the passage. "Sometimes, not always, but sometimes they sound ripped without being placed in context."

I played the whole thing again, this time nailing the high B squarely.

"Great," he said, grinning. "Let's try Berlioz."

In the parlance of trombone auditions, "Berlioz" means the "Hungarian March" from the composer's *Damnation of Faust*. It's one of the most challenging excerpts because it combines so many difficulties of trombone playing in one passage—phrases that start on downbeats but sound like pickups, tricky rhythms, the need for precise intonation in the scales, and a note that is both the end of one phrase and the pickup to another (your choice). Not to mention that there is no musically sensible place to breathe. All this stuff you have to keep in mind at once. If any of it slips, the excerpt goes south—and so does your audition. Imagine the circus performer spinning eight plates on top of poles, and you have the idea. What is so frustrating is that it is *much* easier to play with an entire section in performance. The orchestra keeps the rhythm, and you can spread the breathing issues around the section. The "Hungarian March" wasn't meant to be played alone, but for auditions, alone is how we play it.

"Remember," Dave said by way of introduction. "At every audition I've seen or sat on, whenever they call for this piece, there's one guy on the committee quietly tapping out the eighth notes. Get out of rhythm from him, and out you go. Just like the 'Ride.'"

I nodded and played the march straight through.

"Pretty good," he commented. "Breathing is good, right after the dotted notes. Your rhythms are right on. Just be sure you don't lose the *sense* of syncopation as well as the *fact,* that kind of tumbling down the ladder effect in those scales. Try it again."

I did so, searching for that rhythmic thrust that is not printed on the page but that can make this piece electrifying in performance.

"Better," Dave observed after I finished.

It *was* better. I could tell by the way my body nearly rose from my seat as I was playing.

Next came Strauss's *Ein Heldenleben*. Usually, they ask for the battle music, which has to be at once loud, heavy, yet forward moving. I used to have a lot of trouble with this excerpt because, as with the "Ride," I played it as if I were carrying the entire trombone section by myself. The problem with putting out so much volume is that it requires too many breaths to sustain the line. This is not an issue in the orchestra, where you can sneak breaths when the other trombones are playing, but it is when you're playing alone in an audition. Committee members want to hear a piece of music played like a piece of music. You have breathing problems? Hey. Everybody has problems. There are wind and string players on the committee who have problems playing pages of music that are black with notes. They're not going to have sympathy for trombone players, whose parts are a tenth as difficult as their own. Besides, there is always someone, probably several someones, who can give them exactly what they want while ordering Chinese takeout. I needed to be one of those someones, and for a long time I was not.

Until the Bavarian bass trombonist.

I never actually met this gentleman. Rather, I heard him at a concert by the Bavarian Radio Orchestra a few years ago. He was one of those exhibitionists who likes to "give away" his part by playing it on stage while his colleagues are warming up before the concert. Of course, he ran through the entire battle music. He wasn't practicing—one player can tell whether another is practicing or showing off—but he taught me something by playing the entire line lyrically and smoothly, as though it were an independent piece of music. Nothing was forced—not a hint of bombast—yet the sound was huge. He made it seem so easy, and in doing so, lifted the veils from my ears. After the concert, I raced home and played the entire part just the way the Bavarian did, allowing the natural volume of the bass trombone to carry the line. *Ein Heldenleben* has not bothered me since.

Dave was pleased with my effort, though he found some rhythmic details to stew over. "Dotted eighths and sixteenths, always. No triplets," he said urgently, pointing to the page in question. As for the quarter-note triplets that *were* written later on, "Even. Always even. Each one the same length. Broad. No out of place accents. And be careful you don't cut that C-flat off too abruptly. Remember. It's the first note of this arpeggio." He directed my attention to the tenor tuba line that picks up where my C-flat leaves off. "That C-flat is the middle of a phrase, not the end. Even when playing alone, you have to suggest there is more of this line coming." He picked up his horn and demonstrated, and sure enough, the subtle way he tailed off on the C-flat did suggest there was more to come.

William Tell. "You're practicing this slowly every day with the metronome, listening to every note?"

I nodded.

"It's important that you do so," he advised. "This excerpt slips away if you don't stay on top of it."

I played it. He grinned. I conquered.

On to the Bruckner Seventh Symphony, a piece where the trombones never seem to play all that loud until the finale yet is exhausting anyway. "Keep those double dots consistent," Dave warned, pointing to the jagged rhythms in the Finale. "And don't be shy on that low E-flat. That's one you can sit on. Almost like the E-flat in Shostakovich Eight," the one that seemed to roar like a beast from the bowels of the earth.

Then *Lohengrin*, with its treacherous opening triplets that you dare not triple tongue lest they be rushed, and those grace note-like sixteenths that in no way can be late.

Till Eulenspiegel—William Tell in triplets, with a high A to boot.

And so on.

"Good. Real good. Great, in fact," Dave complimented after we were done. "Just the usual things to keep on top of. I'll hear more next time. Are you playing a lot of tenor gigs?"

There is a lot of debate in the trombone world over whether one should double on tenor and bass trombone. The instruments are similar, but the bass's larger bore and bell require more air, and its bigger mouthpiece calls for a different kind of lip-set (or embouchure). Dave is against this kind of doubling. The effort to serve two masters detracts from devotion to either one, he says. Tenor. Bass. Pick one and specialize in it. Still, Dave is a realist who understands that not all his students can afford to be purists. With only so much bass work around, and with tenor players taking gigs on bass, I had to accept work where I could get it. I'd have grabbed a job on trumpet if I thought I could have pulled it off.

"Go easy on that a few weeks before the audition," he cautioned in reply to my reluctant nod to his question. "You don't want to be tightening up."

I nodded and started packing up. It was a good lesson.

PRACTICE

Two months to prepare. Two months of practicing excerpts over and over and over and over at all kinds of speeds, all kinds of volume. Tearing them down measure by measure, note by note, and putting them back together, only to take them apart again because I missed something, and then repeating the process of building them back up. Preparing to be ready for anything. *Can you play that faster? Louder? Softer? Still softer? Less on this note? More on that one? Longer here? Shorter there?*

String players accomplish this task by moving a bow and fingers. With one exception, wind and brass players do it by controlling air flow and especially by moving fingers. Trombonists follow suit as far as air is concerned, but instead of fingers, we constantly shift a cumbersome slide over a length of about twenty-nine inches, a method far less efficacious than moving fingers. The result is an instrument that, to put it crudely, can play fewer notes per second than can any other instrument in the orchestra.* In that sense, technically speaking, the trombone is the most difficult instrument to play.

Fortunately, composers have taken mercy on us by writing parts with fewer notes and less complexity than those for other instruments. After spending twenty years playing trombone parts, a mere glance at all those black spots on a string, woodwind, or trumpet part makes me blanch. I remember a trumpet audition where the winner won the job because he was the only one who could competently play through all the excerpts on the list. We give the devil his due, though, because every note we do play is that much more easily heard, defined, and criticized, and the loudness of our instrument turns up the microscope that much more. The result is a bunch of people with musical Obsessive Compulsive Disorder. Trombonists obsess over a high B, the spacing of a triplet, or the evenness of a four-note run. This tends to limit our musical perspectives, especially if we haven't played a given work. For

---

*Technology has helped trombonists by creating auxiliary valves (one for tenor trombones, two for most basses) that help negotiate some difficult passages. Valve trombones are valve instruments like trumpets, but play an octave lower. Technology has yet to create a good sounding valve trombone.

a trombonist, "Brahms First Symphony" means a trombone chorale in the finale. The Mozart *Requiem* is one of the most sublime pieces ever written, but the trombone solo in the "Tuba Mirum" is all that many trombonists know of it—until they play the *Requiem* on a gig. The greatest living exemplar of this phenomenon is Ronald Fraser, former principal trombone in San Francisco, whose claim to fame was his ability to "drop the needle" at the beginning of a trombone part in the middle of an LP (that's a vinyl record for modern day readers). When I was a sophomore at New England Conservatory, I made my own contribution to the lore. I was going on in the student lounge about "Mahler Three," otherwise known as the three tenor trombone solos in the first movement of Mahler's Third Symphony. Someone mentioned the solo for alto in the fourth movement. "What alto solo?" I asked. "There's no alto trombone solo in 'Mahler Three.'" (But there is one for an alto singer in the fourth movement.) Then there's my discourse on the difficulties and techniques in executing the two-note bass trombone glissando in Bartok's Concerto for Orchestra. I once knocked an alcoholic trumpet player off the wagon for a week with that one.

Personally, I think that trumpet player just wanted those five beers, but if anything could turn me into an alcoholic, it would be the "Hungarian March" from Berlioz's *Damnation of Faust.* It's not just that we're obsessive. Playing some of these things on the trombone is hard even for the best of us, and the Berlioz is Exhibit A. First, it's that peculiar syncopation and those cascading scales. I repeat them over and over so often that I sometimes go to sleep with them dancing in my head. Then there is that turn in the first scale. It goes from fourth position D to fifth position C-sharp, back to D, then to second position E. For some reason that I cannot explain—just these notes in this rhythm in this particular sequence, I guess—the sudden jump of two positions throws my timing off. If I'm not careful, I don't get all the way up to the E. Do it wrong a few times, and I get used to hearing it wrong. I have to concentrate on my wrist and listen like the devil to keep this from happening.

Then there's *William Tell,* written at 108 beats per minute. Practice it at 76 so I can concentrate on hitting each note of its odd-accidental scales squarely and in tune. Play one measure at a time, sometimes three notes at a time, working for precision. Then gradually speed it up, always striving to retain steadiness of pitch and rhythm, to 108, 112, 116, faster than I'd ever play it in a concert. It is an exhausting process, on some days requiring a half-hour to complete to my satisfaction. Then I'd play into my recorder. On playback, I'd listen for each note, groaning at the occasional fluff or off-pitch note I hadn't noticed before, knowing that audition committees, eager to pare down candidates, hear such flaws better than recorders do, and no mistake is too minor or too occasional for them to jump on. Start over. How can anybody expect such inhuman precision from a slide instrument? Don't these people know Rossini had the valve trombone in mind when he wrote these crazy scales? What do string players do to work out all the notes they play? We trombonists have a few of these passages in our repertoire. They have hundreds. Then again, they don't have to maneuver a clumsy slide all over the place.

Finally, it's perfect.

Change of pace. Schumann's *Rhenish Symphony*. Very *legato*, yet resonant and soft. An excerpt I love to play because it is so beautiful, even out of context.

La Gazza Ladra. Back to Rossini's odd-accidental runs. These lie better for the instrument than those of *William Tell*. Still . . . Concentrate! One uncertain pitch, and you're out. Listen to the recording. Beat the time exactly. Every single note in place.

Scheherazade. Watch it. I'm late getting off those ties in the big theme at the end. How long has that been going on? And watch those triplets. They're starting to get uneven again. What the hell's happening to me? Sometimes I think that for all my practicing, I'm getting worse. . . .

And so it goes. Franck D Minor Symphony; Schubert Ninth. And fifteen more. Some days, time and chops don't allow me to get through all the excerpts. No matter. The "woodshedding" starts to pay off. One excerpt after the other starts sounding good, even to my recorder. As each rounds into shape, I slack off on it to concentrate on the others. Working this way, finally, with a week to go, things are sounding pretty damn good.

LOUNGE

"Going to Detroit?" Glenn Savage, a tenor player, with whom I gigged sometimes, asks. He was a tall, slim man, solidly built with curly blond hair and glowing blue eyes. Very handsome was Glenn Savage, and a mocking curve to his mouth made it clear he knew exactly how handsome. Glenn was a pretty good trombonist, lacking only the ability to bear down until everything was perfect. Not for him was Beverly Sills's observation that the well-prepared musician is never too nervous before performing because he or she knows what the outcome will be. Glenn belongs to the "you never know school," where one nods hopefully before an audition, even though he had not once run all the required excerpts perfectly in the practice room. "Hey, man, you never know." *Maybe those notes I've been missing all week will miraculously come out under the worst kind of pressure and scrutiny.* That they and several others usually do not, merely leads him to seek the comfort and assurance of *Better luck next time* and its little brother, *It only takes one.*

There are a lot of musicians like Glenn Savage. Insurance agencies and real estate offices are full of them.

It had been a few months since I'd seen Glenn, but I was practicing at the Boston University music school that night, so it was no surprise to run into one of the guys. When I answered his question about Detroit, he replied, "I figured. George Finney's going."

"I suppose Sam Roy and Carter Simpson are, too."

"Probably. I heard Sam is, anyway."

"Well, at least I'll have company."

I said this as if I meant it. Collegiality is required by the auditioner's code, but I wasn't all that friendly with those guys, and frankly, I wished they'd stay home. When it comes to auditions, the fewer the merrier.

"Sam had to send a recording," Glenn was saying. He was talking about a pre-audition recording. Once, orchestras listened to almost anyone who wanted to audition. Some still do, but with the increasing number of applicants, many of the larger ones require pre-audition recordings from players without some designated experience or a strong recommendation. Those things are a pain to make, though modern re-

corders make the task a lot easier than in the old days of tape recorders. It was best to hire a professional back then, and some people think
it's a good idea now. And even then, most recordings aren't accepted.
Sam Roy was lucky. Of course, he was good, too. "I assume you didn't
need a recording," Glenn asked.

"No, I didn't. So how are you doing?" I asked, changing the subject. "I heard you went to Indianapolis a couple of weeks ago."

"Not well. *Bolero* went south, but that's no shocker. But Mahler
Three? Can you believe I smashed two notes from the opening triplets
to dust?"

"Gee, that's too bad. Any idea who got the job?"

"Yeah. Ray Washington."

"The guy from Iowa?"

"The same."

"Hmm. I'm surprised. I didn't think he was that good."

"He isn't. But you forget how good an auditioner he is."

So I had. Ray Washington was one of those musicians who plays
auditions better than gigs. Every once in a while an unwary orchestra
hires someone like Ray, usually to its regret, not to mention that of
more deserving players who didn't get the job. A lucky orchestra dis-
covers its mistake before the newcomer's probation period lapses—
often one year. After that, it is difficult to fire players. The others are
stuck with that mistake. Rarely does such a player move on, and the
union usually sees that he or she is never fired, at least not without a
fight. "You think he can hang onto the gig?" I wondered.

"Who knows? He's not *that* bad. And it's Second. Lead would be
something else, but he might do okay on Second. He plays in tune, and
that's the name of the game on Second."

I never subscribed to the idea that Second Trombone was a haven
for weak players, particularly after a conversation I had with Ray
Weathers, the BSO Second Trombone for thirty years. I was subbing
with the orchestra for a week, and during a spare moment asked Ray
why he had never auditioned for a First Trombone job. He replied that
he would find no better orchestra than the Boston Symphony, and besides, he loved playing Second. I was trying to think of a diplomatic
way of asking if that was because there was less pressure in playing Sec-

ond when he continued: "Second is no walk on the Charles. It doesn't have all the solos and high notes, but it has its challenges." The most obvious were the need to support the sound of the First and to balance the intonation between the First and Bass, but he didn't even mention those. Instead, he said something that stuck with me. "The real sound of a section starts with the guy in the middle. You show me a good trombone section, and I'll show you a good, maybe a great First and Bass. But you don't get a *great* section without a great Second Trombone." It's true. Every great section I know has a great Second, but not all of them have truly great players on First or Bass. And though he didn't add this, Ray Weathers is a great Second Trombone.

Of course, such subtleties would be lost on Glenn Savage, and I was in no mood to argue the point. "You ever hear from Rich Wise?" I asked instead.

"Rich? He moved out to Arizona for a teaching job. He'd blown three in a row, and his wife was getting sick of the whole business. They have a kid, and she wants another. And you remember what Rich always said."

"Yeah. If you haven't made it when you're thirty, forget it.'"

"Good advice, too."

"Yeah? Then how come we don't take it?"

"We're not thirty."

"No. We're thirty-two." I said, laughing, not entirely from mirth. I reached into my pocket for change. "Want a Coke?" I asked, on my way to the machines.

"Why not? If my playing doesn't rot the damn horn out, maybe the Coke will. Then I'll be at peace."

"Crave to slay your master, do you?" I teased as I fed the coins.

He nodded and stared threateningly at his horn lying trustingly next to him. I handed him his Coke and took a seat across the room.

"We are slaves to metal," I mused as I sipped my drink. "I remember visiting a plant where they make trombones. Do you know what a trombone looks like before it becomes a trombone?"

"A thumbscrew?"

Glenn caught me in mid-swallow, and I choked some of it up. "Right," I finally managed to utter. "And thanks. My shirt needed that." I rubbed it dry as best as I could. "No. It's sheet metal. Nothing but plain old sheet metal. You've got to be really stupid to allow a piece of sheet metal to rule your life."

"But we do love it so," Glenn reflected, staring at the ceiling. "And love makes us slaves."

It was so. Since it was also too philosophical for a guy preparing a piece of sheet metal for an audition, I changed the subject. "Speaking of stupid, I hear Bud Weaver's going back to school." Bud was the kind of guy who always found a way to blurt exactly the wrong thing at precisely the wrong time to absolutely the wrong person in the dopiest, loudest way possible. A trombonist needn't be brilliant enough to produce a dissertation on the use of the trombone in Italian opera—he just has to play the trombone in Italian opera—but it's not as if orchestras want Goofy in their trombone sections, either.

"Yeah. He's going for his doctorate. Can you believe that? In Performance."

"Performance? What's a doctorate in Performance going to do for him?"

"Well, for one thing, it allows a dope like Bud Weaver to be called Doctor," Glenn declared, his blue eyes twinkling.

What could I do but laugh? The future Doctor Weaver will have trouble reading his diploma, and I'm talking about the English words.

"I went to the BSO Bruckner Eighth last night," Glenn was saying. "Carl sounded great, of course" he continued, referring to Carl Goldberg, the principal trombone and Glenn's teacher. "Say, did you know? I was over at Carl's house the other day."

I sighed. Glenn was always name dropping and bragging how "in" he was with the trombone players in the orchestra. All except Dave, whose playing he claimed he didn't like and, it just so happens, with whom he had two undistinguished lessons. Glenn was that way with women, too. A few years ago, we were playing in a small summer orchestra. Near the end of the season, we heard of a principal and bass trombone opening in the North Carolina Symphony and drove down to audition. (Those were the days before we had money to fly.) Along the way, Glenn kept me awake with tales of his conquests of every female member of our summer orchestra, save the woman I was going with and her best friend. Obviously, Glenn was smart enough to obey the rule that if you're going to tell lies about people, don't include anyone with whom your listener can check. Now I got to hear about how the Goldberg kids were growing up, that Carl and the Mrs. were rebuilding the back room, and how willing slave Glenn lugged drywall, nailed it up, and sucked in its dust. He made the project sound like the building of the Pyramids. "Carl's getting into golf, too, these days," he concluded. "I may play with him sometime."

"Glenn, you don't play golf," I reminded him.

"Not yet, I don't." His blue eyes turned suddenly serious. "Hey, he's a good guy to know." He downed a slug of Coke. "You still studying with Sims?" he asked, burping his disdain for Dave. "He coaching you for the audition?"

Here we go again. "Uh huh and uh huh."

"Well, I'd say *he* could use a little coaching. Every damned trombone chord of the Bruckner was bass light. The finale sounded like two men and a boy. Can't he put out some sound once in a while and not be so damned *tasteful?*"

This was old territory. "Sure. Then after the artillery moves up, maybe they could move a division in along the left flank and storm the ramparts, or whatever the hell it is divisions do."

"Do it right, and they wouldn't need a division," Glenn shot back. "But enough frivolity. When did you break up with Jane Morgenstern?"

I jumped. "Who said anything about me breaking up with Jane?"

"You did."

"*I* did? Exactly when did I say that?"

"You didn't. You demonstrated. About ten days ago when I saw you with Rita Olson."

"Oh." I grimaced.

"Does Jane know?" he sounded almost concerned.

"No."

He smiled. "Well, she won't hear it from me." Gossip though he would about his own liaisons, Glenn never reported those of others—probably because they would detract from his own, but I was grateful for his promise and thanked him.

"Well?" he said.

"Well what?"

"Rita? How was she?"

"How do you know she was anything?"

"I know Rita. She's always something."

"Well, maybe this time she wasn't."

"Come on."

I hesitated, but Glenn knew when there was a story lurking about, and I needed someone to talk to. He was hardly my confidante of choice, but there was that one good quality about him, so . . . "Jane and I had a big fight that night," I began after checking to see no one else was within earshot. "She was irritated that I was always working or practicing. Accused me of being more interested in the horn than her." I paused nervously. This was not the kind of thing I should be discussing with anyone.

"Well, aren't you?" Glenn winked knowingly. "Isn't that the problem we all have with women? They have horns, but *they're* not horns." For all his irreverence toward hard work in his chosen field, Glenn did not like dating non-musicians. I feel the opposite. Non-musicians remind me there are other things in life than excerpts. Still, there are difficulties, and this business of spending a lot of nights alone practicing is one of them.

"You know, sometimes she really exasperates me," I said bitterly. "I bust it to get a gig—this is my career, you know. You'd think she'd understand that, instead of giving me all this stuff about finding a 'real' job . . . A real job." I repeated the words in disgust. "A real job doing what? Teaching school? The public schools are no place for a musician. 'Those who can't do, teach,' right? Teaching scales to sixth grade kids is like admitting I failed. You know something? I was glad when they cut that job. Who am I to be teaching something I haven't really done myself?"

"Hey, you don't have to tell that to me," Glenn said assuringly. "But have you tried to explain this to Jane?" he added with surprising empathy.

"As a matter of fact, I did. The next night I went to the Black Marble, picked up Rita, and went to her place. So you see how that went."

A sly grin crept across Glenn's face. "Except I still don't know about Rita. How was she?" The real Glenn was back.

I glared at him. "Jesus, Glenn, you're nothing but sensitive."

"Hey. I'm just doing research. You know what they say about trombone players."

"Yeah. There's a whole joke page on the Internet." We both laughed, me against my better judgment. "It was a one-night thing," I admitted. "I could never do it again. That's all."

"You're sure? About never doing it again, I mean."

"Yeah. Besides, Rita feels the same way about me. She's not one of those lost women sleeping with different men because she has no soul. Rita does it because she's having a blast."

"Really? I've been putting off giving her a call for too long."

I shrugged. I had a feeling Rita was more selective about men than Glenn wanted to know. "Anyway," I continued, "Jane and I made up. She said she knew I had a big audition coming, and this was no time to get on my case. Then I felt even more terrible."

"Now all you have to hope is Rita is no blabbermouth."

"She isn't. I got off easy this time."

"Unless someone saw you."

I winced. "Gee, you're comforting."

Glenn held up his hands. "I'm just stating the obvious. It's not like you can afford to ignore the possibility."

"No, I suppose I can't," I conceded, my voice trailing off. "Not that I could do anything about it anyway."

"Say, didn't I hear Paul Stauffer went on the road with *West Side Story?*" Glenn piped in quickly.

"Yeah, I think he did," I replied just as readily. "And so did Maury Chovis. . . ."

And so it went until it was time to get back to the practice room. "How about listening to my stuff for a few minutes?" I asked.

Glenn looked at his watch. "Sure. Why not?"

Glenn would never be much of a coach, but an audience of one, even when that one is Glenn Savage, would make me bear down more than I would in an empty practice room. It might also give me some valuable feedback.

I played everything straight through. Glenn didn't say much other than, "Bigger, man, louder. Nail that sucker."

"Sounds great, man," he said after I squared off the last note of *Lohengrin*. "Just keep it huge. Wake 'em up."

Maybe not such valuable feedback. Now you know why they call him "Primitive Glenn."

Still, I thought I sounded pretty damn good.

JANE

"I thought I wasn't going to see you before you left," Jane said, through a crack in the opened door.

On my way home, I had stopped at Jane's. In doing so, I tripped over something else we don't have in common—our sleeping hours. Jane was wearing her blue bathrobe.

I smiled. "It's in one week, Jane."

"That's about how often I see you these days," she countered curtly. Apparently, things weren't as smoothed out as I had thought.

"I know," I said, though she was exaggerating. "I'm sorry."

Jane Morgenstern was four years younger than I. Nevertheless, she was one semester from graduating with a Ph.D. in physics along with two years of college teaching under her belt. She was poised to be more successful next year than I was for my whole life. This was grating on her, not because she'd out-earn me, but because she craved stability and had gone with a trombone player long enough to know the life of a musician is the antithesis of stability.

My dating Jane started out as strictly a physical thing. Not much over five-feet two and small-boned, she was attractive in a way that was at once cute and smoldering. Her nose and mouth were distinct and well defined, set off as they were by a dark complexion and brown, doe-like eyes that spoke even when she was silent. Her pert, well-shaped figure and thick black hair that flowed naturally to her trim shoulders, combined with a demeanor that was at once mysterious and sophisticated to lend her an exotic allure I found irresistible. I was stunned when she agreed to go out with me the first time, and positively floored when we went to bed together that same night.

Afterwards, I assumed she would come to her senses, regret the entire evening, and refuse to see me again, but I was too enthralled not to call her the next night. She agreed to go out with me again. She even seemed eager. By the end of that second evening—morning, actually— it was clear there was a powerful physical attraction between us. Of course, we differed in more ways than we were similar—she not being a musician was just one of the reasons my friends had started a count- down on our relationship—but so far, we had lasted six months. Jane had many qualities I never realized I valued so highly, particularly her intellectual curiosity and worldliness. Both contrasted sharply with my own narrow focus. (What attraction I held for her, I have no idea.)

Now that very focus threatened to break us apart. I could see in Jane's big sad eyes that she was growing weary waiting for me to find some *achievable* goal. She was very open about her belief that I was in- dulging myself with a quixotic quest for a decent-paying orchestra job, and she was not overly impressed when I made the semifinals in two of my last four auditions. All that meant was I had done my best and fin- ished behind five to ten other players. "When Vince Lombardi said, "'Winning isn't everything. It's the only thing,' he could have been talk- ing about auditions, couldn't he?" Jane was no sports fan, so I have no idea where she came up with that gem, but I do remember thinking it was a fine time for her only reference to sports during our entire rela- tionship.

"So how's it going?" she asked as I continued to stand in the doorway of her apartment. The words were friendly, but her tone was flat. Jane never wore makeup, so her unpainted appearance suffered not at all from her accustomed look. Even in her floppy blue bathrobe, her darkly natural good looks shone provocatively. She had unlocked the door, but it did not escape my notice that she had not asked me in.

"Pretty well," I answered. "I'm sounding good, if that's what you're asking."

"It is."

"Then . . . pretty well." I hesitated. "Aren't you going to invite me in?"

"Well, I have to . . . Of course." She stepped aside and let me pass.

It was only when I was in the light of her living room that I could see how drawn she looked. Could she have heard about Rita, after all? "I'm sorry," I told her, not exactly sure about what.

"It's all right," she said. I noticed she hadn't taken a seat. She flashed a sad little smile that made me want to reach for her. "I'm just tired," she admitted. "And I have to get up to teach a class tomorrow."

I could see that she was. Tired, that is. This wasn't about Rita, anyway, I was fairly sure of that, but there was something bothering her.

I nodded. "If I can just have a glass of milk, I'll be on my way. I'll see you tomorrow."

She shook her head wearily. I was enthralled by the way her black hair swept over the shoulders of her light blue robe. She smiled as if embarrassed. "Of course, you can have some milk," she said. "But you can't see me tomorrow. I just learned they're sending me to a conference for a week in Atlanta. I leave tomorrow morning right after my class. And you have to go to work."

She was correct about that. Another day punching a computer in the insurance office. "A conference?" I returned, surprised. "But you're only an instructor."

"Yes. It's supposed to be an honor," she called from the kitchen.

I suddenly felt clumsy. Instead of congratulating her, I was almost accusing her. "I'm sorry, Jane. Of course. It is."

She returned with my milk. "It's all right."

I shook my head and drank the milk quickly. "Geez, what a track we're on. You're being honored. I'm still trying to get hired."

She shrugged as if to intimate it was my decision to be in such a spot. Then she took a seat beside me and very slowly began rubbing her fingers over the back of my hand. Her touch and her nearness sent my senses reeling. I really wished I didn't have to leave. "What is it they say before these things?" she asked. "Break a leg?"

"Right." I chuckled.

"Nice sentiment. Okay. Break a leg."

"I think it has to do with performers dipping their leg when bowing before a clapping audience. The idea is, if you're 'breaking your leg,' they're clapping, and you must have done well."

For a moment neither of us spoke. The tension was still there, but it softened palpably as she placed her head softly on my shoulder. I put my arm around her in response, as always entranced by the slight feel of her shoulders—so childlike, yet resolute. When she gazed up at me,

I wanted to sink into her deep brown eyes. Her dusky soft voice was so soothing, so hypnotic, I could have drifted off to sleep as she talked. Of course, I could not. Whatever was bothering Jane when I arrived was still bothering her. Otherwise, morning class or not, insurance office or not, it might not have been time to leave. Though I sensed she wished it were otherwise, it was time for me to go. Besides, it wasn't fair to keep her up. When I returned . . . then we would talk.

She followed me to the door, then lifted her lips to mine. Even so, at nearly six feet, I had to bend over to reach them. She had somewhat generous lips for one so small, and the kiss that followed was as sweet as I could imagine a woman could deliver, all the more surprising because it was not particularly passionate even as it was loving and affectionate. It was also, if such things could be felt through kisses, kind of yearning and sad. Perhaps dangerously so. I wasn't sure.

"I'll call you when I get to Atlanta," she whispered and sniffed softly. "I'll miss you."

"I'll miss you, too."

"Break a leg," she said quietly, almost plaintively. There was a confused look to her expression that I couldn't translate other than as sadness. I left her, wondering what that look meant and not daring to ask.

I was tired as I drove home. Jane's news about going to a conference hit me hard. Though she knew little about what I was about to undertake, I didn't relish being without her companionship that week. I needed someone who cared about me, and whom I cared about, to talk to before having to rise to another challenge. Damn it. I wanted Jane around. I had *planned* on having her around.

And then it hit me with a rush. I *was* tired. Tired of working part-time in an insurance office for short money because I needed all those hours for practice. Tired of having to use what money I had for lessons and auditions. I was tired of flying all over the country to compete with a hundred other talented players for what was, after all, nothing but a full-time job that paid a living wage. Tired of chasing contractors for two-bit gigs. As much as I liked Dave Sims, I was tired of being extra nice to him and the rest of the section just to get an occasional sub gig tossed my way. Tired of being nice to everybody because I never knew who might get me a gig and tired of going to parties with boring musicians to remain in the circuit. I was tired of looking over my shoulder wondering who the new hotshot bass trombonists at the conservatory were. Tired of feeling lousy when I didn't get a gig I wanted and tired of hating whoever did. I was tired of not enjoying orchestra concerts because I wanted to be up there playing, and just as tired of compulsively comparing myself against whoever *was* up there.

And Jane. I was tired of gazing into her worried eyes, knowing she was wondering what was wrong with me. Tired of having to explain why, at an age when others are finding themselves in life, I'm searching harder than ever. Tired of wondering how long she'd put up with all this before giving up on me, and tired of wondering whether it was already too late.

And now something new. Jane was going to a conference. I knew what people did at conferences. I had never worried about Jane that way. Now I'd been doing it for a whole five minutes, and I was tired of that, too.

I was tired of everything.

WARM-UP

Given how low on funds auditioners usually are, we spend a lot of our money on plane flights and hotel rooms. We fly because we don't want to drive for many hours before playing an audition—unless we plan to arrive two or three days ahead of time, though most of us can't afford to leave our jobs for that long—and we stay overnight in a hotel to get a good night's sleep before the audition. Knowing there are reasons doesn't make it any easier to come up with the money. This little excursion to Detroit was going to set me back nicely.

That night I called Jane in Atlanta. Her conference over, she was to leave for Boston the next morning, and she sounded tired. There was that something else in her voice, too, but once more, I dared not dwell on it. I had a terrible fear that something may have happened at that conference, something that had been coming for a long time. Maybe she wasn't alone in that hotel room. Maybe someone from home called her and told her about seeing Rita and me together. Whatever the case, twelve hours before I was to play an eight-minute performance that could change my life was not the time to find out what was bothering her. I sensed she felt that way, too. By common consent, it seemed, we limited our conversation to how things went at her conference, my flight, and similar banalities. Finally, it was time to go.

"I miss you," I told her.

"Me too."

"I don't really like staying over in strange towns."

"You do a lot of it."

"Not because I want to."

Silence. "I know. I'm sorry."

"See you soon?"

Hesitation. "Yes." Silence. Then, "Good luck, Greg. I mean, break a leg."

"Thanks."

We hung up. I felt worse than I did before I called. I wanted to ring her back and get all this out in the open but fought the impulse. Now wasn't the time to find out I was about to lose her. Better not to be sure. I felt angry. How dare she be so diffident, knowing I was staying in a hotel in a strange town, only hours before I had to play? Would she always undermine me so?

I dared not think about her anymore.

The next morning, after getting out of my cab in front of the downtown auditorium where the Detroit Philharmonic played their concerts, I stood for a moment across the street and stared, imagining what it would be like to call this building my workplace. The structure was new and typical of the arts centers cities are erecting these days, its lines sharp and lean with a lot of glass and gray. I imagined the hall inside sounded the same way: clean and a bit sterile.

I didn't pause too long. Daydreaming is not something you want to do before an audition. Auditions require concentration, concentration calls for discipline, and daydreaming is anathema to both.

As soon as I stepped inside, I could tell I was walking into a professional operation. The lobby was emblazoned with red carpet, and white pillars with gold trim; the few items of well-chosen furniture were made of dark wood and brilliantly polished. The chandelier cast a burnished aura overhead. You could almost wallow in the elegance. The area was quiet now, but I could imagine it bustling on concert nights. Upon two marquees were notices of upcoming concerts. The one for the coming weekend included Janacek's *Overture to Véc Makropulos,* the Elgar Cello Concerto, and Holst's *Planets.* What an odd array of music! Pretty nice blow-out for trombones, too. No other program was as adventurous, but the Detroit Philharmonic was performing some pieces I'd love to play: Nielsen's Fourth Symphony, Shostakovich Ten, *Hary Janos.*

Yes. This was definitely something I wanted to do. I could feel the craving, the very need, deep in my stomach.

But enough of that. Time to suck it up. Concentrate. I had turned myself off during the flight and the cab ride, suspending thought, emotion, and energy for one supreme effort. Now it was time to release that energy. There would be no more daydreaming.

It was then that I noticed the crudely lettered signs, so out of place amid the surrounding splendor, that indicated the route to registration. I followed them to a table at the end of a hall, where two efficient-looking young women waited to sign me in. Three other players were registering, none of whom I recognized. When we finished, one of the women stepped out to accompany us downstairs. In a way, I wished she hadn't. For all the glamour of the setting, I was still a poor man looking for work, and I felt uncomfortable in the company of orchestra personnel who appeared as gracious and as much a part of the surroundings as this woman did. In such circumstances, I end up making inane conversation or remaining dumb as a stone. Today, I wanted quiet, and so, apparently, did my companions. None of them was wearing an expensive suit, either. Men looking for work. That's what we were. Clearly well trained in dealing with tense auditioners, our escort respected our wishes and refrained from small talk.

When we reached the practice area, she quietly directed each of us to our warm-up rooms. "You're in Room 16," she said to me.

And then I heard it: the all too familiar cacophony of a horde of bass trombones resounding through the halls like rowdy knights issuing challenges to Valhalla. That onslaught of sound is a moment of truth for many auditioners. Before arriving at the site, candidates work and practice alone or with a teacher, competing only with their own standards, the teacher's appraisal, and the unforgiving re-utterance of a recorder. We are aware of the competition, but only as an abstraction, not real people. Now, all of a sudden, there are bass trombones and bass trombonists everywhere, and myriad thoughts rush at you amid the wild juxtaposition of excerpts. How could so many people take up this instrument? Where did they all come from? What am I doing in such an insane line of work as this? All those excerpts I've been killing myself to master, analyze, understand, integrate into the fabric of the music—just me and the horn, one excerpt at a time—now they're all around me, blaring two at a time, three at a time, ten at a time, never together, all different styles. Some of them sound damn good, too. I always knew there were good players out there, but to *hear* them. . . . *Are my attacks that clean? My sound that big? Should I be playing the Bruckner as fast as that? The Schumann that slowly? What the hell's he doing with the Hindemith? That wasn't on the list! Why's he playing that part of Bruckner Seven? Did he hear they're asking for it? I never looked at it!*

If it wasn't the excerpts, it was the endless chattering, the shop talk, and the endless drone of name-dropping.

"I saw Dick Tedesco yesterday."

"Billy Engler called me last night, in fact."

"When I was talking to Pete Wolfinch. . . ."

A few interesting tidbits came my way with the gossip. They had so many players that they were using a split committee to hear them all. Charming. A lot of auditioners *and* a split committee. Sometimes that brings in the "luck of the draw" as far as which committee you play for. I also learned the identity of three auto-advancers, i.e., players who were allowed to skip the preliminaries and go right to the semis. Auto-advancers are often invited to the audition by the orchestra, and I suspect that was the case with these three, but I never found out for sure.

Randolph Cohen was the bass trombonist in the New Jersey Symphony and a pretty good sometime freelancer across the bridge in New York. Randy had been placing well recently. I wondered why he was auditioning so much, since he seemed to be doing pretty well where he was. But then the Detroit Philharmonic was better than New Jersey, and he wouldn't have to freelance any more. Randy might have been invited to the audition by the orchestra. Wouldn't have surprised me.

Don Wilson, Phoenix Symphony, he of the best bass trombone sound I ever heard. Don had made so many semis and finals that if they voted for bass trombonists the way they did college football teams, giving points for second and third, he would be in a top orchestra by now. Probably should be, too, when you think about it. Anybody who could finish so high so often had to be a great player. Not good. Great. Consistency such as Don displays under that kind of pressure should not be sneered at. Still, every committee wants to hear greatness for themselves. Only first in any given audition counts. And Don hadn't finished first in twelve years.

Richard Gulasarian. *He* was auditioning? I thought he was playing in an orchestra in Europe. I *wished* he were playing in an orchestra in Europe. Richard was good. Too good.

Three strong candidates that I knew of going in, and, in the case of Wilson and Gulasarian, two very strong. And more to come. It was all too much to comprehend.

My practice room. It was time to get into my practice room.

Before I could get my door open, however, Brad Wallace caught sight of me from the end of the hall. "Greg, how's it going?" he called out over the din. "I just heard you lost your teaching job. Sorry, man."

"Sorry to hear about you, too, Brad," I returned reluctantly. Brad had been playing in the New Orleans Philharmonic when it folded. He was a big guy who kind of reminded me of Dave Sims, with his relaxed folksy manner, though soft-spoken Dave would never allow himself to get as wired as Brad usually does. "Tough way to lose a gig." As soon as I said that, I regretted it: losing gigs was not something I should be talking about, no matter how it happened.

"Yeah, well . . ." Brad's voice drifted off. "Actually, I ended up okay."

"Really? Good to hear it," I said, hoping that was all I was going to hear.

"Yeah," he hurried on. "Just after the orchestra broke up, I picked up a job at Tulane University. Would you believe it, they were expanding their music department right when the orchestra kicked it in. I'm their new professor of trombone. Can you believe that? Me? A professor? Anyway, it's true. I teach lessons, a brass class, and some other

stuff. Not a bad gig either. In some ways, it beats the hell out of playing. I still do some freelancing, but this college teaching stuff is a lot
better than I thought it would be. True, you pay the price of having to
observe some music faculty types. Now isn't *that* an education. You'd
be amazed at how little some of them know about music. They can
give you names and dates, but have they ever actually *played* anything?
Not since high school from some of the things they say. There's a guy
who teaches opera who didn't know Puccini wrote his lowest brass
parts for a big bass trombone, not tuba. But who cares about them?
The kids are cool, some of them anyway, and once you get tenure,
you're set, and then you don't give a damn who's cool. No more worrying about your job taking a header, you know what I mean? You
know, Greg, you ought to think about getting your doctorate. Then
you can forget that public school crap. College teaching's where it's at."
He looked nervously about. "Tell you the truth," he said in a consid-
erably lowered voice, "the way things have been going, it makes me
wonder what the hell I'm doing here, going after an orchestra job
again. Amazing, how some of us never learn. I got it made, and I'm
putzing around here, looking for a ticket back to the unemployment
line. Lot of ways, I'd just as soon get this over and get back to New
Orleans, you know what I mean?" He glanced at his watch. "I hope
they finish on time. I've got lessons scheduled tomorrow," he added
importantly.

Realizing Brad was probably good for the rest of the afternoon,
with a few minutes aside for his audition, of course, I meaningfully
pushed open the door of my practice room.

"Say, what are you doing gassing with me?" Brad blurted even
more volubly than before. "You're one of these *serious* musicians. I'll let
you go and warm up. Good to see you, man," he added, grabbing my
hand. Suddenly, he looked down the hall. "Hey, Gene, wait up," he
called out. "Haven't seen you since Utah." He was gone, but not before I had looked into his eyes.

Brad Wallace would kill to win this job.

But then, so would I. It was time to start warming up. But not before smiling ruefully at Glenn Savage's stories about how a couple of
old-timers got their jobs. Thirty or forty years ago, ten or twenty can-

didates for a job was a *lot*. According to Savage, Jeffrey Barksdale, the great Principal Flutist in New York, and Richard Styles, the tubist in Cleveland both began triumphant auditions for those orchestras by declaring they were the best players in the place and that the rest of the candidates might as well go home. Given the source, I was never sure of the veracity of those tales, but I could never disprove them either. Just once, I would love to pull a stunt like that. A lot of good it would do me, given the crowds and regulated processes of modern auditions, but the memory would sure feel good on the flight home.

There are probably as many ways to warm up for an audition as there are players. Some play long tones and slurs endlessly, rarely touching on the excerpts, never letting anything louder than a *forte* escape from their bells. Others warm up a few minutes and then run the entire audition list, often at a volume louder than necessary, as if to intimidate the competition. Many blow a few notes, wander through the halls, then return to blow a few more. Some play etudes or solos or make things up. A few hardly warm up at all. Most, myself included, warm up gently, then work on trouble spots, though I doubt last minute practicing accomplishes much. If we don't have those accidentals in *La Gazza Ladra* perfectly placed by now, we won't by the time we're called upstairs. So why bother? Maybe it's just to prove to ourselves we can still play before we have to prove it to someone else.

The mouthpiece felt good on my lips right away, a good sign. Playing the trombone is an athletic undertaking—good trombonists usually have a little extra muscle built up at the corners of their mouths—and it's important to feel the strength and flexibility of your lip and facial muscles as soon as possible. When the sensation is right, you can feel yourself controlling and forming each note in your mouth, much as a pitcher wills a pitch up to the plate or a basketball player "guides" the ball into the hoop. When you're right, the instrument is an extension of your personality and the muscles around your face. That's the way it felt. My sound was warm and dark, good even for a practice room, and I tingled with anticipation. Today, I would give my best.

After fifteen minutes, the time had arrived for the first in a series of trips to the water fountain. This has been a ritual since my first pro-

fessional audition, when I suffered an attack of "dry mouth," an afflic-
tion that occurs when nervousness denies adequate fluids to the
mouth. The feeling is similar to what you experience in the dentist's
chair with that suction device in your mouth. Dry mouth can trans-
form a confident player into one who struggles to survive three excerpts before the dreaded "thank you" sounds from behind the screen.
There are several ways to deal with it. Mine is to drink water regularly
until I'm called. Before I play, I spend almost as much time in the
bathroom as in the practice room.

It is during these ventures from the sanctity of the practice room
that I observe another dichotomy between auditioners: those who do
not socialize with the competition, and those who do. For players in
the first camp, conversation conflicts with their concentration, human-
izes the competition, and reminds them how much of it there is. (During my first trip to the water fountain, I ran into established bass
trombonists from the orchestras in Syracuse, Memphis, Phoenix, Sa-
vannah, and Oregon.) Many of the non-socializers are natural hermits,
but for the more outgoing among that group, a walk to the water fountain is riddled with irresistible pieces of gossip from the trombone
grapevine.

I am not quite as reclusive. I was especially gregarious during this
audition, when uncertainty about Jane threatened to break my concentration if I remained alone too long. "Still playing that Holton?" I asked
Joe Pirelli, a freelancer out of Chicago, whose black, lawyer-like mustache caught my eye near the coffee machine. Joe wasn't a big guy, but
he was trim and had enough presence to stand out in a group. He also
was one of those players who, if he ever decided to give up this insane
existence we call professional music, was smart enough to make something else of himself. Joe and I aren't friends, actually. We live a thousand miles apart, but having met and chatted through five auditions,
we have achieved a good-natured acquaintance. With eight other players milling about the lounge at that moment, it required little urging to
seek each other out.

"Yeah," Joe replied. "And you? Still blowing that kluge job?"

"Yup. Only I got the bell lacquered, finally." I showed it to him.

"Bet that set you back," Joe observed, whistling.

"About $200."

"Wow. You really like the sound better with it lacquered? I was thinking of taking the lacquer off mine."

I shrugged. "All I can tell you is that when I got this bell without lacquer, it sounded kind of wooly. I was figuring on getting it lacquered eventually, but 'eventually' became immediately after I heard a bunch of guys with unlacquered horns warming up at the Minnesota audition. They all sounded like foghorns. As soon as I got back I had it done." Joe was competition. Why was I telling him this?

"Interesting," he replied, rather absently. "How many guys went to Minnesota, by the way?"

"About a hundred and twenty. Hey, that's right. You weren't there. What happened?"

"I saw the list," he replied.

Right. The Minnesota list had everything but the violin part to Strauss's *Elektra* on it. Most orchestras, Detroit included, put out lists with ten to twenty standard excerpts to see how well people played music they would encounter regularly on the job. Lately, with so many players responding to ads, some orchestras are trying to limit the field by including virtually the entire orchestral repertoire on their audition lists. The idea is that those not prepared to play *everything*—those not at the peak of their game, in other words—would stay home, as Joe did. "The Vaughan Williams Tuba Concerto was the clincher," he explained. "I hadn't looked at that thing in years, and besides, I was kind of out of shape when the audition was announced. Nobody thought Feldstein was really going to quit and go to law school. I heard he was disgruntled, but I thought he was just going through a phase."

"He'd had it with practicing and the pressure, was the way I heard it," I said. "And he was bored. All the measure counting and sitting out movements and pieces got to him, I think."

"Law school isn't boring and pressured?"

"Not in the same way, I guess."

Joe shrugged. "I suppose. So how did it go for you in Minnesota?"

How I played at Minnesota was a subject I preferred not to talk about, but Joe and I had shared plenty of war stories. There was no reason to duck his question. "Lousy," I replied. "Cracked the low B in

'Bourgeois'" (*Bourgeois Gentilhomme* by Richard Strauss) and blurped the high C in *Petrouchka.*"

"Gee, that's too bad. How did you do on the Vaughan Williams?"

"I nailed it. Maybe that was the problem. I played the VW so well, I let down and stopped concentrating. Real amateur job. Anyway, I never got out of the preliminaries."

"That sucks all right." Joe looked genuinely sorry. "And you were just coming off the semifinals in Utah."

"You didn't play all that badly in Utah, either, didn't you say?"

Joe shrugged noncommittally: "Yeah, well . . . Not bad. Not great."

Just then, the signal that the third act of Wagner's *Lohengrin* had begun sounded down the hall.

"Sal," Joe declared. "I'll give you odds."

"No bet."

Sal Terranova was one of an obnoxious breed of trombone players who liked to blow licks in the halls and listen to the sound echo. He was an active New York freelancer, young, brash, and, worst of all, good. If anyone were ever going to pull a "Barksdale" or "Styles" at an audition these days, it would be Sal Terranova. The consensus was that Sal was going to hit one and soon. Whenever he showed up at an audition, people prayed. *Just don't make it this one, Sal.* Unless they didn't go, in which case, Sal was their man—*one more great player out of the way*—ignoring the fact that great trombone players are like cockroaches. Get rid of one, and ten more enroll in the conservatories.

"Gentlemen." Everyone's head turned expectantly in the direction of the deep baritone voice. Sal was one of those people who could give you Mahler Two with his voice or with his horn.

"Hi Sal," was Joe's reluctant greeting.

"Sal," I echoed, less than enthused.

"Hey, Sal." Jed Morgan, another New York freelancer—just hanging on, I'm told—had just walked up. I didn't know Jed and Sal were friends. Actually, they probably weren't. Jed was probably just trying to latch onto a winner.

"You guys geared up?" This from Sal.

"Like well-tuned racing cars," Jed assured him.

"Then we should all meet in the finals," Sal declared portentously.

"Without a doubt," Joe returned. He grimaced. I'm sure he wished he hadn't said that.

Sal stared at Joe for a second. I don't know what he expected from Jed and me, but I doubted he thought Joe was going anywhere. We all awaited Sal's rejoinder, forgetting that braggadocio and wit are not necessarily companions. To prove it, Sal spun on his heel and pointed himself back into the direction he came. "Gentlemen," he called over his shoulder as he retreated to his practice room. Just before leaving the scene, he cut loose with a machine gun burst of *Till Eulenspiegel* that could have blown a half-dozen snipers out of the trees.

"I wish just once he'd forget where he was and do that in an audition," Joe muttered.

"Don't. It'd probably give some dumb committee ideas," I countered.

Jed nodded and was about to leave, when we were joined by another old vet of the audition circuit. "Barry," I addressed him, "I haven't seen you, geez, when was it, since the San Francisco Ballet, Murray won. Where the hell have you been?"

"Out of commission," Barry replied. "I bagged the horn for two years soon after that. Got sick of not getting anywhere."

"Apparently, you're over it," Jed observed.

"Naw. I just needed an excuse to see you guys." He chuckled. "No, really, I was fooling around a year ago, and stumbled on one of those Shires trombones with the dual bore slide." He was talking about a slide design where the tube that goes into the bell is larger than the one from the mouthpiece. "Changed my whole outlook on trombone playing. Every horn I ever played before was stuffy, no matter what I did with mouthpieces, lead pipes, valves, whatever. Then I found this baby," he said, holding up his horn proudly. "I started practicing again just for fun, and before you know it, I was playing like hell's angels. For the first time in my life I was pushing air into a horn without having it shoved back into my face."

"Sounds good, Barry." This from Joe.

Barry shrugged. "Hope they think so upstairs," he said wistfully. "But, hell, if they don't, I got time. I've only been back playing a little over a year."

Another candidate, a young kid I didn't recognize, walked over. "Say," he said to Barry, "is that one of those dual-bore Shires?"

And off they went, the kid, for his part, extolling the virtues of a brand new Edwards that had come onto the market."

Apparently, Sal's *Lohengrin* had been a call to assembly—or maybe it was his leaving the lounge—for ten more bass trombone players appeared, each with a horn under his arm. Eighteen players milling around talking horns, teaching, and names was too much metal and flesh for comfort. When a conversation about mouthpieces with extra heavy cups broke out nearby, Joe and I greeted the newcomers and headed back to our practice rooms. Before parting, we wished each other luck. Of course, neither of us meant it.

On my way back, I saw two guys leaning awfully close to a practice room where somebody was playing the downward scales of the "treaty" motif from *Das Rheingold*. One of them was Carl O'Leary, late of the Rochester Symphony. Carl had lasted one year with the RSO before Burt Davey, the principal, made it his personal mission to get rid of his bass trombonist for reasons no one could completely determine, since O'Leary was a pretty decent player if an obnoxious one. One of Davey's ploys was to complain about O'Leary's intonation. That can get underneath some people's skin very quickly. As a rule, each party thinks he's right, but generally, the stronger personality and position—Davey's in both cases—wins.

One night the orchestra was playing Bartok's Concerto for Orchestra, a piece containing a gliss from difficult-to-articulate low B up to F that requires a tricky valve change. Compounding the challenge, the bass trombonist plays very little up until that point, so he's not exactly in the flow of things. Worst of all, the gliss occurs out in the open after the entire orchestra stops playing.

On stage, just before the Bartok was to be played, Davey and the Second Trombone (whose name I forget but who knew where his bread was buttered) started playing glisses from their low C up to F (not having B on the tenor). "What are you guys doing?" asked the miffed O'Leary, who missed the gliss in dress rehearsal to a loud snicker from Davey. "It's just an exercise," replied the grinning Second Trombone. Sure. Carl pulled off the gliss in both concerts, but they were hair-raising moments for him.

Eventually, Carl came to hate going to work—quite a feat on Davey's part, since Carl O'Leary was said to make other people feel the same about working with him—and in a fit of pique quit the orchestra. The story goes that he regretted the move later, realizing too late that you shouldn't give up one playing job before you get another. He's been out in the cold, and bitter, ever since.

Carl O'Leary was a guy I tried to avoid at auditions, and I chafed at my inability to do so now. The young guy with him I didn't recognize. Probably, one of O'Leary's disciples. Carl and I greeted each other with cold nods as I passed by, but before I was out of earshot, I learned they were doing what I thought they were doing: standing outside someone's practice room and denigrating the guy's playing just loudly enough so he could hear. "Listen how he's playing that scale," I heard Carl say. "You think he's ever even *heard* this opera?"

Carl tried that ploy on me once, only the piece I supposedly hadn't a clue about was Hindemith's *Mathis der Maler.* Because Carl's jabbering was breaking my concentration, I decided to cut him off immediately: "Actually, you're right," I declared, sticking my head out my door. "I *haven't* heard this piece." I paused taking in Carl's nonplused reaction. "From the audience, that is. But I've *played* it. With the Boston Symphony. Last year." It was true. Carl's jaw dropped to the ground and stayed there until I closed the door, his companion having abandoned the scene forthwith. I heard nothing more from Carl and assumed he moved on.

The hall was less busy the next two times I ventured out. My warm-ups were going well. Seeing Sal took something out of me, but I controlled my reaction. There was always going to be "somebody," and you can never tell how that somebody will do. In Montreal, I was wandering the halls and heard this absolutely gorgeous bass trombone sound singing over the cacophony of everybody else. "Donald Wilson," I told myself. I headed for the room from where the sound was coming and, sure enough, it was Don. I said hello, and we talked awhile. Don was a real nice guy, impossible to dislike, despite being formidable competition, and I didn't try, but afterwards, when I retreated to my own practice room, my tail dragged between my legs, and my spirit was crushed. Donald Wilson has the most beautiful bass trombone sound in the world. How was I going to compete with *that*?

As it turned out, I didn't. Well, I did, but the result was that I just missed the semis in Montreal. Rather than feel good about doing so well, I kicked myself for being intimidated by Don Wilson. A normal performance on my part, and I would still have been playing. Don made the finals, as usual, but he didn't get the gig. Too late, I recalled the words of James Dearling, the long-time Second Trombone of the New York Philharmonic. Dearling was a very large, kindly man, and his words came out slowly in a voice as rotund as its bearer: "Rhythm is a must. Intonation is a must. And it helps if you have a good sound, too." Poor Don Wilson got it backwards. Maybe that's why he "just missed" so often.

Well, Sal Terranova had rhythm, and he had intonation. Maybe he *was* going to win one sooner or later. I just couldn't afford to believe it would be *this* one.

A knock sounded on my door.

"Come in."

Now what?

The face that appeared was that of another trombonist, a stranger. "Oh. Sorry." My visitor's drawl was a thousand miles south of where I was sitting. He was affable looking, medium height, about thirty and dark, with short black hair and big brown eyes. His mouth gave off a crooked smile that almost made me laugh. If he wasn't holding a bass trombone, I might have liked him. "Ah thought you was Joe Murphy," he said by way of introduction.

"Joe? Haven't seen him." My words may read as curt, but I did my best to be pleasant.

"Ain't seen Joe since Dallas," he said.

"Dallas? That was four years ago."

"Yeah. Ain't that something? I kept missing him on the circuit. Joe and I were really good friends at Indiana" (or more fully, the trombone factory known as the Indiana University School of Music). "Say, that's an interesting horn you got there. Never seen one like it. What is it?"

I checked my watch. What the hell. I still had time. "It isn't any kind, really," I replied. "The slide is Bach, the valve is axial, and the bell was made by a local guy back home."

"Really. Who is he?"

I told him.

"Yeah. I heard of that guy. Makes nice bells, they say."

"He does. They're heavier than most."

"As heavy as Monettes?"

I shook my head. "Nowhere near."

His own horn looked unusual, with the widest bell I'd ever seen. "What's yours?" I inquired, curious in spite of myself.

His face broke into a mile-wide grin. "It's a gen-u-ine Boudreau," he announced proudly.

"Boudreau?"

"As in Lucien Boudreau, of the Bogalusa Boudreaus. Call me Lou."

"You built it yourself?"

"I did at that," he answered clutching his creation as though it were a kitten. "I got this baby right where I want it," he declared proudly. "I just do this," he made a soft clucking noise with his tongue, while flicking his index figure to the back of the room, "and *poof!* Peel the paint right off the back wall."

"Impressive" (if you're designing a sand blaster). I might have asked to try it, but you don't fool around with different horns just before an audition.

"Ah sure hope so," he returned, suddenly sober. "Because Ah'd sure as hell'd like to get out of the Starkville Philharmonic. If I don't get one of these jobs soon, I'm goin' to turn to makin' trombones for a livin'."

"Bad gig? I haven't heard much about Starkville."

"The worst. Count yourself lucky y'all don't know. Sixty players, per-service contracts, run outs all over the state by bus, and a conductor who don't know squat about any of the scores and blames people in the orchestra when he makes a mistake. Which is all the time." He lowered his voice to an exaggerated whisper. "Piece of advice. If by some chance Ah do get this gig, don't bother goin' for my old job."

"I'd be better off making horns, right?"

"You got that right. Well, see ya. Say, never did get your name."

"Greg Lawton."

"Well, Greg, good to meet you. And best of luck to ya up there."

"You too."

The time was 9:50 A.M. My escort to the practice rooms said she'd come for me at 10:15 A.M. Twenty-five minutes to concentrate. Even meditate. If another visitor showed up, I could not be as accommodating as I was with Lucien Boudreau.

For the first time since I had arrived, I felt my heart pounding. It might have been worse if I hadn't taken that beta blocker an hour ago. Beta blockers are usually used by heart patients to reduce the flow of adrenaline, but they are useful to musicians for the same reason. You need a little adrenaline or you'd go numb up there, but in my case, a little too often becomes a lot, and I get so nervous my lip shakes, producing a vibrato that would turn off Lawrence Welk's audience. Early in my freelance career, I used blockers on gigs. I stopped when experience allowed me to handle myself better, but I never could wean myself from them on auditions.

Preliminaries

"Mr. Lawton?"

I glanced at my watch, then up at the woman who had appeared at my practice room door. It was fifteen minutes after ten. The committee was running on time. A first class operation, indeed. A feeling of lust ran through my body that made me shudder. *God, how I want this job.*

"All set," I responded. My horn was out. My bag was locked up. I was ready to go.

"Follow me, then," the woman invited. If I had to at that moment, I couldn't describe her, other than to say she was very competent and very nice.

We walked up two flights of stairs. I was in decent enough physical condition, but I'm glad she came early. I'd hate to walk into an audition short of breath from climbing stairs. In spite of myself, "March to the Scaffold" from the Berlioz *Symphonie Fantastique* kept running through my mind. Bad image. The hero of *Symphonie Fantastique* was marching to the guillotine to have his head chopped off. (*Try not to think of that grotesque clarinet figure depicting the head bouncing down the scaffold stairs. I'm taking an audition, not walking the last mile.*)

"After we arrived at a point down the hall from the audition room, my escort informed me I still had ten minutes. "After you play, you may return downstairs," she continued. "We should be announcing who will play in the semifinals this afternoon." She pointed to an empty room and instructed me to wait inside. That was so I wouldn't hear the person ahead of me playing, though I did catch some measures of *Ein Heldenleben* as I stepped into the room. Pretty good, too. I wondered who it was.

Once the door was shut behind me, I could hear it no more. It was the first time since I had arrived at the arts center that I didn't hear someone playing a bass trombone.

Concentrate!

Five minutes later, my escort reappeared at the door. "Mr. Lawton?"

Beta blockers or not, a surge of adrenalin lifted me out of my chair. As I followed the woman down the hall, I suddenly found it difficult to concentrate. I was ready for this, however. A counselor I had been seeing explained it was because I couldn't keep my "essence" together. "Most of you is holding that horn," she explained, "but part of your consciousness is sitting with that committee, judging you, listening to you, questioning what it is they/you are hearing. Some of you is also back home, waiting for your return, anticipating the report, maybe the explanations. It's not like when you're in that practice room, bearing down with your entire being, and yet that is exactly the environment you must replicate. You have to gather yourself, concentrate." Needless to say, she thought it unwise to socialize at auditions.

We came to a door on the right side of the hall. My escort opened it, stepped back, and allowed me to pass inside. *Into the belly of the beast.* The room was wide, like a big conference area. It was impossible to tell how deep because a row of white screens extended almost to the sidewalls, cutting off my view. The audition committee was no doubt seated on the other side, probably at some long conference table, notebooks at the ready.

Just before I entered, my escort had cautioned me not to speak once I was inside and to walk as silently as I could. That was to keep the audition committee from determining my gender and race.

Once inside, I was greeted by a man in a gray suit, whose smile was doing its best to put me at ease. Probably, he was a member of the orchestra, but not necessarily. "This is Number 71," he announced to the committee behind the screen. "If you like," the moderator said to me, "feel free to softly play a few notes." The reason for the accent on "softly" was Mitch Saunders, the long-time bass trombonist in the Philadelphia Orchestra. One of the major consulting teachers for auditioners, Mitch used to tell students to jump-start glaze-eared committee members who had heard the same excerpts seventy times with an improvised-on-the-spot *tusch* (vernacular German for an impromptu fanfare). Mitch was a gruff, good-natured old bird and a really nice guy, who probably knows more about bass trombone literature than anyone in the world. The problem was Mitch had a lot of students taking auditions, which meant he had set off a rip-snorting *tusch* festival. Twenty years ago, a crew of Mitch's students showed up at an audition in Cleveland. The orchestra had just started using screens, so the committee was unprepared for the first three calls to arms. The bemused moderator wasn't sure what to do, but he apparently figured that if Mitch's first three students had been allowed a *tusch*, it was unfair to restrain the others. The result was an intermittent audio fireworks display: the committee never knew when one was to go off. "I hadn't heard that many bugle calls since the army," an oboe player on the committee said.

Hence, "Softly."

But what do you play "softly?" In a Buffalo audition early in my career, I tried to settle myself down and nervously played a couple of scales. When two notes of a D major scale come out flat, I tried again and chipped the F-sharp. By then I figured the committee took me for a loser, and I went on to prove them right.

Dave Sims always said that you don't wake up a committee with a warm-up. All that does is try their patience. "You do it with great playing. So many guys go in determined not to make a mistake, and that's not what it's all about. We're not sitting behind that screen waiting for some guy to clam so we can cut him short. Do you enjoy teaching a student who hasn't practiced? You *want* him to sound good, and that's what audition committees want, too. I've seen grateful smiles when

someone lights up the room with some real music. That's your goal—
to make that committee smile."

So I kept it down to a few quiet long tones to get a feel for the
room. That the sound was very good allowed me to relax. (I later
found out that both rooms used by the two committees were of near
equal quality acoustically.) After I finished, the moderator explained
the procedure. "In front of you are the excerpts you will play in the order you will play them. Start each one at the left red bracket and continue to the right red bracket. When you finish each excerpt, turn it
aside and start the next. Continue until I tell you to stop. If you have
any questions, signal me with your hand. Don't call out." His voice and
manner were pleasant, if flat in affect. He had spoken these words
dozens of times and was obviously tiring of it. *Number 71?* I hoped the
committee wasn't tiring, too. *Maybe just one little* tusch?

After he concluded his remarks, I nodded, careful not to speak.

"Good luck," he concluded and backed away.

The first excerpt was the solo from the fourth movement of Beethoven's Ninth. An easy one to start with. All you need is a good full
sound, smooth vocal attacks, and the understanding that you're playing
along with the male voices in the chorus, not sounding Hagen's call to
the vassals in *Gotterdammerung*. Think of yourself as part of the chorus,
not the orchestra, Dave said. That's exactly what I did, and to good effect.

The "Hungarian March" was next. Make sure those first two notes
don't sound like pickups. Maintain the forward thrust of the syncopation. Don't hold the dotted rhythms too long or make the following
eighth notes too short. *Exact rhythm.* Don't rush. . . . I hit the opening
A square and played the rhythms so crisply I could almost feel my
body swaggering. But don't swagger too much. Remember to give full
value to those quarters and halves at the end. Don't rush them.

Brahms First Symphony. Another easy one. *Don't oomph the low C.*
. . . I felt as if I were the bass line of an organ chorale.

The "Ride." My first "exit opportunity." The main theme appears
in the key of B Major and later in B Minor. *Maintain the Walkure rhythm
at all cost. You cannot let up on a single note.* I had to be careful that the live
acoustics didn't make the rhythms run together, yet I dared not over-

compensate by playing the notes too short because the effect could be brittle and choppy. *Keep it menacing. Portentous. Place the eighth exactly. Always the skip. Concentrate! (Didn't Wagner know that sharp keys are awkward on the trombone?) Don't let two measures go by before establishing the rhythm. Get it from the top.* All right. Solid forward thrust off the pickup, slight push on the downbeat, and off. . . .

. . . When I finished, everything about what I heard and what I felt in my body seemed right. I glanced at the moderator and was rewarded when a fleeting smile lightened his practiced grisé. Those guys don't usually give themselves away like that, so maybe he hasn't heard it sound that good in a while.

I could feel my heart pounding a little too much. I had cleared the first hurdle and was getting too excited. *Bear down. Don't let up. Concentrate.*

Ein Heldenleben. It's a solo, not an orchestra part. Remember the Bavarian trombonist. I played it through, almost lyrically. Some very bombastic music darn near started to sing. I was feeling pretty good about myself when the moderator raised his hand, signaling me to stop playing. He was able to see around the screen from his vantage point, and had received a signal. My heart sank. *That's it? But I had played so well.* I wasn't sure if I thought those words, or actually cried them out. I looked around nervously. *I can't play any better. If this isn't good enough . . .*

A voice sounded from behind the screen: "Could you play that again in a more martial style?"

I almost gushed in relief. Committees don't usually ask you to play something over in the preliminaries unless they are taking you seriously. This wasn't a question of ability but of interpretation. Fortunately, I had left myself some leeway by playing the part so lyrically. It wasn't difficult to play it again with a little more punch.

"Okay," I heard from behind the screen when I was through. "Go on."

Another test passed. If the committee wasn't pleased with what they were hearing, I would have been gone.

Hary Janos featured me at my best: big attacks, big sound, with just a hint of a burr on the tone to lift me off the tuba underneath, and a solid high B. A winner.

Scheherazade. The big 6/4 section of half notes followed by quarters. Every note must be heard equally, one growing from the other. "Think of the half notes as the big kids," Dave once said. "The rhythm takes care of them. Your job is to look out for the little kids." Deep breath. Relax. Big meaty half notes followed by equally powerful quarters. I could feel the room resonate with my sound.

La Gazza Ladra. There were three sections, each consisting of runs, all different. Only the last two were bracketed in red. A rush of panic gripped my throat. I had fallen into the stupid habit of practicing these excerpts in order, from the first section to the last, and had grown used to hearing them that way, with the tonality of the first section orienting me to the others. Now I felt as if I were called upon to start a book from the middle. How could I have overlooked that possibility? This was the second time a quirk about *La Gazza Ladra* threatened to trip me up. One of my early auditions used a different edition than the one I had practiced. There wasn't much variation between the two, but knowing I was approaching something unfamiliar had unhinged me. . . . I didn't play much longer. Of course, that was pre-Dave Sims. Dave was a stickler on familiarizing oneself with all editions of a piece. I was never caught like that again. Until now.

I lifted my horn. *Wait.* I had done well up to this time. The committee could sit tight for a few seconds. I stared at the first set of runs, playing it my mind, exactly in tempo. Only after I finished "playing" did I pick up my horn and play for real. The ruse worked. Every note was dead on. I just had to remember not to overemphasize the quarters or get too loud. This was Rossini not Verdi.

Schubert Ninth. They asked for the trombone calls of the first movement, not the bass trombone solo in the Finale. No problem. Keep it noble, always noble, and the dotted rhythms accurate.

I felt even better than I had at Utah. I could have played all day.

Till Eulenspiegel. Just make sure to get the pickup in triplet rhythm, don't be late off the upbeat, plenty of contrast on the accents that make up the theme. A lot to remember, but it was too late to spook me with that now. I even played it a tad faster than usual. Not like a Sal Terranova machine gun in the hall, but then I wasn't performing a circus act. I finished with a flourish. It was just right.

It was also the last excerpt on the stand. I had played them all.

"Thank you." That was from the moderator. He placed his finger on his lips, perhaps fearing my good playing would cause me to forget the rule of silence. I smiled and walked with great poise out of the room.

After I returned to my practice room, I really wanted to tell everybody how great I played and that I had played *everything*, but you don't do things like that unless you're Sal Terranova. . . . Unless they come to you, of course, as Joe Pirelli did.

"How did it go, man?" he asked.

"Good."

"How far did you get?"

I beamed. "All the way."

His eyebrows leaped. "Wow," he exclaimed.

"How about you?"

"Kicked out after *La Gazza*," he replied sadly.

"That's not bad."

"It's not good, either." He smiled and left my room. No one who has not made it wants to talk to someone who, in all likelihood, has.

George Finney from Boston dropped his head in next. We didn't talk long, either.

Deciding I could use some fresh air, I threw my horn into my gig bag and headed outside for a walk.

WAIT

When I returned to the lounge, it was teeming with bass trombone players, most of them quiet, as they awaited the announcement of their fate. Very few candidates had left. This display of unbridled optimism never failed to amaze me. Not all these guys played well enough to believe they made the semifinals. Yet they remained, hoping there was something among those split notes that intrigued the committee enough to want to hear more. Many years ago, when five or six players showed up for a job, that kind of thing happened. At Mitch Saunders's audition for the bass trombone job at Philadelphia forty years ago, the conductor, who had no clue what he was asking, put up the extremely high and difficult *first* trombone solo from Ravel's *Bolero*. Mitch couldn't play it very well, of course. When the audition was over, he chalked it up as shot and left the building. After a quick supper, he was all ready to drive home when he decided to call the orchestra "just in case." Thus began one of the more famous tenures in the history of orchestral trombone playing.

In those days, it paid to be an optimist, but not now.

It was during this waiting period that I finally ran into my other Boston colleagues, Sam Roy and Carter Simpson, neither of whom thought he did well. Of course, neither had left. The level of conversation rose a bit, as people became restless. It was the first time all day that the orchestra had fallen behind schedule.

But not for long. The woman who had accompanied me to my audition appeared in the lounge. The room turned silent, as if a huge vacuum cleaner had sucked all of the words out into the street. I doubt if she ever had such close attention paid to her as when she proctored auditions. "First, I want to congratulate you on a wonderful audition," she announced. "It was a very difficult job for the committee to pare down the list. Please believe me when I say that. Some of you played extremely well." *Some of you.* She cleared her throat. The tension was so thick you could almost see it. To her credit, she was not acting like someone who enjoyed the power she was holding. If anything, she seemed as nervous as everyone else. "The following players will please stay and prepare for the next round. This is the complete list." Suddenly, I felt very vulnerable. There were over forty bass trombonists in that room who thought they had a chance.

What made me think I was one of the lucky ones? Odds. Always the odds.

She began with the three auto-advances: Randolph Cohen, Richard Gulasarian, and Don Wilson.

Then ...

"Salvatore Terranova." Of course.

"Herbert Vanderkelen." *In and out Herb,* I called him. He'd play well for a time in an audition, but more often than not, he'd sooner or later suffer a glitch or two that did not escape a committee. Herb's the kind of guy who might win an audition if he stayed hot long enough, and then falter on the gig. He is a terrific sight-reader, though, and he's good at the short-term playing a freelancer does—lucky for him, since freelancing is his line of work in Los Angeles. I was surprised he advanced, and glad because he was a good bet to blow up somewhere along the line.

"Morgan Schmidt." The bass trombonist from the North Carolina Symphony. I had spoken to him briefly when I first returned from my preliminary. He said he didn't think he had played all that well. Probably, he didn't, but he was the exception that proves the rule, as they say. The one guy who managed to throw the committee a curve, probably by the eerie stateliness he inserted into his style. I always thought he was lucky to get into North Carolina, if you can call playing for an orchestra that tours a rural state as much as they do lucky. Humph. The semis would take care of him.

Meanwhile, he takes up a spot.

"Jessica Reynolds." A newcomer. There were five female candidates in that room, but it was obvious who Jessica Reynolds was. She was the tall sturdy blond woman across the way with the beaming smile, yet strangely nervous glimmer of fear around the eyes. She looked a little too old to be a student, but I'd never heard of her.

It suddenly occurred to me that a lot of names had been called, and mine was still unmentioned.

"Harris Mackowski." *Harris who?* Who the hell is Harris Mackowski? *Another* newcomer. Suddenly, I heard a high tenorish whoop. The person who made the sound was a young man—boy, really, with short blond hair and freckles, standing five feet to my left. This one probably *was* a student. Terrific. His first audition, and he makes the semis.

The woman reading the names looked over the crowd and lowered the list. She had read eight names—more than I expected for a semifinal. A murmur of disappointment rumbled through the room in response, as the crowd, most of it disappointed, began to break up.

I was stunned. Sick, really. Jane was right. The odds *were* too great. I played my butt off today, probably the best I ever played. If that wasn't good enough, then I have no idea what good enough is. *You played fine. It just wasn't what they were looking for.* That's what my counselor says I'm supposed to think at times like this. *You can't stop believing in yourself. Another time, another orchestra, the story could be different. It only takes one. What's important is you get the audition.*

Every time I get an audition, people like my counselor congratulate me for "getting the interview." And why not? In their world, getting the interview means they're competing against five or six applicants. In mine, it's seventy. Or a hundred. Or more. For maybe one or two, at the most three, openings a year.

I need a new counselor.

Slowly, I bent down to pick up my bag. I had scheduled my flight for nine o'clock to leave time for the semis and finals. Obviously, a foolish thing to do. Now I had seven rotten hours to kill in a town I couldn't wait to get out of. Get out of? I wouldn't even consider visiting the place, let alone live in it, but for its orchestra.

Time to call the airline. Check to see if they had an earlier flight.

"Excuse me! Excuse me!"

I stepped aside, but no one made their way past. The plea rang out again: "Excuse me! Excuse me!"

The call was coming from a distance. A female voice. I saw a woman waving her arm. It was the orchestra official who had announced the semifinalists. "There's one more name," she announced. "I just looked at my list again. I'm so sorry." Her voice was shaking.

Everybody froze.

One more chance.

"Gregory Lawton."

If I had had the strength, I would have pumped my fist into the air and roared, but I couldn't move a finger, let alone my entire arm. My body had turned numb.

"That's you," I heard from my right. It was Boudreau.

"I think it is," I said stupidly.

"Congratulations." He grabbed my hand and shook it with more enthusiasm than I could have mustered in his position.

"Way to go, man." This from my left. It was Joe Pirelli. He meant it, but he was rueful, too. I think Joe expected to do better at this audition. "Thanks," I said softly. I was suddenly feeling very modest.

"Will all the semifinalists come over here?" the official's voice called out over the buzzing.

She was easily accommodated, as the room was beginning to clear out. No further miracles were in the offing. I stole a glance at Brad Wallace, the college teacher concerned he might have to stay over and miss teaching his lessons the next day. The sadness around his eyes and the tightness around his mouth told me everything. Poor Brad.

Without further hesitation, I sidled over to hear what the woman from the orchestra had to say about the next round.

"First, my congratulations," she said when all of us were gathered and feeling very proud, I assure you. She then described the procedure for the next round, which would begin at two o'clock. When she finished, she smiled for the first time since she had entered the room, probably with relief. "Good luck to you all," she concluded as she left us.

We wished the same to each other. (Yeah, right.) For a few minutes, we stood around for some small talk, but it was clear everyone was anxious to go his or her own way. There would be no shared lunches among this group.

On the way toward the stairs, I walked by a bunch of players on their cell phones. Generally, such calls are made to wives, girlfriends or airlines, and judging from the snatches of conversations I was picking up, these were no exceptions.

". . . just didn't have it today, Gail."

". . . thought I played real good. It just wasn't what they wanted to hear."

". . . it's coming. It's coming . . . *next* time."

". . . Look, Karen, we'll talk about my taking that job when I get back. Don't you know what I've just been through?"

"Do you think I can get on that two o'clock flight? Yes. That's right. I was originally booked for nine."

Joe Pirelli was still in the lobby when I arrived upstairs. I planned to grab a sandwich and be back in the arts center no later than one-fifteen. "Play well, Greg," he wished upon seeing me.

"Thanks." I started for the door. "Lunch?" I asked, feeling sociable all of a sudden.

Joe shook his head. "I just phoned the airlines. They have an earlier flight, so I'm going to hustle out and catch it." He sounded down. I really think Joe did expect to do better.

I understood. "Better luck next time, man," I said, shaking his hand.

He smiled. "Just you play well this time," he admonished. "I'm getting tired of seeing you at these things."

"At that moment, Jessica Reynolds walked past us. She smiled at me nervously, but did not pause to chat on her way out the door. Sal was just behind her, but it was obvious they weren't together. "Gentlemen," he intoned, much as he had earlier.

"Sal." This from me.

Joe nodded.

"Good group," he said, grinning. "They're going to get themselves a bass bone today, I do believe."

"You think maybe it'll be you, Sal?" Joe asked innocently.

"Hot damn, maybe it will at that," returned Sal. "Well, break a leg, Greg," he added as if he had just realized I was standing there. Then he strutted out the door.

"Pompous jerk," muttered Joe.

"Yeah, but a good player. If I don't get it, I sure as hell hope he does."

Joe laughed. "I know. I just don't know if it's because I want to get rid of the competition he presents or just get rid of him." Joe lifted his thin shoulders in an aimless shrug. "On the other hand, the people with this orchestra seem nice. I'd hate to wish Sal Terranova on them even if it is in my own best interests."

"Yeah, better you wish me on them instead."

Joe turned serious. "I will, man."

We walked out of the building together and were just about to go our separate ways, when I thought of one last thing to ask him. "Say, do you know anything about this Jessica Reynolds or Harris Mackowski?"

"Not too much about Reynolds, except that I heard her warm up when I got here. Big sound. Very smooth and musical. She wasn't playing anything hard, so I can't tell you about her technique. She looks real nervous, though. I figure she's gone about as far as she's going to. Mackowski, I've heard stuff about, but it's third hand. He's a young hotshot from Chicago. Bit of a clone of the Chicago Symphony section. Big sound, strong sustained tone, ton of technique for a kid, and boiling with confidence. Obviously the word hasn't spread to you guys back East."

"I guess not."

"The word is he's like the pitcher you want to get to in the early innings, because if you don't, he's going to mow you down later."

"Meaning, if I'm going to take one from him, this better be it."

"Or the next one. When he grows up, he's going to be tough. Or so I'm told."

Joe paused. I sensed he had more to say, and I didn't want to rush him. I liked Joe Pirelli as much as I did any bass trombonist, and I don't think it was because I believed he was never going to really make it, either. Joe was just a genuinely nice guy. Too nice, maybe, and too intellectual about his playing. There's a point in performing music where you have to stop thinking and simply put out, and I don't think Joe Pirelli is ever going to reach that point. "For what it's worth," he went on, "one of your strongest competitors is Sal, but you know that. Gulasarian looks and sounds like he's got it together, too. Worse, he's loose. He'd like this job, but he's doing okay in Europe. He doesn't really need it. It's even possible he will not take it if he gets it. That he's just using Detroit as a tune-up for a really big audition. Wilson's always a threat, of course. As for Vanderkelen and Cohen, I don't think so. Vanderkelen looks more relieved than reinforced by making the semis, and Cohen just doesn't sound that good to me. To be fair, though, I really thought I'd beat those two out, so maybe I'm not an impartial judge. Mackowski, I told you about. Reynolds I told you about, too, but keep in mind I was reading a lot into her nervousness. In the end it may not mean a thing. In which case, she could be a threat. She sounded awfully good, the few minutes I heard her." With that, Joe pulled out his hand one last time and grasped my own. "Go for it, man. You can win this one. You really can." We shook hands, then Joe hailed a passing cab.

I walked slowly toward a restaurant I saw across the street. It wasn't until I was seated that I realized I hadn't touched the ground once on my way over. I felt so terrific about myself that I almost didn't order anything, but I thought better about that. I didn't want to find myself hungry in the middle of the semis, but God, I felt good. I had made the semis before, but never while playing so well. Maybe things would turn out even better this time.

Just then, I remembered that Joe had not mentioned Morgan

Schmidt. The lack of completeness bothered me in an obsessive-compulsive sort of way, but there was no matter to it beyond that. I knew what Morgan's story was, and I wasn't worried about him.

After eating, I thought of calling Jane with the news. But I knew how she felt about these things. Besides, I didn't want to go into the semis with something strange in her voice dogging my concentration.

SEMIS

The semifinals of an audition have a very different feel from the preliminaries. In the first round, there is an air of desperate festivity about the cacophony of trombones blaring from every direction. Many players have no chance of advancing, and deep in their heart of hearts, they know it. Usually, they're among the ones who blare the loudest, visit the lounge most often, and exchange the most conversation. By the semis, however, the pretenders are gone, the prep room is emptier, everything is much quieter, and the atmosphere is more serious. Everyone who is there thinks they can win this job, regardless of what they thought of their chances earlier. For the rare advancer who came to the audition on a lark, it is no longer a lark.

A great deal of pride swells up in this room. All nine players have won an endorsement of sorts. It was easy to tell who the oldest hands were. Gulasarian and Wilson expected to be here. Each represented a serious threat. Gulasarian, dapper as always with his attractive mustache and dark eyes, was actually reading a book. Don Wilson and I talked awhile. He seemed down. Depressed. Of all the semifinalists, Don was the most jaded. Now in his forties, he was running out of gas as far as preparing for the rigors of an audition was concerned. I was surprised he was even trying for Detroit, good orchestra though it was. I figured he'd either go for one of the elite groups or not bother, but then maybe the poor guy just had to get out of Phoenix. Sometimes, I wondered why. It wasn't a bad orchestra at all, but I heard Don just didn't like the people in it. Not to mention the town. Cohen and Schmidt were not as experienced, but both obviously had won an audition before. As if seeing themselves as logically paired, they were talking quietly in a corner. Terranova, Mackowski and Reynolds were at the opposite extreme in orchestra audition experience, though Sal had done a great deal of professional playing. The young Mackowski seemed surprisingly cocky. Of all people, he was talking to Sal, who was simply boring holes into the kid's forehead with his eyes. I had no doubt that Sal would have thrown the kid into a cement mixer if he could have—and if he was worried enough about him to bother. Clearly, Mackowski had no idea what he was up against. Joe was right about him. The kid might be dangerous, some day, but not now. I would sell my horn for scrap if this guy went any further. Jessica Reynolds sat by herself, still looking ill at ease, as though this were the last place she expected to be. Joe was wrong to worry too much about her this time around. Like Mackowski, she was too young. She might be a threat some day, but you can't keep it up through three rounds of an audition against good players if you're as pale looking as she is.

The orchestra representative reappeared with instructions about the semifinals. (I can now tell you her name was Karen Landry and that she was an attractive blond with vivid blue eyes.) The format would be essentially the same as in the preliminaries, except there would be excerpts included that were not on the original list plus some sight-reading. (Some orchestras include these items to see how well a player responds to new music and to music he may know but has not had a chance to prepare as thoroughly as the excerpts on the list.) We would also play the Bach "Sarabande." Then she gave the order of our performances, chosen at random. I was to play fifth, after Vanderkelen and before Wilson. Finally, she repeated the earlier instructions about not speaking during the audition.

The wait to play the semis sped by as if in a dream, marred only by the huge beaming face of Sal Terranova (Number 2) after he returned to the practice area. Trombone players are not the most circumspect of characters—at least not those in this group—and I thought I had a good idea of how the others before me had done, as well. Cohen looked downcast. Schmidt had a kind of "oh well" expression on his ruddy complexion.

When Vanderkelen walked off with Ms. Landry, I began my mental preparations. It was time to pay more attention to what I was about to do than what my opponents had done. Still, I couldn't help but notice that when he returned, Vanderkelen rushed to (I presume) his practice room, eager to talk to no one.

Now it was my turn to accompany Ms. Landry. Once again, she proved to be quiet and diplomatic, though this time I felt an air of respect I didn't notice the first time around. Karen Landry was probably one of those ex-musician orchestra employees who realized early on that the combination of talent limitations, the large number of people who played her instrument, and the paucity of playing jobs did not add up to great employment prospects. Jane would call them the smart ones. Maybe so, but they were musicians at heart, and something told me Ms. Landry would love to trade places with me, if only for a moment.

The semis were held in the same room as the preliminaries. At least, that's what I thought at first but something was different about it. Because I didn't know the building very well, I thought at first that maybe my escort had led me on a different route? Then I noticed: the room was the same, but the screen was just a little closer to me. It was also higher off the ground, enough so that I could see fourteen pairs of feet in a row below it—the audition committee, no doubt. I wondered why the change. Maybe to get away from an air conditioning duct? It did seem a little cooler. Funny. Maybe something that didn't bother anyone earlier was bothering them now. Nervous as I was, there had to be a cloud of tension hanging over the committee, as well, making them more acutely sensitive to disturbances. It was no cinch to pull the nine most outstanding players out of a pack of a hundred, but it helps that the top players tend to show themselves quickly, as do the weaker ones. It is more difficult to determine who is the best player out of a small select group that is close in ability.

The same man who moderated the preliminaries took me off Ms. Landry's hands, smiled almost shyly, pointed toward the lone stand in the middle of the room, and took me through the same instructions as before. When I nodded, he announced me to the committee: "Number 5!"

I played a few soft notes as before. The screen was closer by only a foot or so, but it would have made me feel a little crowded if the room weren't so large. I took a deep breath. This was not my first trip to a semifinals, but I never felt as good as I did this time.

The Bach was first. I loved the way the sound of the piece filled the room. The low C's poured out of the bell. I quivered a bit on a measure of Hindemith's *Symphonic Metamorphosis,* which came next. This was one of the unlisted excerpts, but it was so common on auditions, that I was familiar with it. (Whoever I heard practicing it earlier either found out it was going to be on the semis or was just showing off.) I thought they might ask me to play it again, but they didn't. I wasn't sure if that was good or bad. They asked for the "Ride" again, and I repeated my earlier performance. This time they did ask me to play it again, faster and lighter. That made the piece more difficult, but the room acoustics were clean, so it was easy to separate the notes.

It was just after I started the "Ride" for the second time that I spotted the shoe tapping beneath the screen. Not just tapping, but tapping in perfect rhythm to what I was playing—like a conductor's baton. *Very nice.* Suddenly, it was a snap keeping a steady tempo. I wondered if anyone else had noticed what was going on.

Sight-reading was a handwritten, somewhat clunky modern etude with a lot of awkward intervals plus a lyrical line tossed in the middle. It wasn't much musically, but it was a good medium for my solid, consistent approach to the instrument. After that came Wagner's "Procession of the Gods into Valhalla" from *Das Rheingold.* This they wanted to hear as smoothly as possible, then more broad and measured. Both styles were difficult to pull off in the low register and *fortissimo.* This excerpt is easy to drag in tempo, but the tapping foot made things easier. (I played it on my regular horn rather than the contrabass the orchestra had supplied. I don't think I suffered from the choice. I was never all that comfortable with the contra, and I didn't like playing strange instruments.)

Tchaikovsky Four was next, the 9/8 section from the first movement: *Walküre*-ish in rhythm, but balletic in feel—a tricky combination. Then they asked me to demonstrate just how loudly I could play the big Russian tune in the finale. This they followed with a request to play the *Rhenish* as softly as possible. Then the *Lohengrin* third act prelude.

Finally, there was *William Tell.* As I studied the part waiting for me on the stand, I couldn't help but think of Harry Eastman, a friend from my conservatory days and now the great principal of the Chicago Symphony. Harry was one of those "can't miss" players with talent who practiced eight hours a day. One day I went with him for his audition for the National Symphony. (I was visiting Washington, DC at the time.) As it turned out, I was able to wait for him outside the audition room while he played. Harry did fine on the first three excerpts. Then he started *William Tell.* No problem, I remember thinking. Besides having ground the excerpt into fine powder in the practice room, Harry had just played the piece five times in two days in a series of children's concerts. He had the thing memorized backwards, I swear.

Harry stumbled through the first run, did it over better, then completely fell on his face on the second. End of audition. Yessir. Even the great ones fall sometimes. *Practice your butt off. And even then, you never know.*

This was hardly the time to think of such things. There are people like Sal for whom *William Tell* is a display piece, no more difficult than a B-flat major scale, but I'm not one of them. For me *Tell* is one of those excerpts where every note and motion has to be ingrained in my body. After all the work I put in on it, it should have been, but that knowledge has never prevented a small lump from forming in my throat every time I play it in an audition. Doing as well as I had so far put that much more pressure on me. Funny. I was in this same position during the preliminaries, poised for triumph, with the treacherous *Till Eulenspiegel* sitting on that stand, and I wasn't fazed. This time I was afraid to lift up my horn. I took one last look at the part, took a deep breath, did my best to shake Harry Eastman from my brain, and played.

Again, the foot was a great help. Its owner had such a fine sense of rhythm that it was ridiculously easy to time my leap off the long notes into the runs. I pretty much had the excerpt memorized, so it was a simple matter for my eyes to drift from the music to concentrate on— and be hypnotized by—that metronomic foot.

It happened during the held note before the fourth of the six runs. The fourth run is a repetition of the third except that it ends up on a B rather than an E, and I was on autopilot after flying flawlessly through number three. The foot continued to tap when suddenly, in the middle of the long B, it paused on an upbeat, stopped, and proceeded to scratch what I presumed to be an itch on its owner's calf.

Only my endless drilling on this excerpt saved me. Half my mind was stunned, frozen, but the other half kept functioning, and I managed to get through it. But how well? Did I lose count holding the long B and drop a fraction of a beat? I really didn't know. After the foot stopped beating, I was playing in a daze. The notes came out, but I wasn't entirely sure who was producing them.

After I left my last note echoing in the room, I stood still, paralyzed. My body turned suddenly cold, my face bloodless, the way it had when I went into shock after being injured playing softball several years ago. My knees shook, and I had to struggle to remain still and recover. *William Tell* was the last excerpt on the stand. What was I supposed to do now? Stand there? Leave? Maybe it wasn't that bad. I honestly didn't know. I was about to offer to play it again, when I remembered the admonition about not speaking. I turned to signal the moderator. Perhaps he would pass my request to the committee. Then I hesitated. Was this such a good idea? If the excerpt didn't go that badly, offering to play it again might put some doubt into the committee's collective mind.

Then a male voice called out from behind the screen. "Could you play that again, please?"

Well, there was one decision I didn't have to make. I waited for further instructions—faster, slower, louder, and softer?—but there were none. I guessed they weren't trying to see if I could do something differently. They just wanted to hear it again. The message was clear. My last attempt was not up to everything else I had done, so the committee wanted to know. Was it a slip? Or was I starting to unravel? Was the real me—a Me not up to the orchestra's standards—about to emerge?

I looked back at the music. There would be no more watching feet. The whole audition—the rest of my life—could be riding on the next few notes that came out of my horn. Given the importance of the moment, I was amazed at how the nerves I felt before my first *Tell* had dissipated. I felt an eerie calm, as if I had just passed halfway through a hurricane and arrived at the unearthly tranquility of the eye. But I dared not wait too long. The quiet of a hurricane's eye is transitory. The terror would soon return.

Besides, I had nothing to lose.

I raised my horn and put out the best *William Tell* I ever played in an audition, in a practice room, in a concert—anywhere. Every note was clear and in tune, I lingered not a whit on any of the ties, and the final downward figures drove to the end in a fury that left me exhilarated.

I waited. For the first time, I could barely hear some mumbling behind the screen. Then, "Again?"

Again? *That* wasn't good enough?!

"A little louder?"

I breathed a sigh of relief. This was better. I had passed.

I played *Tell* three more times. Louder, faster, then the original tempo, lighter. All were fine.

Finally, "Thank you."

It was over. I had slipped once but recovered. I left the room confident I had borne up well. The slip might even have helped me. It showed I had grit and could recover from disaster, an important trait in any orchestral wind player.

There were only four players after me, but I did not wait around for them to finish. I had some time to go outside, and that is exactly what I did. I was walking on air. There was no way I could sit still in the waiting room studying the competition. Besides, what good would it do?

I walked up and down the busy downtown street, impervious to traffic and street noises in a way I could never be to the blare of fifty trombones. Again, I thought of calling Jane. I *wanted* to call Jane. But the same dark thoughts that stopped me before tugged at me again, so I didn't.

We reassembled backstage to hear the verdict. There was a minimum of chatter and no questions about how much of the list they allowed any of us to play. Everybody plays the same things in semifinals unless someone is really bad.

Finally, Ms. Landry appeared. "My congratulations to all of you again," she said to us. She looked tired, but there still was that ready smile radiating empathy. I doubt she was chosen for this role by accident. "This time there will be four of you going to the next round," she announced. "And this time, I won't forget anyone," she added, casting an embarrassed glance in my direction. "The finalists are Richard Gulasarian, Gregory Lawton, Jessica Reynolds, and Donald Wilson." Two no-surprises, me (who knows what I was), and a finals first-timer who was a real shocker.

Actually, there were two other shocks: Terranova out and my remarkably calm reaction to my own success. It was as if I expected to make it. I didn't know I had it in me.

The look of astonishment on Terranova's face was indescribable, at least by a mere trombonist. If it were possible to be shot in the heart and still be alive and standing, Sal Terranova could submit himself as Exhibit A. For the first time since I had known him, his mouth was open, and no words were coming out. Even his natural swarthiness had deserted him. Pale as Jessica Reynolds was, he was whiter still.

At that moment, it struck me just exactly how good Sal Terranova thought he was. He really did expect to win this thing, and easily. Sal thought he was a *phenom*.

Now there are phenoms in this business as in any other. A few years ago, everyone knew Clarence Weber was going to win Toronto and later New York, and that Fred Horrigan was a dead lock on every audition he took until eventually he settled in Cleveland. Wherever Clarence, and later Fred, showed up at an audition, everyone else just mailed it in. The International Trombone Association could have declared a national holiday when these two finally reached the top and dropped out of the audition circuit. So players like that do exist, but for Sal to think he was one of them . . . and then to watch him slink out like that. . . . It really was amazing.

Now there were four, and I was one of them. I should have been happy. I *was* happy—no I was thrilled. This orchestra liked me! They liked what I did. They *approved* of me. They might even *hire* me.

Not that this was going to be a cakewalk. Two serious competitors were still around. Blinded by Sal, I had not entirely taken their measure, but from the outset, Don Wilson and Richard Gulasarian were excellent candidates to win this thing. And though I still insisted on believing her inexperience would tell in the end, some of Joe Pirelli's words about Jessica Reynolds began to take on importance, as well.

Nor was that all. Until now, I had been comfortably positioned in terms of experience. I had enough to know what to expect, but not so much as to be jaded. This was no longer true. Wilson and Gulasarian had been in finals plenty of times. I had not, even once. From now on, everything that would happen to me would be occurring for the first time. In that respect, I was no better off than Jessica Reynolds.

AND THEN

The format for the finals was quite different from the earlier rounds. To begin with, it was held on the main stage in Detroit's Philharmonic Hall. There was no screen, so the committee, which now included Music Director James Da Costa and Assistant Conductor Philip Lesser, could interact with the players. Also, we would play some excerpts with the orchestra's low brass section so the conductors and committee could hear how we sounded with our potential colleagues. Not all orchestras do this, but many do, and for good reason. The greatest player in the world can blend poorly with a given section. There's the matter of sound, of style, even of personality, that goes into the mix. For a section to sound good, all elements have to mesh. If they do not, and there are plenty of orchestras where they don't, you can end up with a section of three good but unmatched players that sound nowhere nearly as fine as one with three lesser but well integrated performers.

I was the second to play, after Reynolds. As I soon learned, she would be a tough act to follow. My escort brought me up too early, and standing outside the door leading into the hall, I was able to hear Reynolds and the Detroit trombone section playing one of the big fanfare passages from the finale of Bruckner's Eighth. Her rock steady sound, sitting on the tuba and supporting those two tenor trombones the way it did was very impressive, indeed. *My God.* She *was* good. This I did not need to hear, but it was too late to pull me back. The Bruckner was her last piece, and I was summoned on stage a few minutes after she walked past me on her return to the prep room. She looked as nervous as she always did, but no more than I was at that moment.

So that was the way it was: three great players, not two. But then, this was the finals. What did I expect?

Though I had played several concerts in Boston's Symphony Hall, stepping into a new auditorium usually drew a silent gasp from me. The stage was wider and deeper than that of Boston's hall. A single music stand stood at center and slightly upstage. Off to its right were four chairs and four music stands. The golden wood of the floor felt solid beneath my feet as I crossed the stage. Ms. Landry completed her task by turning me over to the moderator who nodded in greeting.

The lights were hot, but not overly so. I liked them. They reminded me I was playing in a real hall this time. Their brightness kept me from appreciating the expanse of seats in the auditorium to my right, but it was just as well. The last thing I needed was to be overwhelmed by the auditorium the first time I stepped into it.

I played my usual array of soft notes, this time to test the acoustics as much as to get loose, and was pleased. The sound was warmer than I expected from the appearance of the building outside. New buildings tend to produce a more clinical tone than the great older ones like Boston's Symphony Hall, but this one was different. A chill ran down my spine. I really did want this job.

"Mr. Lawton," Lesser addressed me as I took my position on stage with the committee in front of me. "You will first play two excerpts so we can hear your sound in the hall. Then you will sit with your hoped-to-be future colleagues and play more of the literature with them." The two excerpts I was to play alone were the opening hymn from the *Tannhauser Overture* and then *Ein Heldenleben*.

I had played *Tannhauser* in a hall like this once before, and the feeling of power while intoning the hymn was overwhelming. I almost felt as if I were the voice of God. I had to watch out for that here. Wallow too much in majesty, and tempos drag. There is another issue, one that comes up on many excerpts. In the orchestra, the entire trombone section plays the *Tannhauser* hymn in unison, so the best approach to volume is to allow the entire section to share the load. The result is smoother and more imposing than if one or more of the players simply blasts away. Playing it alone is another matter. Often the tendency is to play louder than I should to recreate the sound of the piece as I have it in my head—with three trombones. That is almost always a mistake. You can never make up for two missing players, and it is unmusical suicide to try. The problem is, the conductors and committee probably have that same sound in their heads, so if I were to play at a volume suitable for section playing, it might seem wimpy to them. The trick is to find a volume that fills the hall just enough to satisfy them and to find it quickly—in no more than two notes.

As soon as I started playing, Da Costa began conducting subtly with his right hand. *Oh oh. This is tricky.* This time it's the *conductor* who's beating time. I thought it wise to stay near his tempo even if he didn't know he was setting it, and I did so. Still, I was careful—a good idea, as it turned out, since Da Costa started and stopped beating pretty much at whim. But I was on to him, and he caused me no problems. Maybe, I thought hopefully when I finished with *Tannhauser*, he'll screw up someone else.

Ein Heldenleben lent a different sensation. So many notes not meant to be played solo in a huge hall, but the Bavarian bass trombonist had done just that. The problem was, I played this passage lyrically in the preliminaries and was told to toughen it up. Reverting to my earlier style could lead any committee member with notes and a good memory to conclude I didn't take direction well. That's not good. More than one conductor has observed that orchestras are not democracies.

After the last notes echoed through the hall, I waited expectantly. I thought it had gone very well. The big hall hadn't sucked up my sound, so breathing wasn't as serious a problem as I feared, but you never know, especially when no one, including the moderator, says anything.

At that moment, Lesser, perhaps sensing my uncertainty, did something that surprised me. He smiled. "Very good, Mr. Lawton," he said softly. I think he meant it. His words settled me down more than a bottle of beta blockers ever could.

With that, we moved on to section playing. Malcolm Strassman, the Principal, Second Trombone Corey Murphy, and the tuba player, Bill Steinberg walked in from the opposite back stage from where I entered and took their seats in the chairs next to where I had been playing. Lesser introduced them. Each took my hand and greeted me by my first name. They seemed like nice, everyday guys. I reminded myself that they too had once stood in my place and endured this same exhaustive examination. In fact, for all intents and purposes, they were undergoing scrutiny now. Da Costa may have been concentrating on Bass Trombone, but he'd hear First, Second, and Tuba as well. It was in no one's interest to elicit anything but the best from any candidate on Bass.

Strassman sounded his B-flat for me to tune. I blew several B-flats softly, listening carefully to match the pitches. I had no doubt the committee was examining me even then. If I settled on a B-flat that was even slightly removed in pitch from Strassman's, regardless of how well I adjusted with my slide later when playing, I was cooked.

(Or was I just being paranoid?)

Finally, I played one that seemed right on. Taking a deep breath, I nodded I was ready.

Lesser nodded brusquely. "Brahms First," he announced.

Now if someone were to tell me that the first excerpt I was going to play with the section was this one, I would say, great. Let's do it. I had played the piece in concert three times; I played the excerpt well in the preliminaries. It held no demons.

Well, guess what. All of a sudden, I wasn't sure how loudly or heavily to attack the first A in the chorale. Honest. Something that simple, and I was unsure how to proceed, knowing that I possibly could be accepted or rejected on the basis of how balanced and in tune that first chord sounded. It could have been a terrible quandary, but for the fact that Lesser was going to conduct us. I had to be alert for his downbeat so there was no time to fret.

His downbeat came. Almost without thinking, I responded with a solid but smooth attack on the A. We held the note for two beats, during which time I could hear Strassman's high A just a bit louder than I anticipated. The pitch, thank God, was right on. As subtly as I could, I increased my volume to match the lead until our sounds were very much alike. I had prepared myself to blend with this section by listening to a few of their recordings, but hearing a recording is not the same as playing. When the low C arrived, I placed it firmly, perhaps with a bit more impact than Dave would have advised, but it seemed to fit the style of the Detroit section. By the time we reached the last chord, the sound was full and resonant, yet peaceful. I tell you: I liked the way the Detroit section played with such a unified warm sound that glowed over a big orchestra without cutting. I doubt Glenn Savage would have approved; I could also see why Lucien Boudreau, and perhaps even Sal Terranova, didn't get this far.

"Could you play out a little more?" I heard from the seats. It was

Da Costa. Being American, he spoke without a foreign accent, but there was every evidence that the singsong affect of his voice was cultivated. "It's a very nice sound. Very nice. But a little more, please, and just as round. I want as firm a foundation to this chorale as I can get without it being too loud."

This request surprised me. I thought I had balanced perfectly. Apparently, I was wrong. We played the chorale again. This time it sounded a tiny bit heavy to me, but Da Costa looked pleased.

Next, was the broad trombone recapitulation of the main theme near the end of *Scheherazade.* Here the tenors take the top octave and the bass trombone and tuba the bottom. The tuba player, Bill Steinberg, would join us for this excerpt. (There is no tuba in the Brahms.) I was curious how he would affect my sense of balance.

By this time, I was not surprised to find that Steinberg was a "big" player who pushed my volume. This opening to *Scheherazade* was most imposing, and I would have been shocked if Da Costa wasn't happy with it.

"Very good, Mr. Lawton," I heard from the seats again. This time it was a committee member. "Could you play it a little broader?"

Really? I always thought of myself as a broad, round player. Obviously, I was going to have to make some conceptual adjustments if I got this job. Not that that was a problem. The issue was making these adjustments before I ended up *not* getting the job, as in while I was still auditioning.

Scheherazade again. When Lesser nodded approval, we moved on to a work that was not on the list: the big trombone interlude chords from Janacek's Sinfonietta, one of the most dramatic moments in a very dramatic piece. The sound had to ring out resplendently, with the accent on ring, and the changes in the 2/4 bars from eighth note to dotted quarters had to be made exactly together. Remembering the Brahms, I was sure to put a little more weight on my bottom part.

"Good," observed Lesser. "But I want to hear a bit more accent on the downbeats." I nodded. This was not good. I suddenly realized that Strassman had been playing as Lesser asked and for some inexplicable reason, I had not matched him. Chastened, I adjusted for the next attempt.

"Fine. Better," said Lesser.

Beethoven Nine was next, not the solo, but the fugal section near the end. This would be the first excerpt where the trombones did not play rhythmically together. Strassman entered first, on alto trombone, with his high D firmly and a bit more lightly placed than before. I was the last to step in, which gave me a good opportunity to hear how Strassman and Murphy phrased the half note-quarter note rhythm of the 6/4 bars. Only a fool would do anything but imitate them exactly. When we finished, Da Costa was half way up to the stage. "Two things," he began as he approached me. "I want a lighter texture here. You too, Corey," this to the Second Trombone. (It was interesting that he picked out Murphy, the only member of the section he had not hired. Did that mean anything? Who knows?) "A little less," he went on. "Not so much accent on the half notes where they're followed by quarters. And in that measure where the quarter is tied to the half, be very precise where you place the quarter note B after that."

Up until now, I did not mind all these instructions, but here I was puzzled and a bit irritated. The things he mentioned were things I had made it a point to do. What exactly was he asking for? I assumed he wanted things lighter this time because Strassman was playing an alto trombone. Or maybe it was because it was Beethoven. I stole a glance sideways at my colleagues, but no hint of explanation was forthcoming from them.

We played the passage once more, this time with Da Costa conducting. When we finished, I could not tell if he was more satisfied or not. He said nothing and returned to his seat.

Lesser called for the next excerpt, the opening to the finale of Tchaikovsky Four. The tempo was unusually slow. This was no problem, and when we got to my solo downward scales starting on A and E-flat, I projected them cleanly with a big sound. This time, I caught the maestro in a nod of approval. Finally got one right.

By now, I wasn't sure what to think as to how things were going. I knew conductors and committees put candidates through their paces, but I couldn't tell if what was happening here was testing or correcting. That made me nervous, especially when I didn't always pick up from Lesser's conducting everything he said he wanted. Either I was impervious, not used to his direction, or he wasn't clear or expressive enough. We moved through two more excerpts: Tchaikovsky's *1812 Overture* and the *grandioso* part of the finale from Elgar's *Enigma Variations.* In the Tchaikovsky, Lesser played around with tempo and dynamics and asked for different balances. Here I didn't get the impression he was being critical, just curious as to what I could do. The Elgar presents a different problem for the bass trombonist. Here, the tenors play a chorale-like march under which the bass articulates downward, dotted eighth-sixteenth note scales that sound almost out of place. Anything but the most accurate rhythm, and they *do* sound out of place. When we finished, Lesser smiled. "Good," he said and sounded as if he meant it. I thought it was good, too, and I was beginning to feel more comfortable following him.

"Two more," the conductor said, smiling again.

The Schumann *Rhenish* went as well as I thought it would. Lesser played with tempos and balances, but always it sounded good. Again, Strassman was playing an alto trombone, and I lightened my sound just a bit while maintaining volume, especially in the solo lines.

Finally, the Bruckner Eighth finale I heard Jessica Reynolds play earlier. By this time, I knew what was expected from me in literature of this kind. The bass trombone sound had to almost, but not quite, growl, yet at the same time be heavenly smooth and sonorous. Jessica had done this well. I dared do no less.

It was just right. We played it once, and it sounded as if there were no Heaven—on earth or anywhere else—that could have refused admission to this low brass section. If ever I felt I was going to fit in with this orchestra it was after the third and last passage of the Bruckner was over. It was just one big sound, enormous and powerful, and much of the reason it sounded so good was the guy on bass trombone.

"Thank you, Mr. Lawton," Lesser said when it was over. I could tell by his now friendlier manner that he was impressed. "Very nice playing."

Strassman gave me his hand. "Nice job, Greg," he said as if he meant it. Murphy and Steinberg were equally complimentary.

I floated two feet off the floor back to my case. There may have been an uncertainty here and there, but I solved them. All in all, I had given the Detroit Philharmonic my best shot.

Jessica Reynolds and Don Wilson were the only ones in the waiting area when I returned. Just the two of them, and one more upstairs playing. I was that close to joining this orchestra.

Though Don and I knew each other, we talked little. He didn't seem nervous, just resigned to waiting. For him, it was a question of someone deciding that for once no one else had played better than he. Jessica Reynolds seemed completely out of place. Had I not heard her in the Bruckner, I'd have said she was out of the picture, but . . .

Gulasarian reappeared in about a half-hour, meaning he had played no more nor less than I. "They'll be down in a few minutes," he informed us in that businesslike tone of voice of his, as he very carefully returned his horn to his case. Gulasarian was the consummate professional, a man who always wore suits to these things as he did now: a man who *had* a job already and was just looking around for something better—or different. I was glad I didn't take Gulasarian into such strong account earlier. I might have found that calm, assured bearing intimidating. I had a feeling that if I didn't win Detroit, he would.

I have to tell you that the forty minutes the four of us sat in that backstage room were the longest single period I had spent at any audition. Even the hour or two before a preliminary, when you sit around, practice, talk, concentrate, whatever, was a pleasant idyll in comparison. Before an audition, you haven't done anything. It's all ahead of you; anything can happen. Once you play the finals, it's all behind you. Everything is different. Suddenly, you can do nothing more. Your fate is no longer in your hands. It's all over, in the books. You can't take anything back. Even your euphoria about making the finals is gone, replaced by the realization that if you don't win it all, everything that went before was meaningless. Jane was right. Making the finals does mean nothing. Did you get the job? That's the only thing that counts. Winning *is* the only thing.

As I sat there, I studied the countenances of Richard Gulasarian and Don Wilson. Their expressions were markedly different. Wilson didn't look too happy. I wasn't sure if it was because he was jaded from getting this far so often, or because he didn't play his usual very well. If I had to guess, I'd say it was the latter. But Gulasarian. What was it Joe had said about him? That he wondered why the guy even took this audition? He would have expected him to be pointing for something higher up the ladder? But Gulasarian did take the audition. Maybe he was tired of being overseas and wanted to come home, in which case Detroit would do him very well until something better came along. All I knew was Gulasarian was sitting back, his legs crossed, staring into space as if he hadn't a care in the world, looking quite satisfied. Either he's got this thing made, or he doesn't care.

"Do they usually take this long?" The questioner who broke the heavy silence was Jessica Reynolds.

Gulasarian shrugged. "I waited like this for two hours, once," he informed her. His dark eyebrows lifted slightly behind his brown-rimmed glasses. "Other times it's ten minutes. Who knows?" Gulasarian's stare returned to space, but not before his tone of voice had given him away. He was a lot more nervous than he wanted us to believe. Why? Because he really *did* want this job and wasn't sure he had played well enough to get it? Or was it that he had played very well and was now worrying that one of us—*which one?* I wonder—may have played just a bit better? Now I had no idea what was up with him.

I didn't want Gulasarian to win the job. If it wasn't going to be me, let it be Wilson. At least that would create an opening in Phoenix. If Gulasarian (or Reynolds, for that matter) won, nothing new would be created because it was hard for Americans to get auditions in Europe these days, and Reynolds had no orchestra job.

One thing about Jessica Reynolds's question: it broke the ice. What followed was small talk—to be honest, I can't remember about what, but I do know you wouldn't be interested. I know I wasn't. But it passed the time.

Ten more minutes went by. Either Da Costa and the committee had taken a long break, or they were split on their choice. Usually, this is of no consequence, since it is the conductor who makes the decision, sometimes with strong, nearly equal input from the principal, albeit after committee input, but every orchestra does things differently. Perhaps Da Costa was presiding over a split committee and didn't want to act unilaterally without movement below. Maybe he and Strassman were the ones who were split. Or maybe he just couldn't make up his mind. Whatever the case, the wait was nerve-racking. Was Gulasarian telling the truth when he said he once waited two hours for a decision? How did he stand it?

Eventually, you tire of small talk. Your mind drifts. Despite your resolve not to do so because of its inherent futility, you play every note of your audition over in your mind. That glitch in the Hindemith *Symphonic Metamorphosis* during the semifinals. Did they remember that? Was it still bothering them? Jesus, it was just two notes. All those times I had to balance a little more in the finals: had they cost me? I knew the finals are where they push applicants to see how flexible and resourceful they are, but was that what was going on in my case, or were they really uncomfortable with what I was doing?

Was I even one of the ones over whom they were split?

Frankly, the only good thing about all this agonizing was it kept my mind off my uncertainties about Jane.

Suddenly, the normally collected Don Wilson began to pace around. "This is getting ridiculous," he muttered. "I really don't want to stay over because they can't make up their damn minds." His mouth froze as soon as he heard what he said. He could have been just as concerned about catching his plane if he won this thing, but something in his tone told me that wasn't the case. No. Don Wilson was just hanging around, playing out the string, a dreamer, like some duffer in the preliminaries who cracked two notes in the *Till* run and two more in *William Tell* but is staying around in case the committee happened to be overwhelmed with his tone in the Brahms First.

I may not have finished first or even second, but something told me I finished no lower than third.

"Me neither." This was Reynolds again, referring now to her own plane reservation. She too did not think she had won this thing. "Do they ever have people play again?" she asked.

"Sometimes," Wilson replied.

Gulasarian said nothing.

Suddenly, three figures appeared from around the corner. Two were Malcolm Strassman and Corey Murphy. The third was a tall dark-haired woman I didn't recognize. She turned out to be Carol Wolcott, the personnel manager.

The entire room held its collective breath. This was it.

This time there was no ceremonial about the fine audition we played. "Will Mr. Gulasarian come with me?" The speaker was Carol Wolcott, and that was all she said.

Maybe they were going to inform the runners-up first, like in the Miss America contest.

No. Ms. Wolcott was smiling . . . at Richard Gulasarian. Now he was smiling, too. Two questions answered at once.

As Wolcott and Gulasarian walked down the hall, Strassman came straight for me and motioned for me to accompany him down the hall. Murphy approached Wilson and asked Jessica Reynolds to join them.

It was time for post audition counseling.

"You finished a very close second," Strassman informed me softly. A crisp looking man, just under six feet, in his late forties, Strassman was graying, and his wire-rimmed glasses were probably thicker than the ones he wore a decade ago. Still, his was a strapping figure that appeared not to have added much poundage in middle age. Though informally dressed, his clothes were tasteful with every fold tucked in. He looked more like an accountant than a musician. Strassman had been in Detroit a long time. At one point, he was a *wunderkind,* thought capable of rising to the absolute top if he kept the fire in his belly burning hot enough. As it turned out, he took one more audition after arriving in Detroit, barely missing in the finals, then stopped looking. Either the fire had gone out, or he realized the Detroit Philharmonic was a terrific orchestra that had been fortunate enough to have a string of good conductors. (They even made some excellent recordings.) The orchestra may have lacked the glitz of the so called "Big Five" (or Ten or whatever the number was), but that appellation can be misleading. In any case, Strassman was doing very well, and obviously, that was enough for him. "The committee was split evenly," he was telling me. His eyes and a five o'clock shadow added that he was very tired. "Normally, the final decision is the maestro's with strong input from me as the principal, but the committee's opinion is important too, and when it's split, everything takes longer." He shrugged. "Even the maestro was torn by this one. In the end, the choice was made as much on intangibles and instinct as anything we could put our fingers on. Some thought Mr.

Gulasarian's sound matched ours just a bit more. There was also a sense that he was more experienced, judging from how flexibly he adjusted to our style."

"Without having to be told," I concluded. Some of what Strassman had just said came off as mumbo-jumbo, but there was no misinterpreting him on this point.

Strassman nodded. There was a sad look in his eyes, and I wasn't sure where it was coming from. It was clear, however, that, mumbo-jumbo or not, he was selecting his words very carefully. "Have you ever made the finals before, Greg?" he asked.

I shook my head, no.

"Good. I mean, well, I made two finals before landing this job. Each time, I thought the next time would be it, but it turned out that when that next time came, I still had something to learn about the repertoire and about auditioning."

"Until that third time," I put in.

Strassman smiled. "Exactly." He drew closer. "Believe me when I tell you: your time will come, as well. Just keep doing what you've been doing."

I thanked him. There were a lot of things I wanted to ask him. At the same time, I struggled to beat back the stupid impulse to tell him Gulasarian probably wasn't going to hang around Detroit long. But of course, everybody who made an orchestra like this one had the New York Philharmonic or the Philadelphia Orchestra in mind, so there was nothing unusual about Gulasarian. "One thing," I said.

"Sure."

"Is there anything I should be working on? Anything, that if I did it, would have put me over?"

Strassman put his hand to his chin. His fingers began to rub against the stubble on his face as if he was unaccustomed to going this long without a shave. He thought a moment before responding. "I really think it was a matter of experience," he said, measuring his words carefully. "Mr. Gulasarian has simply played more concerts. He was in two good orchestras in Europe full time, you know. You were so close in every other way. If I had to say something about your playing, it would be more in your approach to auditioning. I'd suggest playing a little stronger at the outset and defining your attacks more, but this is really nitpicking. Another orchestra might say exactly the opposite. You can drive yourself crazy worrying about it. When it comes down to it, you're good. You have the sound and the style. You're going to make it if you keep playing like you did for us. I'd almost bet on it." He held out his hand. When I took it, he gripped mine harder than I expected. "Nice job, Greg," he said warmly. "Good luck to you."

"Thank you."

Before he walked away, Strassman gave me a last lingering, and dare I say it, disappointed look.

And that's when the real cause of Strassman's difficulty became clear. Detroit's principal trombonist was trying very hard to be diplomatic. When Strassman said that as principal trombone he had considerable input to the final decision, he was understating the case. In most orchestras, the principal player is the second most important person an auditioner has to please, and in this case, I *had* pleased that second most important personage. Unfortunately, Gulasarian had pleased *numero uno*. In a word, the conductor and his principal trombone were split: the man listening and directing, Da Costa, preferred Gulasarian; the man who actually had to *play* with the new bass trombonist, Strassman, preferred me. No wonder there was such a delay. Da Costa knew his First Trombone was not getting the bass trombonist he wanted. Whatever time was consumed sorting that out was probably spent on assuaging Strassman's feelings.

Too bad. *Too . . . damned . . . bad.*

The most frustrating part of this whole business is, depending on the kind of person Strassman was, Gulasarian could end up wishing he never got the job. These conductor-principal splits are not healthy. Unless it is for a principal position, once an audition is over, the conductor usually moves on, and the section leader becomes the new player's most important person. As Carl O'Leary found out, it's not easy playing with a principal who doesn't like you . . . regardless of what the conductor thinks, especially during your probationary period. Gulasarian could be moving on sooner than he thinks. And it would serve him right.

If you think I'm just being bitter . . . well, you're damn right. I am bitter. You have no idea how frustrating this is. The worst part of it all is that I'm probably wrong. Richard Gulasarian is a much better player than Carl O'Leary, and Malcolm Strassman seems a much more decent sort than notoriously nasty Burt Davey. There's not going to be a Rochester Symphony scene in Detroit. If Gulasarian leaves, it's going to be because he was lured by the bigger money of one of the "Big Five" orchestras. And don't be so sure he will leave, either. From everything I've seen, this Detroit Philharmonic is a pretty classy operation. The peripatetic Gulasarian may just have found a home—even if he doesn't know it yet.

Why didn't the bastard stay in Europe?

I was so close.

Damn, I wanted that job! Damn!

The final amenities were soon disposed of. We finalists said goodbye to each other and congratulated a gracious Richard Gulasarian who, relieved of uncertainty, was sincerely wishing that we would all soon come to know the happiness he was experiencing. Jessica, looking far less nervous, and even rather pretty all of a sudden, was very pleasant. Realizing from Strassman's taking me aside that I was the runner-up, she made it a point to shake my hand and congratulate me for playing so well. Her grip was more powerful than I expected, and a little stimulating. I looked into her newly sparkling blue eyes and did my best to be cordial in return. There was something about her ample lips and high cheekbones that was enticing, and, I noticed with a touch of guilt, she had more of a figure than Jane.

Jessica seemed in no particular hurry to leave my presence, and I wasn't sure I wanted her to. I suddenly felt so empty. How would Jane take my failure? Not like Jessica Reynolds, I feared. Jessica understood these things in a way Jane never could. Maybe I *was* a fool to date only non-musicians. Jessica was young, but suddenly, she seemed not only prettier than before, but older. There was something challenging—and inviting—about the way she looked into my eyes.

I hadn't noticed at first, but we had been walking together and were soon separated from the others and standing near the elevator.

"There's a coffee shop downstairs, off the lobby," she said. "Are you up for one before you go back?"

Her invitation caught me by surprise, but I had no reason to refuse. Usually, I want to get away from the scene of the crime after an audition, but this time I had to talk to someone. Normally, that someone would be Jane, and I would have called her. But Jane wouldn't understand. And Jessica Reynolds would. "Sure," I replied.

We made small talk on the way down to the lobby and to the coffee shop. I don't remember what was said, only that I was beset by a sea of fantasy and emotions, the most prominent of which was that I was doing something wrong but exciting.

The coffee shop was part of the Detroit arts complex. From the pictures of musicians on its walls, it was a pre- and after-concert hangout. We took a booth in the back. The light was slightly dim, but not so much that I couldn't see a slight flush in her cheeks. I conjured this picture of conducting a long-distance affair with a twist. I lived in Boston. Jessica told me she was from LA. We'd meet at auditions. If today is March 23, this must be Cincinnati.

After we ordered coffee, our conversation drifted naturally to recapping our respective auditions. I was surprised to discover—though I shouldn't have been—that Jessica believed she had done very well. "You know, I actually thought I won. I was so nervous, waiting there, waiting to hear," she admitted. So much for why she appeared so pale after she played. I liked it better when I assumed she had snuck into the finals, did her best when she got there, fell back to earth, and had turned pale from disappointment and relief that it was all over.

We could rehash excerpts only for so long before we moved on to orchestra gossip. I could never talk like this with Jane—not about the music business, anyway. It didn't hurt that I was the one who had subbed in the Boston Symphony, who had been to many of these auditions, and who finished second in this one. I was in control for a change, and it felt good.

But not for long. First, I learned that Detroit was not Jessica's first finals. She had made two others with smaller orchestras I didn't audition for. She actually won San Diego, but it suspended operations the year she was to start and had yet to reorganize. I was growing uncomfortable with what I was learning, so I asked her how she found freelancing in Los Angeles.

"Difficult at first," she replied, "but now I'm breaking through with some good gigs. I'm even getting some studio work. It's not orchestra playing, but I may soon be making a living at it until an orchestra comes along." Clearly, I wasn't in control for long.

As we talked, I found myself studying her more closely. If she noticed, she didn't say so. If anything, I had the impression she was studying me. Suddenly, I noticed that she was looking absently across the room. She seemed to be thinking of something. Then she turned back to me. "Have you heard about Houston?" she asked.

"Jack Mellanby?" I returned, referring to the bass trombonist in that orchestra. The name alone was sufficient shorthand.

She nodded slowly, as if we were discussing a grave secret. "Yes. He was planning to come back next year, but now he's wavering."

"I've heard that before. He's always talking about retiring."

"Yes. But I have a friend in the orchestra who says he's serious this time. According to her, the only reason he's hung on this long is his wife."

"His wife? From what I've heard, they don't get along."

"Exactly. They're getting divorced. My friend says he stayed in the orchestra to get out of the house."

This startled me. Not the news, so much as Jessica was more plugged in than I was. "We'll know soon enough," I acknowledged, hiding my discomfiture. "The ad should be out soon, if it's for real."

She nodded. "I'll see you there, if it is," she replied.

"I guess so."

"Oh. Good." I thought I saw a speck of disappointment at the downturn of her lip. Not everyone would have seen it. I did because I was disappointed, too. I'm always disappointed when formidable competition shows up at an audition.

We talked a bit more. Everything was pleasant, collegial, but my hotel-trotting fantasies had burst like soap bubbles. Jessica and I had things in common, all right. The most significant was that we wanted the same job. Jessica was no longer a potential lover—if she ever was. She was competition, and you don't sleep with the enemy.

I glanced at my watch.

"Got to go?" she asked.

"Yes."

"Me, too."

I called for the check. She insisted on paying for hers. We settled up and left the restaurant.

"See you in Houston," she said when we were outside. She took my hand one last time and squeezed it softly.

"Unless I get out of the business," I laughed. "Or you become top call in Hollywood and make too much money to quit," I added, hoping my words sounded light and not hopeful.

"I doubt either of those things will happen," she returned. She pointed to the row of taxis down the street. "Want to share a cab to the airport?" she asked.

I shook my head. "I have to return to my hotel first," I said.

She didn't look disappointed. I know I wasn't.

We said good-bye, and I watched her walk down the street. She had a sexy walk. The memory of her touch on my hand lingered, but it was too late for that.

My God. Sal, Vanderkelen, Schmidt, Joe, Don Wilson. And now Harris Mackowski.

But the most dangerous of them all may be Jessica Reynolds.

New players. Unknowns soon to become knowns. Like cockroaches, they just keep coming.

I pulled out my cell.

DEAR JANE

"They say I finished second by a hair."

"Oh. . . . I'm sorry. Or congratulations. I'm never sure what I'm supposed to say at times like these."

"Either is okay. They both apply."

Silence.

"Jane?"

"Yes, Greg."

"Are you all right?"

"Of course."

Silence.

"Are *we* all right?"

Silence.

"Jane?"

"Yes."

"Yes, what?"

"It's all right, Greg. *We're* all right."

Silence. "Greg?"

"What?"

"I'm sorry about last night. The way I talked. I must admit I was frustrated with all this, but that was no time . . ."

"I love you, Jane." I interrupted her before I realized I was even thinking the words. It was the first time I spoke them.

". . . I wanted to call you today, but, you fool, your phone was off. You never told me what hotel you were staying in. Detroit's such a big city. I should have called them all. . . ."

"Jane, it's all right. I'm sorry about the phone. I didn't want it ringing while I was playing. I was afraid I'd forget, so I turned it off when I got to the hall."

"I felt so terrible." I could tell by the sob in her voice that she was crying.

"I love you, Jane," I said firmly.

"I love you, Greg. Please have a safe trip home, and I'll meet you at the airport. Then we'll . . ."

I don't remember the rest.

For the first time that day, I smiled.

DREAM DATE

Edgar Vogel often had dreams about women. They were pleasant little dreams with images that lingered like delicious scents of perfume, but they faded quickly, leaving only a satisfying glow to remind him they occurred. They were nothing to worry about, he would assure himself upon waking as he glanced fondly at his wife lying next to him. Dreams about other women were normal for a forty-five year old monogamous man married for twenty-four years, no matter how much he loved his wife.

That was until he started dreaming, not once but several times, about a girl he had taken out a single time in high school. In the dream, she was young, as was he. They would meet, talk, do things together, and experiment with sex as if they had been doing those things all their lives. The dreams grew more real and erotic with each occurrence, and the girl's image did not fade when he woke up. A warm glance at his wife's lush form next to him did not erase their effect, nor did a soft caress on her hips or a kiss on her cheek. He would climb out of bed, eat breakfast, go to work . . . and the girl's image remained as enticing as when he was asleep.

In the minds of the sophisticates who made up the male student body at Pittsburgh's Littleton High, Gretchenanne Kinderhaben was an oddball. She had that strange first name and mispronounced-more-often-than-not surname (to which she would respond in the pedantic manner of a strictly raised, adult-like child, "Kinderhä'ben"). She wore straight, figure hiding skirts and blouses that made her appear uncomfortably older. She was tall, gangly and awkward, as teenagers who haven't totally developed often are. Her lips were full, but usually they were stretched into a serious expression that made them appear as thin as the rest of her. Her most promising features were her long dark hair and sad, slightly off-focus, brown eyes.

Bright and studious, she had few girl friends and no boy friends. She was nice, though, and, in her formidable-unformidable way, approachable. He had noticed her staring at him in Latin class more than once. Good thing, too, for Edgar Vogel, a shy and unpopular young man himself, was in desperate need of a date for his junior prom. Gretchenanne was not one of your more comely girls, but she was not without her attractions, and there was something intriguing about her eyes that drew him to her. More importantly, he was sure she was available. So he asked her. And she accepted.

To Edgar's surprise, they had a terrific time together. Conversation was no problem: both liked music and books, and there were several teachers about whom they could compare notes. When she talked to him with her voice low and sensuous, her dark eyes poured into his, while her fingers fluttered along his wrist, begging him to take her hand, which he did. With her head resting on his shoulder, they danced closely through all the slow numbers, while agreeing to skip the fast ones. None of this was particularly erotic. They explored each other with the innocence of children.

The only thing that spoiled the evening for Edgar was the scornful looks of the "popular" kids and the "look-at-yech-Edgar-with-yech-Gretchenanne" stares that caused him to pull back from her gentle pressure. Soon, though, the heady brew of dancing and slow music formed a cocoon about them. Her scent filled his nostrils, intoxicating him to the point that, as they danced toward the end of the evening, he could not prevent himself from whispering into her ear, "Maybe we can go out again sometime."

Gretchenanne pressed against him and squeezed his hand: "Sure." Her voice choked against his shoulder.

A sudden chill ran along his arms at her response, and he felt a flush on his cheeks. He wasn't sure what was bothering him, and there was no time for rumination. The hour was late, and they had to meet his father for a ride home. As they walked hand in hand out of the gym, discussing their next date—it would be to a movie that had just arrived in town—his anxiety increased. During the ride home, he conversed loudly with his father without saying a word to his date, as he desperately bought time to sort through his emotions.

If Gretchenanne realized she was getting the cold shoulder, she never let on. After Edgar walked her to her doorstep, she paused and gazed up at him, her eyes closed and her breathing coming in quick animal-like gasps. When he tentatively placed his hands on her shoulders, she stepped closer and lifted her lips. Their mouths touched, but at the moment when he should have been feeling the tingle of his first kiss, the scornful stares of the guys at the dance interrupted, robbing him of all sensation, save that of an overpowering urge to get away from her. As soon as the kiss was over, he disengaged himself and bid her good night. Oblivious to his change in mood, she said she was looking forward to seeing him again. Her words barely brushed against his ears as he escaped into the night.

Edgar was disappointed in the kiss, though its failure was hardly her fault. Gretchenanne was nice, and she liked him, but the evening was a mistake. Given his tenuous social position, he should never have asked out someone so unpopular, and he certainly shouldn't have asked her out again. Still, he might have gone through with the date, had "the guys" not ribbed him so mercilessly the next day about taking Gretchenanne Kinderhaben to the prom. It took three days of avoiding the poor girl before he summoned the courage to phone her with an excuse to break their date. Gretchenanne offered no resistance. By this time she knew something was wrong and was expecting such a call. He was relieved at her lack of reaction and never realized how long she cried after hanging up the phone.

Once he had gotten rid of her, he wasn't sure he had done the right thing. They *did* have a good time at the dance, and he liked her. As for the kiss, maybe it would have been better the next time. A spark gleamed in his heart before it was immediately doused by the standards of normalcy and peer pressure that controlled teenagers in the American Fifties. He never spoke to Gretchenanne again.

So why, twenty-nine years later, was he having erotic dreams about her?

*   *   *

One night, while making love to his wife, he saw Gretchenanne's face on his pillow and nearly called out her name. Afterwards, too shaken to sleep, he slipped out of bed and headed down to the cellar in search of Gretchenanne's picture in an old high school yearbook. It was time to confront her likeness. Steeling himself against seeing her portrait for the first time in twenty-nine years, he found the old volume and leafed briskly through the pages. Sexually drained as he was, one look at her teenage image should put things in perspective.

Instead, a hot surge swept through his body when he saw her likeness. Gretchenanne looked exactly as he remembered, but through the eyes of maturity, she appeared not awkward but dusky and mysterious, almost exotic. Her quizzical dark eyes were not unfocused but instead were sad and provocative. He stared at her picture for several minutes, terribly disoriented and vexed by his desire for this strange woman from his past. Finally, he staggered upstairs to bed. Better that than fall asleep on the basement couch and have Virginia find him in the morning with a yearbook on his chest.

He was too weary to dream that night, but Gretchenanne invaded his sleep the next night. This time the images were more sexual, and their lovemaking proceeded to just short of intercourse. He awoke in a cold sweat and reached for his wife who responded by mumbling softly in her sleep. Normally, her presence beside him was reassuring. This time he felt a cold chill at the touch of her body, and his hand recoiled.

That morning he reexamined Gretchenanne's picture, hoping daylight would restore his equilibrium. It did not. Her dark eyes poured into his, as if the photo were alive. Shaken, he slammed the yearbook shut, determined never to pick it up again. It was a promise he kept for two days. On the third, he leafed through the yearbook furiously, like a man desperate to end starvation.

*   *   *

That afternoon, he called Littleton High. He wasn't going to contact Gretchenanne, he told himself. He just wanted to know where she was living. The school kept no such records, but the secretary gave him the name of the representative of his class reunion committee. "She might have that information," the woman told him.

Edgar nearly choked. He remembered the popular Joan Flagle too well—almost as well as the boys in her crowd who taunted him in gym class for being too skinny, too pale, too awkward and all the other "too"s that were the bane of skinny, pale, awkward teenagers. He'd wonder what they told her about him. Judging from the occasional odd look she flashed him in the halls, it was nothing good.

In a way, he was glad it was Joan Flagle he would have to call. If he was uncomfortable in Joan's presence back then, there was damn little chance he would make a fool of himself now by calling her for a girl's address, especially when the girl was Gretchenanne Kinderhaben. Bringing Gretchenanne and himself together in Joan's mind was too humiliating to imagine.

That was it, then. End of the line. Over. Finished. And not a moment too soon for his sanity. He shoved Joan Flagle's number into his desk, slammed the drawer, and returned to work.

Three days later, he had another dream about Gretchenanne. It was the most heated one yet.

He would call Joan from his office, but only after his secretary had gone home. He was taking no chances on being caught. The wait was excruciating. Eight hours passed with all the celerity of a snail crawling up the side of a fish tank. When finally it turned five, and his secretary was safely gone, he locked the door. His hands shaking so hard he had to start over three times, he dialed Joan's number. When it started ringing, he leaned back in his swivel chair, swung his legs on top of his desk, and did his best to effect an attitude of ease and relaxation. He was still worried someone might burst in and catch him.

He promised he would hang up after five rings. Joan Flagle picked up in four. To his astonishment, she remembered him quite affably. For several minutes, they exchanged the courtesies of people who had a place and time in common many years ago but no longer. Soon, he felt comfortable enough to get down to business.

"Yes, Gretchenanne is listed," she told him. She read him Gretchenanne's home address and that of an antique store she owned. There was no derision in her voice. She didn't even ask him why he was looking for Gretchenanne. "I hope that helps," Joan said pleasantly. "If you reach her, say hello for me."

"I will."

"And take care of yourself, Edgar. If you ever get back to Pittsburgh, look me up. I always like to hear from the old gang."

He promised, flabbergasted at how quickly the strata that people cling to in high school are eradicated in adulthood. *The old gang!* He would have enjoyed that little irony, but for the chills running up and down his spine. How dramatically the stakes had just increased. Gretchenanne Kinderhaben, high school memory and picture in a yearbook, was now Gretchenanne Kinderhaben, antique dealer, of Rutland, Vermont.

Vermont. That was two thousand miles from his Denver home. There was no way he would travel to Vermont to fulfill a foolish fantasy. This truly was the end of it.

*   *   *

That evening Edgar was home at the desk in his study, poring over some figures. He looked calm, but inside he was shaking. He and Virginia had just finished a squabble that he had started—and meant to start. His boys were not home for supper, and he was angry because he did not want to eat alone with his wife. Why wasn't he told the boys weren't coming home, he demanded. How dare she not keep him informed of things going on in his own household.

"Mark and Raymond did tell you, Edgar," a stunned Virginia Vogel explained. "This morning at breakfast."

"They did?!"

"Yaiah." The twangy "yaiah" was a remnant of her Australian accent. "Maybe you ought to listen once in a while. You've been a million miles away lately, I don't mind telling you."

"I have?" He tried to sound surprised.

"Yaiah. You have."

"Well, then, I'm sorry." But he wasn't. "Don't you think you could stop saying 'yaiah' like that all the time? It gets on my nerves."

Virginia stared at him, speechless. Edgar had never said anything like that before. Her egalitarian husband was the last person to criticize someone about her accent. Instead of contending with him on the spot, however, Virginia refused to reply. A bright thoughtful person, she was not one to act impulsively. Something was wrong with Edgar, but Virginia Vogel would take no action until she knew what it was.

It was fortunate she had no idea what her husband was thinking at that moment.

He wished she were thinner, though Virginia had gained no weight since their marriage. Sturdy, broad across the shoulders, and almost as tall as her six-foot husband, she was hardly fat. Handsome, statuesque, voluptuous were more accurate descriptors.

He wished she were younger. It was true: the lines in her face betrayed her entry into her fifth decade, but Virginia's light brown, medium-length hair and bright blue eyes minimized the evidence so well that she continued to arouse the admiration of younger male acquaintances.

He wished she'd stop saying "yaiah." It was driving him crazy.

At the end of the meal, Edgar complained again about the boys not being home for supper. When Virginia repeated her observation of his not paying attention, he grumbled about how pressing his financial consulting job was compared to Virginia's work as a public school librarian.

"Now that's not faiah!" Virginia's accent had faded over the years, but when she was angry, as she was now, it became much stronger. "You said you loved the financial business. It was your choice. Don't complain because you're stuck with it now." She slammed her fork on the table so hard it bounced up and nearly hit Edgar in the shoulder. "Listen to me, Edgar Vogel," she commanded once she was sure the fork had missed him. "Very little of what's gone on since you've come home has made sense. Obviously, you're spoiling for a fight. Fine. If a fight is what you want, you'll have one. Only please tell me what we're fighting *about*. You owe me that much at least."

Edgar was satisfied. He had succeeded in making his wife furious with him. Instead of answering her question, he felt justified in storming out of the kitchen to his study.

"Thanks for a wonderful meal," she called out, just before the study door slammed behind him.

But she did not leave him alone for long. Something serious was troubling her normally even-keeled husband, and she was too staunch a woman to allow him to face it by himself. She granted him a few moments of solitude by taking her time piling the dishes into the dishwasher. Then she headed for the study.

At first, he denied anything was wrong, but Virginia wasn't buying that, so he decided to appease her. "There is the Welles account," he began. . . . He hoped it was enough for her to let it go. Edgar hated deceiving his wife, but if she pursued the matter, he would have no choice.

She did not. Not that she was satisfied. Work never upset him like this before. This was more serious than she thought. More cautious than ever, Virginia again decided to leave the room and let him cool off.

After she was gone, Edgar glanced fitfully about the room. Having achieved solitude, he wanted somebody to talk to. He picked up the phone and made several calls. As he talked, he scribbled down some words and figures on the pad next to the phone. They were the same figures he was studying earlier. He pored over them now until he memorized the schedule and fare of every flight from Denver to Boston. He wasn't planning a trip, mind you. He was just going through the motions . . . to see . . . to see what it felt like. Once he had all the data memorized, he tore the incriminating paper into tiny scraps.

By the time he climbed into bed that night, he was tired and eager for sleep. Perhaps he would dream of Gretchenanne again, a prospect he welcomed with equal portions of anticipation and guilt. The only problem was that his wife was in the bathroom rustling about. He wondered what was keeping her.

He found out moments later when she emerged in the pink nightgown he liked so much, the one whose frilly bodice dropped halfway down her ample breasts, its sheer fabric revealing a hint of broad dark nipples beneath. He always wished she would wear this particular garment more often, but, wise in the ways of men, Virginia wore it only occasionally, and so it never failed to arouse him. She smiled broadly as she approached the bed, confident that no matter what the trouble, the nightgown would work its magic.

Edgar's heart sank. Not tonight of all nights. He wanted to get to sleep, and his disapproving frown did the trick by immediately dampening Virginia's lusty smile.

As humiliated as she was once full of desire, she angrily climbed into bed, turned her back to her husband and switched off the light. Only habit and reluctance to make a bad situation worse kept her from storming out of the room and sleeping on the couch downstairs.

Virginia fell asleep immediately. She was a strong woman who recovered from adversity quickly. She would find out what it was that was troubling her husband and do something about it—even if it meant dealing with another woman. There was no need to stay up all night fretting. Virginia slept, if not peacefully, then certainly well.

Her husband's was the sleep of the haunted.

Breakfast the next morning saw a renewal of the tensions displayed the previous evening. Rarely did either Vogel reject the other's sexual overtures, and never with the disapproval Edgar displayed. He felt remorseful, and not just because he had denied her. When he finally managed to fall asleep, he dreamed of making love to Gretchenanne, just as he had hoped. Only this time when he awoke, he didn't reach for Virginia to obtain relief. Instead, his passions burning, he snuck into the bathroom like a guilt-ridden teenager.

Now Virginia was prodding him, trying to find out what was bothering him. She did it gently, patiently, her voice soft, but still she was irritating him.

Wordlessly, he looked up at her in near disgust. The "yaiah"s, her . . . *size* . . . she seemed so . . . *big*. The large breasts. She talked so much and wouldn't stop asking what was wrong.

How could he tell her he wanted her out of his sight?

He could bear it no longer. His skin crawling with anxiety, he waited for her to disappear into the living room, and then dashed out of the house.

On his way to the airport, he stopped to telephone his secretary with instructions to tell his wife he was called away on business—not an unusual occurrence in his job. When he hung up, his groin tingled with the typically male sensation that accompanies doing something outrageous and dangerous. He did not call Vermont. He did not check to see if Joan Flagle's information about Gretchenanne Kinderhaben was current. All he did was pray he could get a ticket on the first flight to Boston.

*   *   *

Until the events outlined above, Edgar Vogel had no reason to doubt he loved his wife. Virginia was bright, strong, and outgoing; she made friends more easily than he and was his link to their community. She was hard working and, like her husband, an incessant reader. (They met in their college library.) Virginia shared herself with the joy of a child giving an ice cream party. Her friends were fascinated with her. Some wondered what she saw in a husband of such contrasting character, but that was unfair to Edgar, whose aloofness was rooted in a lifelong difficulty expressing emotion. He had "looked around" and flirted occasionally during his marriage (he rejected two opportunities for affairs early on), but he believed his behavior was normal for a man who had been monogamous as long as he had. As far as Edgar knew and felt, his marriage was a happy one.

Now, after four hours in the air and four more on the back roads of New Hampshire and Vermont—an area familiar from his college years at Boston University—he wasn't so sure. How happy could he have been if he was driving into the outskirts of Rutland, Vermont in passionate search of a woman he had not laid eyes upon since high school?

Just after he passed the "Welcome to Rutland" sign, he spotted a small rundown diner on the left side of the road. A Public Telephone sign was posted above the front door. His heart pounding, he pulled into the diner's parking lot.

It occurred to him that he could still turn back with no harm done. As he walked toward the diner, he promised himself that if the phone was in use, he would turn back.

The phone was free. All right. If Gretchenanne didn't answer after three rings, he would hang up and turn back. There was no answer at Gretchenanne's house. Undaunted, he tried Clandestine Candles,

Gretchenanne's antique store. Three rings at Clandestine Candles and he'd hang up, then.

A female voice answered on the fifth.

He opened his mouth to speak, but no words came out.

Had he decided to go no further? Had he lost his nerve?

Neither was the case. Edgar was merely reconsidering his strategy. Once he welcomed the shielding properties of the telephone when making first contact with a girl. Now there could be an advantage in confronting Gretchenanne in person without warning. The receiver chanted "Hello" three more times, but he had already decided to hang up and proceed into town.

He was almost to the diner's front door when he stopped abruptly. Had he done the right thing? He glanced back at the phone, still unused. The entire diner was nearly unused. He stood fitfully still a moment longer. It didn't seem right to come upon Gretchenanne in person after hanging up on her like a teenager. Not at his age. He returned to dial the number again.

This time the "Hello" sounded irritated.

He felt foolish. "Gretchenanne? Gretchenanne Kinderhaben?"

"Yes?" She didn't sound caught off guard by his use of the name Kinderhaben. Why had he not asked Joan Flagle if Gretchenanne was married?

"Gretchenanne? This is Edgar Vogel." He was about to continue, "Do you remember me?" but she cut him off with a sharp gasp.

"Edgar Vogel!? . . . From Littleton High? My God!" The line went silent. "Is it really you?"

"Yes," laughing nervously. "It's me. Of that, I'm quite sure."

He could hear her breathing unevenly through the earpiece. "Where are you?" she inquired. The excitement in her voice had changed into wariness.

"In Rutland. Actually, just outside."

"In Rutland?!" she echoed. "What are you doing here?"

"I'm here to see you."

"My God!" The receiver turned quiet. Not even the sound of breathing came through the holes in the earpiece.

"Gretchenanne? Are you still there?"

"Yes. I'm still here. But I don't . . . Why do you want to see me?"
She sounded even more suspicious than before.

"I don't know. I just do. Is that . . . is that all right with you?" He
had never considered that she might refuse to see him.

"I don't know. . . . No. . . . Yes." Her voice was nearly inaudible. "I
guess it's all right. Though I don't know whatever for."

"Good. I have your address. I can be there in a few minutes."

"No!" Her voice was so sharp he had to yank the phone from his
ear. She sounded like a different person, but only for an instant before
she continued in her normal tone: "Not at my house. Here. At the
store. In . . . in an hour." She gave him directions.

"Why an hour?" he inquired when she finished.

"Because that's what I said. In an hour. No sooner. At the store.
Or not at all!"

"All right," he agreed hastily. "An hour."

She hung up without saying goodbye.

It was done, then. There would be no more talk about turning
back. Indeed, having spoken to her, his impatience to see her mounted
with each swirl of his coffee spoon. The diner's shopworn character
and the equally tired-looking neighborhood made it a tough place to
hang around, but he was unable to move. As if it would make any difference. He had always found Rutland depressing. A partially rundown mill town, the city seemed better suited to crabby, hard-hearted
New Hampshire than Vermont.

He wondered why Gretchenanne settled in Rutland. What would
she say to him? In his dream, she was sixteen years old. What had
twenty-nine years done to her? He imagined her to be quite thin, gaunt
even, and past a brief physical prime, nothing like her fantasy image.
And what of her reaction to him? She remembered him quickly
enough. Could she have been carrying a torch all these years?

In an hour he would know everything.

*   *   *

Clandestine Candles was located in a better-kept part of the city on
the edge of downtown. The shop was housed in typically old New

England clapboard with peeling white paint and a large front window that displayed an array of antiques and pottery. Edgar was studying the building from across the narrow street hoping to catch sight of Gretchenanne through the front window. A last-minute fit of irresolution had made him more nervous than ever in his life: he was about to "see" the first woman other than his wife in twenty-four years. When it was clear that Gretchenanne's image might never appear in the window before dark, he took a deep breath and crossed the road, pausing for a last fruitless glance through the front window before entering the shop.

The light inside was dim. His first sense of the surroundings was that of smell—the air pleasantly aromatic with wood, varnish and dust—but when his eyes adjusted, he saw old furniture everywhere: tables side by side from the front of the store thirty feet to the back, with every ancient design of chair imaginable set around them. Along the walls stood stacks of bookshelves—some covered with glass, others open—filled with dusty rows of hardcover volumes. Boxes of old magazines lay scattered about the floor. Three corners of the room were occupied by grandfather clocks whose out of step ticking lent an air of disquietude to the place. No one appeared to be about. He was about to call out, when he noticed a chain next to the front door, like one of those old butler cords he had seen in the movies. He pulled and waited.

Moments later a woman entered from a back door hidden in the shadows. Even in the faint light, he could see she was tall, dark—gangly, of course—yet curiously graceful, with black, slightly graying hair pulled along the sides of her head from where it flowed softly to her shoulders. Though not beautiful in the strict sense of the word, she was not past her prime, either. Time had filled out her once-thin body with an appealingly slender form her youth never promised. She embodied a strong physical contrast to Edgar's wife: darker, not quite as tall, with a slimmer figure and delicate, angular features that spoke more of Southern Europe than Virginia's Northern European ancestry. She was dressed more sleekly as well, in a black, lightly clinging dress. The neckline dropped low enough to reveal a hint of cleavage, and the hem stopped at the knee. Such accouterment was not worn to sell antiques but to stop hearts, and a jolt of excitement stronger than anything he felt looking at her yearbook picture surged through his body.

As she moved closer to him, he was struck by the fullness of her lips. They were not stretched thin by a serious expression but were blooming with a broad smile. "Good evening, Edgar," she greeted him, sounding and looking much more poised than on the phone. "Welcome to my shop. It's wonderful to see you again." Her voice was very soft compared to Virginia's.

He gazed at her, stunned—her relaxed air, the gracious reception, the soft voice, and the fetching dress combining to render him nearly speechless. "Gretchenanne," he finally managed to utter. His mouth was dry and unyielding.

She held out her hand, which he shook weakly. However taken aback she might have been an hour ago, she was in control now.

"Y–You . . . you look very nice," he stammered. "Is that why I had to wait an hour? So you could change?"

Taking no offense at his awkward question, she swept her right hand across the front of her dress. "It's certainly nicer than a sweatshirt and jeans," she said.

"Yes it is," he mumbled. Talking about her appearance made him feel uncomfortable so he changed the subject. "Clandestine Candles?"

She caught his drift immediately. "A strange name," she acknowledged. "I didn't choose it. This store has existed since the Colonial period, though it's been restored since. It's known as Clandestine Candles because it was a candle shop and the site of spy operations against the British during the Revolution."

"Interesting."

"It is, actually." She stepped toward him, eyeing her visitor curiously. "But you didn't come here for a history lesson." She looked even more striking up close. "What *did* you come here for?"

"I . . . I'm not sure."

"Oh? I hope you didn't come very far, then."

"Actually, I did. Denver."

She whistled softly at a very low pitch. "All the way from Denver, and you don't know why," she said teasingly. "That sounds very strange, Edgar. Or very romantic."

"I had to see you, that's all. I'm not sure I understand why myself."

"Well, I certainly don't. It's not as if I were an old flame of yours.

We had one date thirty years ago in high school. That's not a whole lot to build a romantic obsession on."

Suddenly, her appearance seemed like a safe topic after all.

"That's quite a nice dress," he said.

"Yes. . . . So you said before."

"I–I know. I just didn't expect . . ." He lapsed into silence.

"Did you come here to stare at me?"

"I'm not sure. I mean, no. I wanted to see you. Talk, I guess. I hadn't imagined we'd have a . . . a . . ."

"Date?"

"Yes."

"I see," she replied, drawing out the "eee" like a detective mulling over a mystery. "Even now, the word 'date' scares you."

"No, no, no," he interrupted. "A date is fine. A date is terrific, actually. It's just more than I expected."

"Obviously. Well, this is the Eighties. We women can take the initiative now and then."

"Gretchenanne, I'm sorry about what happened back then. I . . ."

She cut him off with a wave of her hand. "Think nothing of it. You don't have to apologize. Besides it was a long time ago."

"But I want to tell you . . ."

"Tell me what?" she interrupted. "That you came all this way to exorcize your guilt over the terrible wrong you did me? I hope that's not it, Edgar, because if it is, your trip wasn't necessary. I managed to get over that little trauma many years ago. I was hoping for something more kinky."

He shook his head vigorously. "No. That's not it at all. N–Not that I don't feel some guilt, I mean, but . . . kinky?"

"Why *have* you come, Edgar?" She was stern all of a sudden.

"To see you, to . . ." Battered by the dual assault of her glamour and boldness, he foundered, with no idea how to proceed.

Sensing she had pushed him as far as she could, she let him off the hook. "Well, you've come all this way," she declared, the lines on her delicate forehead softening, "and as you said, I'm *dressed*, so let's not waste the effort."

"You have something in mind?"

"I know a place I'd like to go, if that's what you mean." She reached for her purse that was lying behind the counter. "For the moment, I want to keep it a surprise, but if you're game, I'll take you there and see how you like it."

"A surprise?"

"Yes. For now. Are you willing?"

He shrugged. "Why not?"

They took his car. When he asked where they were headed, she told him Burlington. "It's not that far," she said in response to his upraised eyebrow. "Besides, it's a pretty ride."

That he knew to be true. On this journey, though, scenery took a back seat to the disturbing presence of the woman beside him, her dress gradually hiking above her knees, revealing legs that were slender, long, and fetching. He found himself sneaking glances at them more often than discretion dictated. He gulped audibly.

"You really don't know why you've come all the way up here, do you?" she said after several miles of Route 7 had passed in silence. She smiled and lifted her hand. He thought she was about to lay it softly on his, and he held his breath in dreaded anticipation, but she replaced it innocently on her lap. "This *is* kinky," she added huskily.

"I wish you wouldn't use that word," his eyes now straight ahead on the road.

"Why not? Because it's accurate?"

"No. It's just that . . . I don't know why."

"All right. I won't use it any more. I'll change the subject. Are you married, Edgar?"

Her question threw him, though he was expecting it some time. "Yes," he admitted before he had a chance to lie.

"For how long?"

"Twenty-four years."

"Any children?"

"Two sons."

"Does your wife know where you are?"

He gulped again. "No."

"What did you tell her? That you were going on a business trip?"

"Essentially."

It was her turn to swallow deeply. "I'm married, too. Twenty years and two daughters. My husband's name is Mark. And he doesn't know where I am, either. That's why I had you meet me at the shop rather than the house."

His mouth went dry again. "So we're partners . . . in whatever crime we're participating in." The words were light, but their tone was quite dark. They lapsed into silence, but, finding stillness more unnerving than conversation, the "conspirators" decided to fill each other in on what they had done with their lives after high school.

Gretchenanne had left Pittsburgh for college at the University of Chicago. Finding big city life oppressive she abandoned Chicago after graduation for Burlington, where she attended graduate school at the University of Vermont. There she met her husband, who was finishing medical school. The move to Rutland occurred when he inherited the practice of his old family doctor a year later. Several years after that, when their two daughters were in school, she bought the antique store.

Edgar had just finished running through his own life, when they entered the motel-lined outskirts of Burlington. He had not looked forward to driving that far but now was glad he did. He had always liked Burlington. It was a small city, but a refreshingly liberal and cosmopolitan one, much more pleasant than Rutland.

Gretchenanne directed him to College Avenue at the center of the city. There he parked the car and followed her to a small vegetarian/Asian restaurant. The place looked unpromising from the outside, but the interior was dark and woody, a slightly exotic version of her antique store. He nodded approvingly. It was the kind of place he never found in Denver.

After ordering, they faced each other with the second silence of the evening, giving him plenty of time to study her. Gretchenanne had become a confident, almost serene, woman, obviously at home in crusty New England. Her eyes were as dark as he remembered them—sad, even, as before, too—yet at the same time, they exuded a strength that reminded him of the stone walls that wended their way through the New England countryside. How out of place she must have been in Chicago! Just as she was in high school.

High school. Thoughts of back then rushed over him. Would he have run from her had she looked as provocative and appealing as she did now? He couldn't imagine doing so, no matter what "the guys" thought. He found himself staring at her low neckline which revealed more than a hint of her small breasts. He had no doubt she knew what she was showing and that he was looking, but he couldn't help himself. He found them so breathtakingly attractive. How he could be so drawn to Gretchenanne, and have married someone so different from her?

Just then, their orders arrived. The doughnuts he ate at the diner were still with him, so he wasn't as hungry as he should have been, but the vegetable/seitan mixture in peanut sauce was unusual and enticing.

Most of the meal passed in silence. Edgar was nervous, and Gretchenanne, sensing this, left him alone. He thought of Virginia and wondered if he would ever see his wife again. All of a sudden, that bothered him. He was seized by an urge to stand up, pay the check, and take Gretchenanne back to Rutland, but the fit passed. The idea of ending his evening with Gretchenanne upset him even more than the thought of not seeing Virginia, and the vision of his wife faded from his mind.

Gretchenanne glanced at her watch. "A few more minutes," she informed him, raising a napkin to her mouth. This business about a "surprise" was beginning to annoy him. She took his right hand in both of hers, squeezed it tightly, and stared dreamily into his eyes. Her hand was lighter and more fragile than his wife's and her touch more delicate. The feeling of it upon his was far more suggestive than that of the awkward high school girl he remembered. He wanted to kiss her, but before he could move, her eyes turned somber, and the lids fluttered nervously. She released his hand as quickly as she had taken it, darting away from him like a moth that had skittered closer to the flame than she had intended.

The waiter came with the check.

On the street, Gretchenanne put her arm in his and led him down College Avenue. Downtown Burlington was teeming with activity, and the high spirits percolating around them blended with Gretchenanne's scent, intoxicating even in the open air, to markedly lift his spirits. He chided himself for worrying whether he'd see his wife again. He was about to embark upon an affair. Fine. People had affairs every day, and they didn't all end up in divorce court. Why should he? And what if he did? What if he and Gretchenanne sought to resume what should never have ended?

All this thinking was making him dizzy. Her scent, her touch on his arm, the way she seemed so comfortable with him and took the lead in a manner he never would have thought possible. . . . It was too heady to contemplate. Better just to relax and enjoy. . . .

Gretchenanne interrupted his reverie by tugging on his arm and pointing to a movie theater across the street.

"We're going to the movies?" he inquired.

She nodded.

He glanced at the marquee: *Two Robert Mitchum Hits: Cape Fear and Night of the Hunter.* A Mitchum revival. He shrugged. Why Mitchum?

She caught the gesture. "You don't remember?" she sounded disappointed.

"Remember what?"

"*The Night of the Hunter.* That was the movie we were to see on the date you broke."

He whistled in amazement. "You knew this was playing?"

"I saw it in the paper this morning. I didn't think anything of it at the time, though I remembered what it was. Then when you called . . ." She twisted a few stray strands of her hair between her fingers. "I don't usually believe in omens, but if there ever was a reason to make an exception, this was it. Besides, they tell me it's a marvelous picture, and I never had the heart to see it. Have you?"

He had. Twenty years ago, in the theater. And since on television. Saying so made him feel like a heel.

She dropped her arm from his. "Then it's time I did too," she declared. She retook his arm and led him inside the theater.

The Night of the Hunter, an expressionistic black and white film and the only movie directed by Charles Laughton, was one of his favorite motion pictures. Under normal circumstances, he would have relished seeing it again, but the coincidence of its showing on this night was disturbing. The air in the theater suddenly seemed chilly. Those dreams. He had never given a thought . . . Now he could not help but wonder. . . . Where had they come from?

They chose a row near the back right corner of the theater. He was

about to ask Gretchenanne if she had been employing some sort of te-
lepathy on him, when the theater lights dimmed, lending a golden am-
bience to her slightly Mediterranean profile. All he could do was stare
at her as she gazed straight ahead, seemingly unmindful of his rapt attention, until the theater finally darkened. Even then, the aura around
Gretchenanne remained. Edgar shook his head in bewilderment that
approached distress. He was no longer sure he could believe in the in-
tegrity of what he was seeing or the elective nature of any action he
was taking. Best now to watch the movie and get hold of himself.

He could not, of course. By the time the robber Peter Graves had
told Mitchum about the money he stole, Edgar was interested neither in
the movie nor the question of whether he was or was not in control of
circumstances. All he could think of was holding Gretchenanne's hand.
Her hands were lying next to each other, one on each of her thighs.

*Grab her hand and get it over with, or sneak up slowly, square inch of flesh by
square inch?*

He looked up with a start. Since when does a forty-five year old
man find it so difficult to take a woman's hand in the movies!? Certainly, it wasn't his wife who held him back. He could barely picture
Virginia by this time. Nor was he hindered by lack of practice. It was as
if he had regressed into the awkward teenager he was long ago.

When Mitchum was playing up to Graves's widow, Shelley Winters, he found the courage to reach for Gretchenanne's hand. Another
eternity passed. At last, she folded her long, warm fingers within his
and squeezed firmly. He sighed with relief and rising excitement. He
wanted to settle for this contact and concentrate on Mitchum's phony
Bible reading that duped Winters's self-righteous old neighbor, but his
hormones gave him no quarter: all he could think of was putting his
arm around Gretchenanne's shoulder. Again, astonishment at his awk-
wardness. And again, desire overcame his reserve. Proceeding slowly,
he snuck his arm across her back, pausing a moment before placing it
around her slim shoulders. This time she moved closer to him, her
warm cheek so near his own that he could feel its radiated heat. The
most crucial event of all was now upon him, and it was not until the
children's pilgrimage down the river that he dared take the step. This
would be it. Once he kissed Gretchenanne, there was no turning back.

And kissing her was all he could think of doing. Drunken by her near-ness, her touch, her scent, his eyes removed themselves from the screen as if by their own will and turned toward her. He leaned toward her, then halted—might she pull away from him even now? She was still staring at the screen, after all. But nothing she had done indicated she would do anything of the sort. Finally, he moved his lips close to hers. Her head turned to face his. Their lips moved forward and touched, at first very softly, then more firmly. Then much more firmly. His mind turned white. This was not like the kiss that misfired thirty years ago at all. This one was exciting and involving. They moved their lips against each other for what seemed like hours until at last, her mouth opened.

They continued to alternately neck and watch for the rest of the movie, not like adults, but as the sexually inexperienced teenagers they once were, curiously, passionately, gently stoking their frustrations, rousing but not fulfilling their desires, as if thirty years of adult matur-ity had gone for naught. He was too inhibited to undo a few buttons on her dress in the public theater, though it was dark and they were sit-ting in the back. He settled for kissing above the neck and stroking her small breasts, feeling the hard nipples under her blouse and bra until the film was over, and the children were safe with Lillian Gish. The an-ticipation of sexual fulfillment was both delicious and unbearable.

When the movie ended, he was jolted by the absence of its light and sound. He pulled away from Gretchenanne, but only for a moment be-fore leaning forward to kiss her again. This time she pushed him away, but he had no time for disappointment. "I know a motel," she whis-pered urgently into his ear. Understanding immediately, he stood up, and scrambled to follow her out of the theater to his car. Before he could start the engine, however, she had slid across the seat and was nearly on top of him. They began necking more furiously than they had dared in the theater, their hands wandering frantically all over each other.

"No!" he heard himself barking, his breath coming in snarling gasps. "Not here! The motel! How far away is it? How far?"

"Only a few blocks," she replied breathlessly, and, truth to tell, in frustration. "Only a few minutes away."

He started the engine.

By the time they arrived at the motel, he had only marginally managed to steady himself in the brisk night air. Putting themselves together as best as they could, he registered as Mr. and Mrs. Edgar Mitchum—not very good aliases, but the letters seemed to inscribe themselves on the card. He paid the bill with cash. Fortunately, they looked like a staid, middle-aged married couple, albeit a slightly disheveled one, perhaps on a second honeymoon, so there were no questions or suspicious looks.

Once in their room, the sensation of being a hapless teenager disappeared. Without hesitating, he took her in his arms and crushed her to him. His first impression was how delicate and incredibly feminine she felt pressed against his chest; he feared he would hurt her until he felt her strength when she reached around his neck. They kissed more passionately and more deeply than before. He wanted to move on, but her mouth and tongue wouldn't let go of him, and they continued as if their lips were locked together. Even when he placed one hand on her breast and held it there for several minutes, he never stopped kissing her; nor did he when he reached with his other hand for the buttons on her dress in desperate search of the reward denied him in the theater. At the same time, he felt her fingers tugging furiously on his shirt, but it was her bodice that opened first. Then—his mouth never leaving her lips—he worked the brassiere clasp along her back. At long last, her freed breasts were bare and burning beneath his hands, the nipples hard and willing against his palm. His passion and concentration on her shocked and frightened him. He groped between her legs and somehow managed to pull them both down to the bed. The sounds they were making were guttural and breathless. He hadn't felt this way with a woman in years, if ever.

And then, in less time than it had taken to flip the metal snap on her brassiere, the fervor was gone. Her lips were suddenly cold and clammy, as if someone had spilled a bucket of water on them. He feared he had gone impotent, but impotence is wanting and not being able. He was able. He just didn't want to, and this time, there was no leaving her on the doorstep with empty promises. Stunned by his barrenness and sense of loss, he pulled away gently, hoping his desire would return, and wondering how he would explain it if it did not.

He needn't have worried. As he relaxed his pressure on her body, he could feel her arms loosening around him. He thought she was reacting to his movements. When he looked into her eyes, he expected to see disappointment. Instead, he was met with a dissipation of passion that matched his own. She looked as stunned as he was. It was as if a huge void had opened between them and sucked the feelings out of their bodies.

The two of them sat together numbly on the bed. He stared at her naked breasts, the dress worked down below her waist. She gazed at his chest, which was exposed beneath his open shirt. They remained fixed for a moment, partly in shock, partly in hope that the sight of the other would arouse them again.

But it did not. He was the first to move. She followed immediately after, despair etched into the lines of her forehead. Wordlessly, they dressed.

"After all these years," Gretchenanne broke the stillness with the amazement of a child who realized she didn't want that doll after all.

"In my case, after all these days."

She looked at him curiously, but was too confused to pursue the matter. "Lucky you," she said simply.

He slumped into a chair by the bed board; she took the seat by the television. "What happened?" he wondered aloud.

She shrugged, the movement almost lifting her slender shoulders out of the low-neck dress. "I don't know. It just went. Poof!" The air exhaled sharply from her lungs, and her words hung in the room like tufts of milkweed. She wiped a small tear from beneath her left eye. "Maybe somebody was trying to tell us something."

"Like what?"

"That you were right when you broke it off when you did." She gestured toward the bed. "If this is any indication of what was in store for us, we didn't have much to look forward to."

He shook his head. "I don't believe that. We were a damned inferno. It wasn't lack of attraction that stopped us."

"Then what?" She crossed her legs the slow way she did in the car, but the gesture had no effect on him.

"I don't know. Maybe we just keep meeting at the wrong time."

"Then when is the right time?"

The irritation in her voice disturbed him—maybe it *was* only he who had pulled back. She seemed about to lash out at him, but instead, she gazed down at her lap, distracted for a moment, before her gaze floated around the room. Her eyes seemed removed from the rest of her. When she spoke, the words came from a space not within her, but from somewhere else, as if she were standing aside and listening to herself. "Yes. When *is* the right time?" she murmured. She stared about some more. "For me, it was twenty-nine years ago. When I had such a crush on you even before you asked me to that dance. I was thrilled. I thought things had gone so well that night that I was going to marry you. I was sixteen, but I thought I knew about things like that. I felt so at ease with you. So much seemed right between us. How you held me. How we could talk. How much we had in common. How wonderful I felt when I was with you, walking, drifting, flying. How you kissed me. I couldn't wait to see you again.

"But you never called." She dabbed again at her eye. "Until you broke our date, and then I was heartbroken. I was such a young and foolish girl that I cried for hours. I stared at you in school, hoping your reason was genuine, and that there was hope for us, all the time knowing there was no chance. You made up an excuse. A lie. The only truth was you didn't want to see me any more. And I never knew why. That was the worst part about it. I never knew why."

Her body stiffened, and her voice was her own again. "But that was twenty-nine years ago. It was a brief episode, and I came out of it. I had boyfriends. I got married. I had kids. I grew up, and thank God I did because young girls are very foolish, and I was sick and tired of being foolish."

She stood up and approached him, her bearing stiff, her arms crossed as she stood over him like his stern third grade teacher. "Now you show up, and my stomach is turned upside down again. From the moment I heard your voice on the phone, it was as if the last twenty-nine years never happened. I felt confused, scared and horny as hell—just like I did back then. I couldn't wait to see you. If nothing else, maybe at last I was going to find out what happened. Then you were in my arms, your hand on my breast, and just like that, it was gone. Edgar

Vogel, lost passion of my youth, turned into a man of straw in my arms, and suddenly, all I wanted was to know what the hell he was doing here." Before he could say a word, she grabbed him hard by the shoulders and shook him hard. "What the hell *are* you doing here, Edgar?" she shouted, her voice trembling with anger.

Edgar was jarred by her assault. For a moment, she *was* his stern third grade teacher, and he wanted to bury his head in his desk. But Edgar was no longer in third grade. Gretchenanne had a right to the truth. And so he told her: about the dreams; about how he had no idea what started them; how sexual they were, and how he tried to fight them off before they took over his mind. "Unfortunately, I was more successful asleep than I was awake!" he concluded, trying his best to make light of his confession.

Gretchenanne's face was red. Her shoulders were slumping and shaking, and the once-steady eyes were rapidly dampening with tears. He stood up, but she raised her hand like a traffic cop, halting him in his tracks. "Damn you, Edgar," she cursed, fighting her tears. "All these years I thought I was a fool for wanting someone who didn't want me. And now I find you actually . . ." Her voice shook uncontrollably. She stamped her foot hard upon the floor in her frustration. Her tears were flowing freely now. "I carried a torch, you know. I admit that now. *Damn* you, Edgar! Why did you run away?"

Instead of responding, he began pacing around the room with his hands shoved in his pockets.

"Edgar! Don't you dare walk away from me. Not again! I want to know why you ran." When he stopped pacing, she lowered her voice, and her words tugged at his heart. "Just tell me why. Then you can go," she said, almost sobbing. "Then I *want* you to go."

Edgar longed to tell her. It had been dammed up inside him for so long. He sat down, and the truth poured out from him. "I had a great time with you at that dance, Gretchenanne," he began. "You were the first girl I could talk to who listened to me, and who didn't expect me to perform or have money or a car. You didn't even mind that my father had to drive you home. And I meant it when I asked you out the second time. It's just that some of the guys I wanted to like me ribbed me about you, and when they asked if I was going to see you again, I couldn't help myself. I said I wasn't. It came out so fast. I didn't even realize what I had said at first. But seeing the satisfied looks on their faces, thinking they would be my friends . . . I had so few friends . . . I couldn't go through with it after that." He shook his head. "The guys," he scoffed. The words grated against his ears. "They never became my friends. I can't even remember who they all were. Hell, I can't even recall their names." He wanted to take her in his arms, but the gulf between them seemed as wide as the expanse from Denver to Rutland. "There *was* a spark between us," he confessed, the words catching at his throat. "I snuffed it out." He walked to the window and gazed out into the darkness of the street. "I don't know, Gretchenanne, but twenty-nine years ago, I may have made the biggest mistake of my life."

He looked up quickly. Tears were flowing freely down her cheeks, but there was a hint of a smile about her lips. "I should have known it was something stupid like that," she said wiping at her eyes. "I should never have let you go without a fight. I was just too damned afraid to try. *Damn* it all!" She kicked hard at an imaginary object on the floor.

Edgar walked over and laid a hand softly on her shoulder. "Don't be too hard on yourself. Even if you had tried, it wouldn't have mattered. An aggressive girl in those days? I'd have run like a deer." He dug at the rug with his toe. "Remember what you said about young girls being fools? Well, young boys can be downright asses."

He took her other shoulder and turned her around to face him. His gesture was an invitation to resume where they had left off, but when she shook her head, no, he retreated without protest to his chair.

Gretchenanne wiped the rest of the tears from her cheeks with a tissue. When she was sure no more would flow, she handed him the tissue. "I'm afraid that if there was to be a time for us, Edgar, it was twenty-nine years ago, not now."

"I know." He dabbed the tissue below his own damp right eye. "I just don't understand why. Most people don't get a second chance because they never meet again. But we have. We're alone. We have the opportunity. Yet . . ." He looked about the room, confused and frustrated. "A few minutes ago, I was ready to chuck it all. Virginia, the boys, everything." He threw up his hands in frustration. "I don't get it. What's stopping us?"

Gretchenanne looked up suddenly, her eyes alert. If she were a cat, her ears would be standing up and curling forward. There was something in what he said. . . . And then she smiled. "What's stopping us is twenty-nine years of living. We're not the same people we were back then, Edgar. That's what your dreams were about: to be able to go back in time as the person you are now, and put what you have learned as an adult to work on early-in-life opportunities. Only you can't. None of us can. Because we have acquired baggage in gaining that knowledge.

"You spoke of chucking it all. For me, that means Mark, Clara and Rachel, plus my friends, my home, my store, and the constancy they bring to my life. I say this even though I know my marriage isn't the most thrilling in the world, my daughters are getting older and don't need me like they used to, my friends are as stuck in their ruts as I am in mine, and running an antique store isn't exactly leading an archeological dig. Even though I know there is something more exciting out there than what I have, I can't walk away from my history and the life I made for myself. I'm stuck with what I've become. And I'm afraid, dear sweet Edgar, that despite what you just said (and it was the most wonderful thing you ever said to me), the same is true of you." She chuckled. "Besides, I still love my husband. He's the only person I know who makes me laugh—you certainly don't—and that's important because I don't laugh very much on my own."

He wanted to reply that it was horrible that she was condemning herself—and him—to a life of boredom and unfulfillment, based on habit, misguided loyalties, a warped sense of sacrifice and outdated Judeo-Christian ethics. He wanted to tell her that what she really meant was she was afraid to take a chance and start her life over. He wanted to say that what she called love was habit. He wanted to say all these things, and he would have . . . if she were the only one who needed to hear them. But he was as tied to his history as she was to hers. And he was unable to inflict any more pain on Virginia. She had devoted her adult life to him and had never done a thing to hurt him. He still loved her and the boys. "You neglected to say that we are stuck because we want to be stuck," he observed.

Gretchenanne placed a hand softly on his shoulder. "It's all right to be what we are, Edgar," she said gently, "and to love whom we love."

He took her hand and squeezed it against his face. She slipped her other hand behind his head, ruffled his hair, then released him and stepped back to the middle of the room. Her slender figure stiffened. "Since we're not going to have an affair," she declared, "I'd say it's time we get out of here."

"At this hour?" he protested. The last thing he was looking forward to was the trip back to Rutland, especially when he was so tired.

"We can't stay here."

He was about to suggest separate rooms, but staying would be impractical. What would she tell her husband—now that she was going back to him? "No, I suppose we can't," he conceded.

They arrived at the door simultaneously. Each waited for the other to go first. It was an awkward moment, as if neither wanted to risk touching the other, but she took the initiative, and he followed her into the hall. They discovered a way out of the motel to the parking lot that did not go past the desk.

"The key," she said suddenly, when they were outside.

He reached into his pocket. "I almost forgot."

He thought they might have to confront the desk clerk after all, but the office was dark. Then he noticed a slot in the front door inviting departing guests to deposit their keys. "I guess they're used to this," he muttered as he dropped the key through.

"Have you had an affair before, Edgar?" Gretchenanne asked as they walked to their car

"No."

"Neither have I."

He led her to the passenger door. "Do you know this evening is the most outrageous thing I've ever done in my life?" he asked.

"Me too."

"What does that say about the lives we're leading?"

"That we're satisfied with them."

He shrugged. "Or that we're boring." He unlocked the car door. "And to think there are people who are going to be glad that nothing happened tonight. Like my wife. Only I don't dare tell her. Besides the obvious reason, it's too damned embarrassing. She thinks I'm a stud."

"She *does?!*" Gretchenanne's eyes opened into saucers.

"Yes!"

She started to giggle.

"I don't see what's so funny."

"Oh, but I do." She was grinning. Before he could say another word, she broke out laughing. It was the first time she laughed all night, and once she started, she couldn't hold back. For a moment he was furious, but then his lip too began to quiver. He attempted to stiffen it, but it was like trying to suppress an urge to sneeze. He tried smiling, hoping the upward motion of his lip muscles would deaden the impulse, but the effect was the opposite: the smile grew to a grin, then to a laugh, until finally, he broke out in convulsions that matched hers. They laughed so hard they stumbled against the side of the car and rolled into each other's arms. Finally, they were weeping.

"What kids we still are!" she gasped into his shoulder.

"I thought you said your husband was the only one who could make you laugh," he said through clenched teeth.

"Until tonight, he was," she gasped.

"Well, at least something new has been added to your life."

"We could have said that if I broke a tooth," she said.

The inanity of the remark made him laugh, and for a moment he thought he was going to break out again, but the time for *that* had passed, and he climbed into the car. Gretchenanne suggested stopping at a restaurant down the road. Edgar saw no point in prolonging the trip, but he couldn't deny the wisdom of a little refreshment before the long drive.

They stayed for two hours, lingering over apple pie and several cups of coffee. Their fit of laughter had washed away the tension the way a storm cleanses the air of a hazy summer day. They resumed recounting their lives since high school, this time in greater—and more humorous—detail, describing not only what they did, but how they felt about it. They laughed easily and often, as though the starkness of the events in the motel had passed from their memories.

They continued chatting on the drive back. Both were tired, but the exhilaration over finding someone new to tell about their lives kept them alert. It was as though each was determined to leave something of themselves with the other. The ride was relatively short, but by the time they turned onto her street, they were friends.

Edgar swung the car in front of a large two-story wooden house that stretched back from the road like a ghost in the black New England night. Gretchenanne reached for the door handle, but he grabbed her wrist before she could pull. "No!" he exclaimed, leaping out of the car and walking around to grab her door handle. "I want to walk you to your door."

She hesitated.

"No one's up," he whispered.

She glanced back toward the darkened house, saw he was correct, and relented. Arm in arm, they strolled up her walk. When they reached her porch, he spotted the names Mr. and Mrs. Mark Smith written under a lighted door bell. "Smith? That's your married name?"

"Yes."

"Quite a switch."

"I still go by Kinderhaben most of the time," she replied. "Why give up something so unique?"

"What are you going to tell him?" he asked. "It's so late."

She smiled. "I have friends."

He took her in his arms and kissed her—again struck by how much more delicate she was than his wife. She responded by drawing closer to him, and he was startled and excited when he felt her tongue poke between his lips. He began to regret their hasty departure from the motel, when suddenly, she pulled back. "That shouldn't have happened," she gasped breathlessly.

He shook his head. "Sure it should have. Twenty-nine years ago." He wasn't smiling, for he knew she was right. The burn of that kiss was a warning. What happened back in the motel was not a denial of attraction between them. It was a reprieve to allow them to return to their lives. The truth was that together they were unstable chemical elements whose electrons were craving to combine, if only once. There would be no fighting temptation a second time.

She rummaged in her purse for her key.

"I don't want to leave Virginia," he declared suddenly. The words were out before he had divined their meaning. Then, "Could you leave Mark?" He watched her eyes carefully.

She did not hesitate: "No." Her eyes said she spoke the truth. She found her key, looked back up at him, hesitated, then kissed him softly and lingeringly on the lips. In doing so, she communicated the last bit of her soul to him that she could spare. "Good night, Edgar," she whispered. "I hate the idea that I'll never see you again." In the dim moonlight he could see a tear forming in her right eye just before she yanked open the front door and disappeared into her house.

Though he was very tired, he moved quickly, remaining on her porch no longer than he had twenty-nine years ago. There was no way he could stay in Rutland that night and be sure he would not show up at her antique store the next day. He ran to his car as if pursued by demons from the inky blackness. Boston was three hours away by Interstate. He made it in two-and-a-half.

When he stepped into his motel room, he was exhausted, but eager to see Virginia again—not so much because he missed her, which he did—but because he needed the comfort he felt when they were together. He longed for her generous figure and the way it felt so strong and lush against his own. He wanted to call her and listen to her voice, but it was too late. She would be asleep. Besides, he wanted to see her, not just talk to her. He had a strange urge to buy a good book in the morning, read it on the plane, and tell Virginia about it. Perhaps he could find one about the power of dreams, contrasts, coincidences, missed opportunities, and whether one ever forgets anything or anyone.

He still tingled with desire for Gretchenanne. He would always feel desire for Gretchenanne, and he would always have regrets over not consummating that desire. Sleep would come with difficulty that night and perhaps other nights because of that desire, but it would come, for nothing can stand in the way of love that has been nurtured by the tender ministrations of time.

No dreams of Gretchenanne Kinderhaben haunted his rest that night.

*   *   *

Virginia Vogel had just finished tidying her husband's study. It was not a job she did very often. The study was Edgar's sanctuary, but every once in a while she went through it. She liked to feel his presence there, and he seemed to appreciate her efforts, especially when he returned from trips and needed a place to relax. On this day, her hands worked by rote, for her mind was occupied by other thoughts. Despite what his secretary had told her, she knew this was no business trip he had gone on, and today she would confront him about it, not with hostility, but with her strength.

The last item she picked up was a volume of capsule movie reviews that had been lying open beneath some papers and folders. Despite her distress, she smiled and shook her head as she examined it. Edgar never watched a movie on TV without consulting his movie bible. The last one he saw, they watched together three weeks ago: she forgot the name but recalled it starred Richard Burton. She closed the book and carefully set it in the bookcase, as if it were the most important book in the world, sure it would behave itself. But the volume had a mind of its own, and its pages split apart at the point where they had lain open for three weeks.

When Edgar picked up the book that evening, they would open to a one-paragraph review of *The Night of the Iguana*. He would notice it and recall that it was the last movie he had seen on TV. And then he would catch sight of the review above it, of *The Night of the Hunter*.

TOBY

Brian Griggs was not having a good day. He had reserved his last hours in New York for a vintage classical LP buying binge, but after chasing all over Manhattan, all he had come up with was one dealer who had gone out of business, another who looked like he was about to, and two private sales that were in no danger of ever starting a business. His third private sale address was at an old Eighty-first Street apartment building. It must have been regal in its day, with its plain concrete base and six red brick upper floors, but now it appeared tired in a way that was quite fitting for someone searching for records pressed in the 1950s and 60s. The lobby's dusky golden glow, slight fog in the air, and smell of decades-old tobacco, actually felt like a trip back to the 1960s when he could buy the records new. The old elevator was far less romantic, and Brian could only cling to the hope that there was something to the adage of slow and (more or less) steady wins the race. By the time the car shuddered to a stop at the sixth floor, his return trip down the stairs was assured.

The dingy hall, with its yellowish walls of old paint and slightly dank odor, was far less inviting than the lobby, but he'd been through worse on his vinyl pursuits. His knock on #608 was answered by an elderly, sad-looking woman in her seventies named Mrs. Ellis. She told Brian only that she was recently widowed, the records were her husband's, and little else, but she didn't have to say any more. Veteran collector Griggs knew the rest of her story.

The collection was Mr. Ellis's pride and joy, but since Mrs. Ellis didn't care much for listening to recordings, he was fine with her selling it, though he made her promise to try a private sale before essentially giving it away to a dealer. That was one of his last wishes, and his wife was loathe not to fulfill it, distressed though she was by the notion of strangers pawing through what her husband loved so much. Her slightly irritated manner led Brian to believe that he was not the first record nut to darken her door—no surprise, since private sale ads are blood in the water to sharks swimming about looking for RCA "shaded dogs," Mercury *FR* pressings, Columbia "six eyes," London "bluebacks," and similar fish. It was bad news, however, because it meant that any meat in this collection was probably stripped to the bone. With the collector's hope springing eternal against all odds, Brian followed Mrs. Ellis into a small apartment that was nicely decorated in an old fashioned style with soft chairs, slightly ornate lamps, and a reddish ambiance similar to that of the lobby. The records were arranged in several columns on the living room floor, making them easy to search, but also blocking the entrance to a nearby hall. Brian had to smile. It would be no more than a week before Mrs. Ellis dumped the whole thing on a record store.

"Anything you want you can put on the end of that desk over there," Mrs. Ellis said, pointing to a sturdy piece of furniture on the far side of the room. She then took a seat on the couch next to the desk and picked up a magazine. Brian usually hated it when sellers hung around to watch him, but this sale was bound to be a bust, so he wouldn't be around long enough to care. He dropped to his knees and began pawing through Mr. Ellis's legacy, but he got through no more than a dozen records when four real paws belonging to a beautiful long-haired cat sauntered in to inspect him. He was about to pet the animal, when he heard Mrs. Ellis scurrying up behind him. Muttering an apology, she scooped up her cat, but not before Brian got a good look at the animal's rich dark fur.

"He's a beauty," he said, looking up at her. "Seal-point Himalayan male, right?"

She nodded, a glimmer of surprise in her tired eyes. "You like cats?"

"Yes. I have a Siamese. What's this guy's name?"

"Harvey."

"Nice. Mine's Sybil."

"That's nice, too," she replied as she put Harvey down and shooed him away. Her message was clear. It was grand that she and Brian both liked cats, but the sooner the young man picked out his records and got out of there, the better.

The collection was not terribly large, maybe a thousand records. It contained many fine performances, but to a collector looking for rarities, it seemed ordinary. After making his way through a quarter of the discs, Brian could honestly say he could not remember a single record that had passed before his eyes. By then, his fingers were flying.

Suddenly, about halfway through the collection, he thought he spotted a familiar black background with big pinkish letters. The sight took a moment to register, and he had to flip back through several records to get to the item that had just caught his eye. As he suspected, he had nearly blown by an RCA recording of Rimsky-Korsakov's *Scheherazade* conducted by Fritz Reiner. At first, he thought it was a worthless late pressing, but the cover looked older than that. He picked up the album, pulled the record out of its sleeve, and was surprised to see that it was a mint shaded dog (literally a dog with a reddish shading over it). How did the shark(s) miss that? He looked the record over carefully, thinking it might be a worthless Canadian pressing, but it was American all right, no doubt a *5S* pressing, the most common of the shaded dog *Scheherazades*. He owned two, but there was nothing wrong with picking up a third. A mint *5S* was worth $50 or more—not a bonanza, but something, as long as Mrs. Ellis was not actually charging $50, which she probably was, since her husband had surely told her about his more valuable discs. Brian searched for the pressing stamp in the run-out grooves, but the dim light made it hard to see. He needed to put it under that lamp along the wall, but the last thing he wanted was to show intense interest in the record, since obvious interest can turn into a higher price. A stolen glance over his shoulder revealed that Mrs. Ellis had grown bored and left the room, so he got to his feet quickly and hurried to the lamp. After he got there, a sharp gasp escaped his throat. The sound horrified him—a gasp was worse than a show of interest—but Mrs. Ellis was still nowhere to be seen. He looked again. He was not hallucinating. This was no *5S*. It was a *1S*, the earliest pressing of the Reiner *Scheherazade*. *1S*'s were extremely rare because most phono cartridges of their time of manufacture could not handle their huge grooves, forcing RCA to issue new pressings with smaller, less dynamic-playing grooves. A mint *1S* is worth at least $500. Brian had never even seen one before. Could he afford to buy it?

He returned to the rows of records, inserted the disc back into its cover, and casually set it aside. Mrs. Ellis might be aware of what the record was worth, but she would have to prove it.

From that point on, the collection yielded eighteen valuable RCAs and Mercuries, three Deccas, and five rare Lyritas for a bonanza worth $3,000. Either he was the first shark in these waters, or the previous sharks didn't have the jaws—make that the money—to pay for this prey. Neither did he for that matter, but he would go through the motions anyway. After adding some "everyday" records to keep Mrs. Ellis from spotting a pattern in his selection, he piled his hoped-for booty on the desk and called out that he was finished.

She returned immediately, wiping her hands on an apron.

"How much for these?" he asked, pointing to the pile.

Without responding, the old woman went through the records twice, counting them both times without appearing to take notice of any particular disc. Brian held his breath. Dare he hope that Mr. Ellis had died unexpectedly and failed to alert his wife to the most valuable part of his collection?

For an exasperating moment, Brian thought Mrs. Ellis was going to count the loot a third time. Instead, she reached for a pencil and piece of paper, stared at the ceiling for a moment, apparently calculating, and then began to write. Brian was not in a position to see what she was putting on the paper, but when Mrs. Ellis started erasing things, he felt sick. *She knows exactly how much these records are worth and is just having difficulty adding large numbers.*

Finally satisfied, she picked up the paper, turned in his direction, and without lifting her eyes from her calculations, announced, "You have thirty-five records. That comes to $175. Five dollars a piece."

His reaction was a small, resigned, and much practiced wince. *You drive a hard bargain, Mrs. Ellis,* it said, but all he declared aloud was, "I have cash." He pulled out his wallet and "reluctantly" handed her the money. She accepted it without any apparent interest and tucked it into a small purse.

There were no further amenities. Brian stuffed his booty into his two cloth bags and followed Mrs. Ellis to the door, accompanied by Harvey. After kneeling down to give the cat a quick pet, he said good-bye and added his condolences for the loss of her husband. Her thanks were almost indecipherable, but the expression in her sad eyes as she took one last look at the records in his bag spoke volumes more. Not only was Brian her first customer, he was also her last. Selling off parts of her late husband was just too painful. She would call a dealer and get it over with in one blow.

After the door shut quietly but firmly behind him, Brian fled down the hall almost at a run, half expecting her to rush out of her apartment yelling, "Stop, thief!" He felt guilty for a moment, but only for a moment. He was a bandit, sure, but he did pay five dollars a record, and five dollars was a lot, at least for those "extra" records, which weren't worth two dollars, let alone five. Any other collector would have done the same, and besides, she'd never know what she didn't get. Hell, that dealer she'll call will give her only a quarter a disc for what Brian left behind. *And would that dealer ever choke if he knew what I didn't leave behind!* That thought brought a smile to his face. There were two kinds of people Brian hated: dealers who charge exorbitant prices and collectors who paid them, driving the prices even higher. He beat them both with one clean stroke.

He looked at his watch. If he headed toward Penn Station, he could catch the three o'clock express train back to Boston and be home around seven. He felt like a desperado who would be wise to pass up the Fourth Street sale and get out of town with the loot, but scores like the one he pulled off sometimes run in streaks, and any collector knows that the most important sale is the next one. The express at five would do, so instead of Penn Station, he headed for the Sixth Avenue subway, which took him to Fourteenth Street. There he got off to walk the last ten blocks amid a huge, good-natured crowd bustling on the streets, as Brian bumped from one body to another like a cue ball. Another time, he might have been irritated by the jostling, but not today.

Brian first caught sight of the homeless man while waiting at a light to cross at the corner of Washington Place and Sixth Avenue. The derelict was camped against a building on the other side, slumped over his knees as if drunk, despondent, or asleep. Surrounding him was the usual clutter of knapsacks, open boxes, and junk that marked homeless street settlements. His legs extended far enough across the crowded sidewalk to force people to find an alternate route to get by him, though no one seemed to mind. Next to his knee was a small box, probably to collect coins from an occasional passerby.

Brian used to give money to panhandlers, but that was before he tired of running the obstacle course of beggars in Cambridge's Harvard Square on his way to work. Every day they were there with their hands out. The last straw was when he saw one panhandler passing his paper cup to a replacement as if it were a relay baton. This is s*hift work*, Brian marveled—a job. And a con. Well, Brian Griggs was through paying their wages. The last time he did so, he was taking a woman to lunch and wanted to impress her with his generosity. As the couple watched the grateful indigent stagger down the alley, the young woman chided Brian for wasting his money on a bum who was "only going to drink it up." Her contempt was palpable. Never was his money more ill spent.

There would be no such waste this time. Brian was so eager to get to his sale that he was caught leaning too far forward on the curb while waiting for the red light to change. When the light for the cross traffic turned yellow, he stumbled into the street and was nearly erased by a huge cab. After barely saving himself, he managed enough of a kick start at the green to jump ahead of the crowd. At the opposite curb, he tripped, sending his body lurching forward and twisting downward to the right. Out of the corner of his eye, he caught sight of an orange, foot-long object stretched against the wall behind the man on the sidewalk. When he regained his balance, he saw that it was a cat lying still. He thought it might be dead until he spotted a collar around its neck with a leash attached. Probably asleep, then. The cat was very thin with a bedraggled coat. Its body appeared limp and old. Upon closer inspection, he could see that the homeless man was gaunt, dark-haired and somewhere between thirty-five and fifty. He didn't look very good either. Next to him was a sign that Brian had missed earlier.

Please help Toby and me get something to eat.
Thank you for your generosity.

Neither man nor animal looked as if he had eaten in days. It was a pathetic sight, but Brian's time was limited. The homeless were everywhere, always would be, and cats die in the streets every day. There was nothing he could do but get upset, and what good would that do? So, okay. He stopped and pulled out all his change—thirty-five cents—and deposited it into the box. One more look at the hapless pair, and he headed for business.

This time, his low expectations were met. The sale was a bust. The guy's apartment was a dusty mess, hardly the kind of place you want to take vinyl records from, so Brian plowed through the collection as fast as he could, bought nothing, and fled down the stairs. Even the polluted Manhattan air was better than that guy's apartment. It was disgusting. What kind of fool would waste his time at a sale like that? But then he remembered the Ellis haul that he was carrying in his bags and felt much better. He couldn't complain. And now it was time to go.

He decided to walk up Sixth Avenue, over on Washington Place, then up Seventh Avenue to Penn Station. It was a trek, but it was still a nice day, and he had the time.

The corner of Washington Place and Sixth Avenue loomed ahead. The homeless man and Toby were still there, and the scene was more animated than before. The man was talking to a "customer" who was throwing some coins into the cup, while the orange cat was on his feet and casually looking about. His collar and leash were still attached, but the animal didn't seem to mind. Probably, the restraints weren't even necessary. Man and cat had probably been together a long time. Even so, the scene brought back pictures Brian had seen on the TV news of roadside circuses where people led bears about by leashes, forcing the animals to stand up on their hind legs to lure cash from passing motorists. Brian tried to let the image trigger some anger, but instead, he felt a strange urge to drift closer to the two. There wasn't much money in the cup. His thirty-five cents might have grown to a dollar or so. That corner sure wasn't lucky for them.

He reached into his pocket. There was a lot of traffic noise at the moment, mostly horns, but strangely, all he could hear was the voice of his erstwhile lunch date. *He'll just drink it up or shoot it into his arm.*

Brian stared at the cat. Toby was sad-looking and so thin that Brian could count his ribs. The animal looked old, and there was not a spot of food anywhere. The voice was right.

That's when he knew what he had to do. Instead of dropping money into the cup, Brian would buy cat food.

He set off. There wasn't much time. He probably never was going to make the five o'clock train because of that dumb last sale, but the seven o'clock—the last for the day—was a must. He couldn't afford to run around all afternoon looking for a box of kibble. Two hours ago, he tossed some coins into a cup and walked away with nothing but vinyl on his mind. Now he was chasing a box of cat food for a feline he didn't know and putting his departure from New York at risk in the process.

Brian found boxes of *Purina Cat Chow* and *Meow Mix* in the first store he tried and bought one of each. After impatiently waiting for the unusually slow clerk to take his money, he hurried back to the man and the cat, determined to complete delivery as quickly as possible. He approached them without the hesitation of his first visit and placed the boxes next to the cat, while taking a closer look at the animal that was lying as still as before. Toby was thin and bony, his orange fur was scraggly, and he was old, sick, or both. Brian wished he could do more than just leave a couple of cartons of cat food with a homeless owner, who at that moment was setting the newly acquired boxes aside, away from the cat. The man's thin lips were twisted into a brief weak smile that seemed askew, as if he were simple or off balance. "Thanks," he said in a soft creaky voice.

Brian stepped back quickly as if the man had struck him. He had hoped the guy was merely poor or down on his luck, but that smile told him the man was either a simpleton or nuts. "You're welcome," Brian replied. He felt out of place, the way most people do around an aberrant personality. Maybe he should find a way to set the cat free, but the poor thing wouldn't survive three days on its own in the streets. It probably couldn't even hunt any more. No. He had done what he could. It was time to go.

His stride carried him twenty yards before he slowed to a reluctant halt. Suppose the man sold the cat food for drug money. What about the sneaky way he moved the boxes away from his cat—unopened—as if to keep their scent away from the sleeping animal? Was he going to eat the cat food himself?

Brian had to go back.

He checked his watch. *Damn!* He didn't have *time* for this. The man would think he was crazy, but why should Brian care about that. Who was *he* to judge?

When Brian returned, the homeless man was pouring *Meow Mix* into a bowl, to the obvious pleasure of Toby who was scarfing up the morsels with a gusto Brian didn't think the animal capable of. The man directed a broad toothy grin of delight at Brian, at the same time taking great care that not a single morsel landed on the sidewalk. He looked no saner—or healthier—than before, but there was no mistaking the satisfaction that his cat was getting something to eat. The man's dark almost black eyes were set deep in his long gaunt face; though smiling, they were glassy. His skin was as pasty as his ragged teeth were dark, and his frame was nearly as bony as his cat's. He too, might be sick, but for the moment, he was all delight.

Brian nodded, then knelt to stroke the happily-feeding Toby's head. He couldn't help noticing how bony it felt under his fingers, and how dry and brittle the little guy's fur was in contrast to the firm flesh and clean, soft fur of his own cat. "He's a real nice boy," he said softly.

"Yes he is," the man agreed proudly.

Brian had said the right thing but still felt out of place. He stroked the cat's head a few more times, then stood up and mumbled an awkward, barely audible good-bye.

This time he made it thirty yards before turning back. Poor Toby was not long for this life. He just had to pet the animal one last time, kind of send him off. "This guy will really think I'm nuts," he thought and this time he worried about it.

But the man merely smiled his twisted toothy grin as he looked up at his benefactor. Brian saw understanding in those glassy eyes. Toby was still eating, as Brian knelt and resumed his gentle stroking. Remembering how Sybil often purred loudly while eating, he probed Toby's thin body for the same telltale vibrations, but he felt nothing but sharp ribs, dry skin, and matted fur.

"He hasn't been feeling well, lately," the man said, as if reading Brian's thoughts.

Brian looked into the man's eyes, where he now saw sadness and concern, as if the man knew he would soon be saying good-bye to a dear friend. Brian recalled his earlier thoughts about whether Toby actually needed his collar and leash. He had seen leashed animals who didn't want to be fettered and leashed animals resigned to their tether. Toby was neither. This cat was devoted to his human, and his human was devoted to him. They were family and probably had been for years.

"He threw up this morning," the man informed him.

And he may again. Brian had seen this binge and purge syndrome before with sick and dying cats.

"I bought him some supplements."

Brian didn't understand this last sentence until the man reached into one of his packs for a jar of feline vitamins. Brian was stunned. This poor man, starving himself, but for two doughnuts in a dirty box behind him, had spent some (all?) of his meager funds on a jar of vitamins for his cat! Brian's shame over his earlier suspicions hurt him inside. "He needs more of that stuff," he said, pointing to the cat food, "than those." Thinking this too harsh, he added, "Just make sure he gets enough food, okay?"

The man nodded.

His hand shaking, Brian bent down to pet the still-eating Toby one last time. At the same time, he deposited a ten-dollar bill into the man's cup to an even more enthusiastic "thank you" than before. Then he stepped back for a final look at the two before hurrying down Washington Place. He turned up Seventh Avenue and didn't look back or stop until he reached Charles Street several blocks from where he started. Again, maddening concerns brought him to a halt. *How can two boxes be enough? I should have bought four. How long will two last a cat?* He glanced at his watch. There was just enough time to buy more cat food, bring it to the man and his cat and catch his train. It would be close, but he could do it.

He turned and started back down Seventh Avenue. His heart pounded, and a spasm of anxiety gripped his chest until he stopped and caught himself. It would take a half-hour to buy food and return to the settlement, and during all that time, he would be anxious over what was happening to him. He couldn't bear it any more. Not for that long. This had to stop, and it had to stop now.

He took a deep breath and let the air out slowly. For the first time in a while, he noted he was not alone on the street. There were people everywhere, bustling this way and that, with concerns and anxieties, just like him. There was no reason to act like he was cracking up. There was nothing more he could do for the man or the cat. They were one each of their species in a city teeming with unfortunates just like them. Cats like Toby were starving every day. Besides, it wasn't just food the animal needed. It was medical attention—if it wasn't too late. Was Brian prepared to miss his train so he could spend the rest of the day finding a vet? Was he willing to pay a large bill to restore the poor cat's health—assuming it was possible? Where would his involvement stop? Would it *ever* stop?

At last, the ache in his chest eased. A few deep breaths, and it was gone. He resumed his trek up Seventh Avenue and toward Penn Station. He had done what he could, and promised to do more when he returned home. Maybe call someone in New York about that poor cat. But who? An overfilled (human) shelter that might not take more animals?

The ASPCA?

Oh no. He knew what they would do with an old sick cat like Toby.

Well, someone. He'd think of someone, and he'd call them.

Brian reached Penn Station with plenty of time to find a "train book" in the book store, a thriller, five hundred pages long. He should have read at least two hundred by the time he arrived in Boston, but he read less than fifty. For most of the ride, he stared out the window at the passing Connecticut towns and inlets. Once, he picked up his bag of records and looked through them, fondled each one, and gazed at the covers.

A long time ago, Brian Griggs had carefully constructed his shield against the distress of the outside world, but the stoutest of barriers is sometimes breeched by the unlikeliest of interlopers. Toby was such an interloper. Brian had encountered four beggars during his walk up Seventh Avenue to Penn Station, and he gave money to each. Once he even went into a store for change so he wouldn't leave a grey-haired, stubbly old man empty-handed.

He never did call anyone in New York about Toby. He meant to but forgot. When he returned home, he placed his new records on the "to be listened to shelf" next to a hundred other such discs. They would be forgotten for a while. Some might not see a turntable for years.

The next day, he gave a little money to two familiar faces in Harvard Square. Both recognized him and were surprised. He did the same thing the next day and the next. The day after that, the two men were standing next to each other as Brian approached. As if on cue, they held their cups out at the same time. The coordination of their movements startled and annoyed him, and he quickened his pace.

The two men shrugged. Someone should have told them. Tiny miracles do their work for only a short time and then vanish. What becomes of the remnants they leave behind is the mystery.

THE ALL AMERICAN

1993

I thought I was the only person left in the building. Band practice ended two hours earlier. Jack the custodian left an hour ago. The only reason I was still around was to sort the band parts for the Spring Concert, and I had just finished. All that remained was a quick check to see that the instrument lockers were closed, and I was ready to leave myself.

The February sun sets early in far Northern New York State, where Commanders Corner sits primly on the St. Lawrence River, so I wasn't surprised to find it nearly dark when I stepped into the front lobby. Indeed, it was so dark that I didn't see the woman in the shadows by the athletic display until just before I walked into the brighter expanse of the lobby near the front doors. I was pretty sure I didn't know her, but it was hard to tell in the dim light.

How did she get in there?

A push on the latch of the front glass door answered that question. Jack had forgotten to lock everything up. It wasn't the first time. He was getting old, Jack was. And forgetful. Of course, I could say the same about myself, so I wouldn't be "ratting" Jack out any time soon. Reminding him the next time I saw him would be enough. Who would want to break into Commanders Corner High School?

Which brings me back to our visitor who was so engrossed in the photographs that she seemed unaware of my presence. She appeared to be studying the pictures of ex-Commando football teams, in particular, the portrait of Jason Richards. I felt like a spy, watching her, but given Jason's tragic demise twenty-five years ago, a strange woman gazing at his portrait in the dim northern light of a high school lobby fired both the imagination and the caution of an old band director. In the world of the Commanders Corner Music Department band room, "mystery" means wondering what happened to a missing second flute part. This was something new.

It was silly, I chided myself—a fantasy born of watching too many spy movies in a small northern town. The woman found the front doors open, had no idea the building was closed, stepped inside, and walked into the display. Of course, that doesn't explain why she came to the school in the first place—nor why she was gazing at Jason Richards's portrait with a concentration that suggested she was seeking an answer from it.

Answer to what, I wondered. What happened to him? Or did she know what happened and was wondering why?

By now I had regressed from spy to peeping tom. It was time to reveal myself. "Can I help you?" My voice rang out through the lobby, apparently startling her, because she turned about sharply. My eyes now adjusted to the low light, I could see that she was indeed startled but I don't think frightened. She was a handsome woman in her forties, of medium height, slim, with fashionably coiffed brown hair and a youthful figure that suffered not at all from her simple attire of white blouse, brown slacks, and loafers. The few wrinkles around her eyes spoke more of maturity and depth of character than of aging. Only a hint of sadness around her mouth betrayed that all was not well.

"I guess everything's closed up," she declared with irritation and disappointment. Her direct gaze, the way she planted herself to the floor, and her lack of artifice made me feel as if I were the intruder.

"Yes, it is," I replied. I felt uneasy.

Her eyes fluttered. She looked tired. "I'm sorry," she said. "My name is Katherine Manley. I came all the way from New York City to see Ronald Harris. He is—or was—the band director here. I don't suppose you can tell me where I can find him at this hour."

"Is?—or was the band director?" I repeated. My uneasiness gave way to interest.

"I'm afraid my information is old," she admitted.

"Well, allow me to update it. 'Is' is correct. I'm Ronald Harris."

"You are?" Her tired features lit up with surprise. She was clearly pleased. "Listen, Mr. Harris, I know it's late. I'm sure you're on your way home, but my flight was delayed, and I couldn't get here any sooner. I have something I want to discuss with you. I promise I won't hold you up too long."

I studied her a moment longer. Maybe my fantasies were not so farfetched. She had traveled all the way from New York to see me? When is the last time a stranger said that? "I see no reason why not," trying to sound casual. I gestured toward the hall I had just walked through and beckoned her to follow me.

Instead of taking my lead, she pointed to the picture she had been studying. "Did you know him?" she asked.

"Jason Richards? Not really."

This seemed to unsettle her. "Are you sure?"

"Quite sure. He wasn't in the band program, so I had no reason to know him."

"You *do* know what happened to him," she pressed. "After he left high school, I mean."

"Yes. He killed himself in his senior year at Syracuse. That's why his picture is set off here. That, and the fact that he was second team All-State, the highest any of our football players ever got."

Instead of replying, she pulled a piece of paper out of her purse and handed it to me. It was crumpled and quite old. "If you didn't know him, why is your name written here?" she challenged.

I looked to where she was indicating and gasped.

> *Someday when you're in Commanders Corner, New York, look up Ronald Harris, the band director at the high school there. He can help you understand.*

I looked at her, nonplused.

"Read the rest of it," she said.

It was Jason Richards' suicide note.

"Where did you get this?" I asked, returning the paper to her. My hand shook as if it had been holding a piece of a ghost.

"I found it a week ago when cleaning out my basement. It was such a horrible time when Jason . . . died. Everything about that time is a blur. He must have left this note in my room, and it fell into the box of books where I just found it. It was stuck in there for twenty-five years!" She placed the piece of paper carefully back into her purse.

"You were his girlfriend?"

"Yes." Her lip was trembling slightly; she bit on it like a frightened child. "Mr. Harris. Why did you say you didn't know him, when you obviously did?"

"Because I didn't really know him. We met only once, during the last week of his senior year. He came down to the band room. He had something to tell me, he said. It took him a half-hour, and I never saw him after that."

"Do you have any idea why he told me to see you?" she asked. "It must have had something to do with what he said to you."

I looked into her slightly teary brown eyes. It didn't seem possible that this crisp, seemingly sensible woman was still in love with a dead man from her past.

"Maybe," I muttered almost to myself as I stared at the old piece of paper clutched in her hand. It seemed to be a magnet for my eyes. "I had a suspicion after I heard what happened," I continued, "but . . . now, after . . ." With a bit of an effort, I tore my attention from the letter and re-engaged her. "Look . . . Ms. Manville?"

"Manley," she corrected, "but call me Katherine."

"Katherine." I pointed toward the hall leading to the band room. "Please. Come to my office. I'm not sure if what I have to tell you will clarify that note, but . . . well . . . maybe it will."

She lent me a grateful nod, and we walked silently down the hall I had just exited.

Unlike the band room where the kids rehearse, my office was full of music lying about, two old clarinets, a sousaphone, several bottles of valve oil, two broken music stands, pictures of the brass sections of two orchestras, and—well, let's just say it was a functional mess, not exactly the suite in a New York skyscraper that I suspected my crisp, professional looking companion would be familiar with. Still, it is the place where I engineered an unusually strong music program for this part of the country, so, instead of apologies, I offered her the old leather seat by the window and slipped behind my desk.

After a shove to clear a pile of music away, I began my tale. "As I said, it was during the last week of his senior year. Jason said he had something to tell me. I was surprised since I didn't know the boy other than as a football player, and that wasn't saying much, since I'm not a football fan. I don't even handle the marching band. He must have known this because he made a point of informing me he was going to play football at Syracuse University. There was something very flat in his voice when he said this. He wasn't bragging. He didn't seem excited or even proud. Then he told me a story about something that happened when he was eight years old." I paused a moment. "You know? It's been thirty years since he sat across from me at my desk in the band room. I haven't thought of Jason in at least twenty years. Yet I remember what he told me as if it were last month."

1954

It was to be the first football game Jason would attend in person. His father had been looking forward to that day since his son was born. Syracuse is over a hundred miles south of Commanders Corner, but Jason's father had season's tickets and was used to the trip. To Jason's father, a boy's first football game was a rite of passage. Sit in the grandstands on a brisk fall afternoon and root for SU. His father's father had taken him to *his* first game at the age of eight. The opponent was Colgate then; it would be Colgate for his son Jason's first game, too.

Jason had no idea what to expect. All he knew was that the ride was a long one and that his father's excitement over taking him to a football game was real. Jason found that odd, given he had never been excited by football on television. It seemed to be little more than a lot of men wearing uniforms and funny helmets running back and forth up a field, crashing into each other. "It's not the same on TV," his father explained, as they watched a game a few weeks earlier. "You don't get the atmosphere, the excitement of the crowd on TV. You've got to be there. You'll see."

At that moment, one of the players crashed to the earth and could not get up. He had to be carried off on a stretcher. Jason started to cry.

"He ain't hurt," snapped his father, clearly disgusted with his son's tears. "They wear lots of padding."

Then why did they have to carry him off, the boy wanted to ask but dared not.

Now Jason was on his way to seeing a game in person. He tried to look forward to the experience. His father didn't take him many places because he was working all the time. This football game must be very important to make him and his mother sit in a car for the long Friday night trip from Commanders Corner to Syracuse.

The family arrived late and stayed at Uncle Dan's house. Uncle Dan would be going to the game with them. Anticipation filled the air at breakfast the next morning. "We'll be leaving at noon," his father announced.

"After lunch?" Jason asked his father.

The elder Richards laughed. "Before lunch. None of your mother's lunches today, my boy! We'll eat at the stadium. That's half the fun of football. Hot dogs, soda, beer." He winked at Jason's mother, who looked away, irritated but unwilling to contradict her husband. "No beer for you, Son. Your mother won't have it." Then he winked at the boy. "You know women."

This time it was Jason who turned away. He wished his mother were going to the game, but in his father's words, this was to be a day for "the boys."

Jason was hungry when the three males left his uncle's house, but his father had promised they'd buy hot dogs and soda right after they found their seats. Jason tried to quiet his growling stomach so his father wouldn't hear it.

It was a typical fall day in October. The trees were aflame in reds, oranges and browns. The air snapped with the vigor of a year that knew its best days were behind it but wanted one last shot at glory. Jason's uncle parked several blocks from the stadium, so they had to walk past rows of student houses, following crowds that were flowing in the same direction. Many were college students, but to Jason they were adults, all either chatting or laughing. Jason could not help but feel their excitement and anticipation.

Maybe this wouldn't be so bad after all. He found himself walking faster. "Easy, Son," admonished his father, who had been discussing the game avidly with his uncle. "We'll get there." There was a glint in his father's eyes. Jason slowed down immediately. He had appeared too eager, like a dog pulling at its leash.

As they neared a grey edifice fronted by wide, steep stairs that rose sharply from the street, Jason heard the roar of the crowd inside. He also heard some loud march music. He held tightly to his father's hand—his major source of locomotion against the crowd-surge tugging against him up the stairs. The hand pulled him powerfully along, almost unheeding of its burden, as if its owner were caught in the mass movement upward.

Inside the stadium, the dull roar of the crowd surrounded him. As they walked around the circular structure, he heard the din of two bands playing in opposition, as if trying to drown each other out. People around him were no longer moving in one direction, but were scattering every which-way, up, down, forward, backward, each looking for and eventually finding a place on the concrete slabs that served as "seats."

"Right up here," he heard his father yell over the bedlam. "These are great seats, right on the forty-yard line. See?" he asked pointing to the field. Though the stadium was quite high, their seats were fairly low, so the field wasn't too far away. "There's the hot dog man," his father said, pointing toward a man carrying a big silver box against his chest. Jason's stomach growled in response.

Finally, two adults and child were settled in, each with hot dog and drink in hand. "You can have a sip of beer, Son," his father said, offering him the cup, "but only if you don't tell your mother." Jason knew nothing about beer other than that his mother didn't want him to have any. He felt guilty disobeying her, but better to go against her wishes than his father's. He sipped the drink, barely managing to swallow it without spilling. "More?" his father asked. The boy shook his head. He preferred his Coke.

Only then did the impact of where he was hit him. The stadium was cavernously huge, like a monstrous bowl, with an acre of green below and thousands of tiny dots of people all around and across from him. In one area across the way, the dots were holding cards that spelled out messages and school names. The roar of the crowd was thrilling, mesmerizing, and frightening. His father and uncle were part of a captive madness—yelling, standing up, and waving their fists in a "charge" motion. Jason might have been overwhelmed too, if he could understand what people were yelling, but the sounds were more groan-like and hollow than words and sentences.

Suddenly, he heard his father's voice in his ear above the din: "Jason! They're kicking off. Stand up!" The puzzled boy obeyed. Since everybody else was standing, he could see even less of the field below than when he was seated. Understanding his difficulty, his father lifted him up high enough to see—a simple task for such a big man.

One of the helmeted figures, like those Jason had seen on television, ran up to a football that somehow was able to stand up on its end. The roar of the crowd grew louder at the figure's approach and peaked into an explosive howl as foot struck ball, sending it soaring into the air until it landed in the arms of another figure, clad similarly to the kicker, though in different colors. The receiver took the ball and headed in the direction the ball had come from. He ran behind people, through people, around people. Some were trying to clear the way for him, others were clawing at him. Finally, he was brought to earth by four figures who wore the same color uniforms as the kicker.

Only then did Jason notice how the colors resembled those of the autumn-hued trees outside. One team—Syracuse, he was to learn—wore orange helmets, white shirts with black numbers, and orange pants the color of pumpkins. Colgate was clad entirely in bright red, like the cardinal he chatted with outside his bedroom window. As the teams moved up and down the field, he was more conscious of masses of colors shifting positions than of individuals. Occasionally, one of their elements broke out of the pack, running desperately for what appeared to be its life until it was swallowed up by the sea of color.

The crowd responded to each burst of action. Sometimes it roared; sometimes it groaned, though Jason noticed that its clamor was louder and more enthusiastic when the orange cloud moved forward. Everyone seemed high-spirited, including his father and uncle, who jumped to their feet and fell back on the concrete slab, up and down with the crowd, like a piston. Jason was impressed by the pageantry, but understood little of the emotions behind it. Occasionally, he asked his father what was going on, but the elder was too immersed in spectacle to respond clearly.

An hour or so passed. Jason was cold and huddled inside his coat.

Suddenly, everyone was leaving the field, heading through what appeared to be tunnels leading to the bowels of the stadium. Jason looked up, puzzled.

"Halftime," explained his father.

Next came the bands. Jason heard them when he entered the stadium and during the game, but he never saw them clearly until now, as they took turns marching up and down the field. They fascinated him. It wasn't the raucous cacophony of brassy marches and show that grabbed his imagination, so much as the instruments. Music had always fascinated Jason, though it was clear from all the yelling and chatter around him that he may have been the only one in the stadium so affected.

"Let's go get some hot dogs," his father suggested.

Jason wasn't hungry any more.

"Jason!" his father urged. "It's halftime. Time for some chow. Let's go."

"Can't I stay here, Dad? And watch?"

"Watch? Watch what?"

"The bands."

"The bands?" echoed his father, clearly puzzled.

"It's all right, Fred," interjected his uncle. "You go. I'll stay with the boy."

"You, too? You're going to watch the halftime show?"

His uncle laughed. "There's a first time for everything."

His father shook his head in a combination of bemusement and disgust. "All right. Stay. What do you guys want?"

His father took their orders—Jason finally agreed to another hot dog—and left. Jason was glad. Uncle Dan seemed to enjoy watching the bands. Jason was fascinated by the trombones: slides darting quickly in and out, like tongues of a row of snakes. He liked the squealing clarinets and flutes, but wondered what chance they had against the edgy brass of the trumpets and the rat-a-tat of the drums. Yet somehow they made themselves heard. Where were the violins, he wondered aloud? Why no violins? He had seen orchestras on television, he said, and they had violins. Uncle Dan explained that bands didn't have violins. Only orchestras did. Jason was disappointed but only for a moment. He would imagine himself playing the trumpet, then. He knew the brilliant sound came from there, and he liked brilliant sounds. He still preferred the violin, but somehow he found the trumpet stirring in a different way. For the first time since he had arrived in the stadium, he was thrilled.

His window of enjoyment was brief, however, for his father returned with the food, and Uncle Dan reverted to football fan. The bands marched off the field, and the teams returned. Jason was disappointed, and his attention wandered more than in the first half. The surging colors meant little to him now. He had no interest in who was winning, though it was obvious the orange team was, given the joviality of the crowd and the lightheartedness of his father. His aim was to endure the rest of the afternoon.

An hour or so later, the players began to mill off the field, and the bands started playing again. With the roar of the crowd sapped, he could hear them better. He tried his best to catch sight of the musicians, but failed because everyone around him was standing and was taller than he was. But he could listen, and he did.

When they were outside and walking more freely, he heard his father's voice more clearly than he had since that morning. "Well, what did you think of your first live football game, Jason?" it asked.

"It was okay," he replied.

"Just okay? The Orange won!"

"The Orange?"

"Syracuse. That's what they call them: the Orange."

That explained the uniforms. "I liked the bands," Jason said.

"The bands?! What do they have to do with it? Syracuse wins, and you liked the bands!?"

"The game was okay too, Dad," Jason said hastily, hoping to gain approval, his voice shrinking with each word, when he realized he would not. "But I liked the bands."

He shouldn't have made that last remark. He made his point the first time. Now his father was upset.

"It's okay, Fred," his uncle said. "The boy's only eight years old."

Jason felt a loosening of the hand pulling him along, as if his father were trying to let him go. Jason scurried on his shorter legs to keep up. "The bands!" he heard his father mutter angrily. Jason was not surprised at his father's disapproval, but was afraid and puzzled. Hadn't his father noticed that his son never played football and never spent much time at his side when he watched a game on TV?

"I'd like to play one of those instruments some day," Jason ventured meekly. He couldn't seem to stop himself. Surely, once his father understood . . .

His father shook his head and kept walking. He didn't look down at his son, not even as he spoke: "Son, it's time we spent some time together. And I don't mean playing musical instruments. (I won't have a son of mine playing a musical instrument.) I mean playing football. We'll toss it, catch it. You'll love it. You'll play football in high school and in college like your old man did. Maybe even here at Syracuse— *also* like your old man did. I was a tackle. Damn good one, too." His father punched his fists together, before reclaiming Jason's hand, pulling him along. "It's in your blood, son," his father continued. "You just don't know it yet. But it is."

Jason was surprised to hear his uncle add agreement: "I wasn't half as good as your dad," Uncle Dan explained. "Never played in college. But I was a pretty good halfback in high school."

"Pretty good?!" Jason's father echoed in mock indignation. "He only set a single game rushing record against Perryville. You should have gone for that football scholarship at Potsdam, Dan. Even if it's a small school, it's still football."

Jason longed to yell that he didn't want to throw a football, but he finally sensed the trouble he was in. With the not yet fine-tuned survival instinct of an eight-year old, Jason kept quiet. His father would forget just as he always did when he promised to do things with his son. It was just talk—throwing the football with his son. Just talk. He hoped so. His father was a powerful man. There would be no resisting his wishes. If his father remembered, he could make Jason play football and forbid him to play a musical instrument. But high school was a long way off. His father would forget. He had to. Because if he didn't, there'd be no musical instrument for him—not as a boy, not in high school. Maybe when he was grown up, but that was even further off than high school. He couldn't even imagine it.

Jason and his father walked in silence, not a word passing between them. Jason couldn't know it, but his father was serious about his son playing football, and if that meant spending more time with the lad, well so be it. Such time was long overdue. The boy was in his mother's company too long. Where else could nonsense like wanting to play music come from? Well, he'd put a stop to that.

At one point in their journey, they were stalled by a crowd that didn't readily budge. With nothing else to do, Jason looked around and caught sight of a sleek, long-haired white cat sitting in the window of a house not more than twenty feet from the sidewalk. The cat's muzzle was feminine in appearance. She studied him intently, and he studied her in return. He felt as if they were talking to each other. She urged him to run while he still could. She had done that, she said. Her first owners hit her, so she ran away. Now look at me. See what a nice home I have?

It is nice, he thought. He liked the regal old wooden structure, with the big front window that gave the cat such a nice view from her seat on a soft blue pillow.

Just then, he felt a strong tug on his wrist. The crowd was moving again. As Jason's short legs struggled to keep up, he wished he could have left his body for just a minute, to pet the creature who had just spoken to him, feel her lovely white fur beneath his fingers. She was as fascinating to him as the musical instruments. He yearned to look one last time into her big green eyes. He wanted a cat just like her, but he dared not ask. Cats were silly, girly creatures. His father would think him a sissy. Maybe when he was grown up, he'd get one. Yes. He would buy a violin or a trumpet, and a beautiful white cat would sit in his room and listen to him play.

1993

The room was silent except for the thud-like ticking of the big school clock.

Katherine Manley's head was buried in her hands, and she sobbed silently. I gave her a piece of paper toweling I had on my desk to wipe her eyes.

"He never played an instrument, did he?" she asked.

"Not to my knowledge."

She folded the towel carefully and held it tightly in her fist. "Did his father hear this story?"

"Not from me. He passed away a couple of years after Jason's suicide. He was never the same after his son died, I'm told. I never met him or Jason's mother. She died a couple of years ago."

Katherine shook her head slowly, as if in thought. "You know, I never met them, either," she said. "Jason didn't talk about them much. I thought it was strange." She looked absently toward the window. It was dark outside. "Now I guess I understand."

We were silent for a moment. The air seemed heavy when I spoke again: "You know, when Jason told me that story, I thought it was one of those interesting anecdotes you never expect from a big football hero. The other side of the coin, that sort of thing. It didn't occur to me it might be a plea for help, and I never quite forgave myself for missing it."

She shook her head vigorously. "You shouldn't feel that way, Mr. Harris."

"Oh, I know, but . . ."

"No. You don't. Mr. Harris, Jason and I were very close. I wanted to get married, but he never mentioned it, never brought it up. That bothered me because Jason was a planner. Our dates, weekends, how we'd study together. He planned everything—everything but our future. Whenever I brought it up, he looked at me with a blank, fish-eyed look and changed the subject. For a while, I wondered if he were seeing someone, but we were together too much for that." She stood up, smoothed her blouse and slacks as if rearranging herself, and walked over to the window like an insect attracted to darkness instead of light.

"Now I really don't understand," I prodded her.

She turned around. Her eyes were wet. "Jason even planned his suicide. He knew in high school that he was going to kill himself. He planned it as far back as then. That's why he told you that story. . . . So that you could explain why. . . . The only thing he didn't plan on was his note not being found for twenty-five years." She rubbed at her eyes, and I gave her another piece of toweling. "Neither of us should feel guilty, Mr. Harris," she continued. "I thought I had failed him, too, but . . . you see?"

"I guess . . ."

"No guessing, Mr. Harris!" Her voice was suddenly firm. Then she caught herself and spoke more softly. "I'm sorry. I didn't mean to be so sharp. But I will never see you after today, and I want there to be no doubts in your mind after I go. I want you to understand that you inferred the true meaning of Jason's story precisely when he wanted you to—when it was too late to stop him from killing himself. Do you see that?"

Yes. Yes, I did. There was something subtly alien about Jason when he spoke to me that day. I just took him for a kid who would have been dismissed as weird by the other kids if he weren't a football star. Maybe if he had seemed disturbed in some way, I would have suspected something, but disturbed was the last word I'd use to describe him. Calm was more like it. And efficient. He stepped into my band room, convinced me that even a football player can appreciate a good band, and left to knock heads in the Syracuse defensive backfield.

I told her all this.

"Then you understand," she said.

"Yes."

She started toward the door, stopped, and turned about. I think she was about to leave and had abruptly changed her mind. "The band room," she stated simply. "Could I see it again?"

I nodded, and we left my office. After I flicked on the lights in the band room, she gazed about a world that was so familiar to me and utterly strange to her. "Were you in your school band?" I asked, not at all surprised when she replied in the negative. I pointed to a desk by some file bins at the far side of the room: "That's where we talked," I said.

She nodded and silently crossed the room. For several moments she stood by the desk, studying it. Then she gently placed her hand along its edge. A cloud of darkness seemed to envelop her. I feared I was to be a witness to some kind of mental breakdown, but as quickly as the cloud had formed, it dissipated, and she gathered herself. Her body stiffened, she wiped her eyes awkwardly, and turned away from the desk, as if to shove it permanently into her past. A moment later she stood back alongside me. "Thank you for your time, Mr. Harris," she said quietly. "I'm sorry if I kept you long, and I assure you I am very grateful. Now I must be going."

Her tone was firm, but I could see a slight shaking in her hands. I assured her that she was no trouble at all and accompanied her back to the front lobby where she paused for a last look at Jason's picture. "Such a waste," she muttered sadly, wiping a final tear from her eye. "Such a nice boy."

We stepped outside into the night, and she offered me her hand: "Thank you again, Mr. Harris."

I was worried. She had expressed concern for my well-being, but what of hers? "Katherine," I spoke up suddenly. "This isn't right. It's getting late. You don't want to make that trip back tonight. Why don't you come to dinner? My wife can set another place. It's no bother, and we'd enjoy having you and hearing more about you." My friendly invitation covered a sudden onset of anxiety. Katherine Manley had reached into my past as well as hers. As quickly as she had walked into my life, I was not quite ready for her to walk out of it.

She ruffled through her purse until she pulled out her keys. "Mr. Harris, thank you so much. But I can tell you everything about myself right here. I'm a lawyer, married twenty years with three kids. I live in New York City. A young man I loved and maybe still love killed himself, and I blamed myself for it. At least, partially. Thanks to you, I know there was nothing I could have done. I just tied up a loose strand of my life. Now I must get back to that life. Any other time, I would gladly accept your invitation. Now all I want is to go home. Do you understand?"

In print, her demurral looks brusque, but standing next to her in the dark on the walkway in front of the school, it was most beseeching, as if she were desperate to escape and was pleading with me to allow her to go. It was clear that she must leave Commanders Corner and never return. Still, there was one more thing she had to know. "You didn't just tie up a loose end for yourself," I told her.

She looked at me curiously and waited for me to continue.

"Jason's life was not a waste. All the time he was talking, he was looking around the band room—at the pictures of instruments and musicians on the wall, at the couple of instruments some kids hadn't put away. After he left, I began to think. The band program was struggling back then. I had been treading water for three years and was thinking of getting out. But if music was that compelling to our football hero, maybe I was missing something. I decided to give teaching another year, maybe even be positive about it for a change. I did and things turned around." I stared back toward the school. "We have a pretty good music program here now, and I've enjoyed building it. I always knew that much of the credit for that goes to Jason Richards, but until now, I never realized how much."

She placed her hand on my shoulder, much as she had on my desk, and kissed me on the cheek. For the first time Katherine smiled. "Thank you again, Mr. Harris," she whispered.

I watched her walk to her car in the school lot. Main Street was empty but brightly lit at that hour, so I could follow her vehicle as it proceeded down the road past our few stores. The last I saw of Katherine Manley was a set of taillights disappearing into the darkness.

MEET NOT CUTE

1987

Not all orchestra concerts are created equal. For some, I would pay a fortune to wrench a ticket from an extortionist moonlighting from his day job of scalping sports tickets. Other concerts could put the sleeping pill industry out of business. A few, like one I attended by the touring London Philharmonic, are a little of both. Mozart's *Overture to the Marriage of Figaro* was a delightful curtain lifter. Edward Elgar's First Symphony under Richard Carleton, the greatest Elgar conductor alive, was magnificent, but sitting through the Brahms Violin Concerto to get to it was like enduring an initiation rite.

I don't know about you, but I have no patience for the look-at-me, star-studded concertos of the nineteenth century. There's something obscene about a soloist strutting on stage with ninety players awaiting his/her arrival like lackeys to royalty. The worst pieces by the best Romantic composers are usually their concertos—Sibelius, Beethoven, and Tchaikovsky, to name three. Even the structurally sound Brahms had to put off developing ideas in the orchestra because of the need to keep the soloist front and center lest some dowager pine too long in his absence. Given the near impossibility of avoiding a concerto on an orchestra concert, that opinion is not widely shared. Soloist worship borders on religion with today's concert-going public to the point where it isn't the piece that's important but who's playing it.

Well, no concerto was going to spoil the Elgar for me, and I looked forward to the symphony with relish. My center balcony seat provided a panoramic view of the orchestra. Some people feel no need to gaze upon the inner workings of the fine watch that is an orchestra, but I find it fascinating. There is so much going on in an orchestra concert—musicians playing, making adjustments to their instruments, reacting to passing events, or sitting and waiting for their next entrance. It's also economical, since those floor seats where you can see only the conductor and front-row players are generally expensive.

I was surprised to find the auditorium nearly full. Elgar is not a big draw in the United States, and touring orchestras don't get big audiences, even on a Saturday night. The incentive for such a large gathering had to be the soloist in the Brahms, a cute little English button named Kara Simmons, the latest violin ingénue to be promoted by the classical music industry. At five feet tall with short blond hair and the face of a pixie, she resembled the short, compact cheerleader who sits atop those bizarre pyramids that have nothing to do with cheering. She looked about sixteen, and though older than that, Ms. Simmons wasn't mature enough to play a heavyweight concerto like the Brahms. Like all prodigies trained from the age of four never to make a mistake, she had all the notes, but even I admit there is more depth to the Brahms Violin Concerto than notes. For that reason, kids should not play Brahms. His power, reflection and grandeur elude them and will continue to elude them until they've had one or two serious setbacks, perhaps an illness, not to mention a couple of love affairs, and nothing I'd heard from Ms. Simmons marked her as an exception.

Maestro Carleton was not one of those conductors who stood on ceremony with the audience. He bounded to the podium, barely acknowledging our presence, and with a slight lift of his baton sent the violins bubbling merrily into the Mozart. Even a mediocre performance of the *Figaro* overture can make me wish the opera were to follow, and there was nothing mediocre about this reading.

For most of the audience, Mozart was but a tidying up before the guest of honor was ushered in for dinner (and Brahms did like his dinner, particularly *wurst*). Ms. Simmons popped out on stage right, her cute, choppy steps keeping her just a step ahead of the long strides of Maestro Carleton. Her blond hair was piled higher atop her head and longer than I remembered from her publicity stills. She looked like a French poodle. Eschewing the usual long gown worn by female soloists, Simmons's emerald green dress seemed to split in the middle

around her waist, rising three-quarters up her bosom and down just below her knees. She would have looked sillier but for the way she thrust
her shoulders backward to emphasize her ample cleavage.

Carleton lifted his arms, looked longer than necessary at the voluptuous Ms. Simmons, and began the introduction, which, as with so
many concertos, was the most impressive part of the piece. Brahms
had created a great opening for a fifth symphony here, but once the
unwanted guest arrived, the circus act would begin. A performer of
maturity can make a strong case for the first movement, but our English crumpet was decades away from achieving that depth. Instead, she
piled notes upon notes with the same color and carefully honed, perfectly neutral expression. Well, big breasts or not, I don't go to concerts to ogle. Out came my hefty copy of *The Count of Monte Cristo*,
which proved diverting in ways Ms. Simmons was not. I was barely
conscious of the second movement, though it was nice enough if the
few measures I caught were any indication. The elephant dance opening of the finale was so goofy—it sounds awkward even in the best
performances—that I was distracted, if only momentarily. The ending
set off a burst of applause and the ritual standing ovation that American audiences routinely give soloists and good weather reports.

The applause died down after only one call-back for Ms. Simmons,
proving Brahms was no Tchaikovsky when it came to curtain calls. After her final flouncing off stage, the hall was silent but for the murmur-
ing and creaking of chair bottoms. My last thought of the erstwhile
soloist was that someone should tell her to take up Sarasate's *Carmen
Variations* and leave Brahms to the adults.

Intermission followed the Brahms so I joined the rest of the crowd
on its exiting feet. That is when I heard an angry female voice from
several seats to my left: "I've never seen such rude behavior at a concert in my life."

I paid no attention. What did such a remark have to do with me?

"Did you hear what I said?" The voice was more insistent.

I turned in its direction and was startled to see the face of a young
woman directing considerable anger in my direction. What did I do?

"If you want to read, go to a library."

I stared down at the "Count" as if he were an interloper I mistakenly invited to a party.

"You turned a page during that beautiful oboe solo in the Adagio, and the paper crackling spoiled the moment completely."

Paper crackling? *That* was what she was talking about? I turned my pages so carefully that even *I* couldn't hear them crackle. How could she? I looked at her sheepishly, but with curiosity. Could she really hear me turning a page? Her gaze was too withering to allow for examination. Her eyes and lips were narrowed into parallel lines, and her cheeks were rouged only by anger. She was a daunting figure, though an attractive one, as well.

I saw no point in defending myself. Better to admit to boorish behavior than stand up for it. I had violated concert etiquette. My duty was to apologize, and I did so profusely.

"Forget it," she snapped. "Just tell me. You won't be reading during the Elgar, will you? I certainly hope not, because there are no decent vacant seats in this hall."

After I assured her I would not be reading, she turned away and sidled to the end of the row, taking the long way toward the aisle in the process. Perhaps she was pushing her indignation just a little bit?

"I didn't hear you turn any pages." This time the voice came from my right, from a much older woman. She was short, neatly dressed in a tweed suit, and a little fussy looking. "I think she's showing off," the woman added in a little voice. "*Very sensitive* and all that." Her disdain was enhanced by a creaky cultivation in her voice and an accent that seemed foreign but was more likely formed by class than nationality.

"Thank you," I responded gratefully. "Still, I guess I was wrong. The problem is that I really dislike the Brahms, and I didn't want to miss the Mozart."

The woman nodded. I wondered if she agreed with my assessment of the Brahms. "I wouldn't let her bother me," she said assuringly. "You were very quiet."

I thanked her again. "Do you know her?" I asked.

"No. I've never sat up here before." She smiled and slowly got to her feet. "Excuse me," she said. "I need to get started. I can't get to the ladies room as quickly as those young girls."

I returned her smile, and she headed for the exit. *Very* sensitive, my new friend had said. *Yes. I agree.* My aggrieved victim protested as much out of affect as indignation.

I saw no familiar faces while prowling the elegant halls and the bar. I thought of taking a seat in the bar and reading the program notes about the Elgar, but I could probably have written them better than whoever did. I've been a serious student of Elgar for many years. I am a member of the Elgar Society, made a pilgrimage to Elgar's home town of Malvern, and even wrote a short article for the Society's journal. I don't think I'm being boastful here. Still, I couldn't help peeking at the long essay in the program while waiting in line at a drinking fountain. "Not bad," I muttered to myself. Nothing new but better than I expected. Assured that Elgar was getting his due, I took a drink and returned to the Count.

I reclaimed my seat early to avoid stumbling over six pairs of knees, including the conceivably frail ones owned by my elderly supporter on my right. I hoped that the woman I had offended would have returned early, her anger cooled so that I'd have one more chance to expiate my sin.

Neither lady was present, so I sought out the Count once more, but not for long. I didn't want my so-called victim to catch me reading again, even if it was Intermission. I put the book away, and gazed absently around the hall with its dark wooden walls, thick red curtains that covered the windows, and the six busts of composers arrayed along them, three on each side. As Intermission drew to a close, I noted with disappointment that the second half audience was three-quarters of its original complement. The rest were satisfied with half a concert and seeing precious little Kara Simmons play her violin.

The stage remained empty except for chairs and instruments like string basses that were too large to be carried off. American orchestra members tend to drift on stage at the start of concerts and after intermission. Europeans usually enter in a collective march that can be quite imposing. The Germans and Russians look like an advancing army, but the British aren't quite as mechanical. Their seriousness of purpose is that of a group of young professionals emerging from a London Underground station. As I awaited this dramatic moment, I wondered why that nice old woman had not returned. Perhaps my appreciation of her sophisticated reinforcement led me to overestimate her musical acuity. Or maybe she was just tired.

Just as I settled back in my seat, the orchestra surged onto the stage. At the same time, I heard the creaking of seats to my left. Miss Sensitive was returning late, no doubt to avoid a confrontation with me.

The ill will between us gnawed at me, and that was not a good thing with the Elgar coming up. I struggled to regain my concentration and succeeded just as the solemn opening march—every bit as good a tune as the famous one from the first *Pomp and Circumstance March*—concluded. Such are the greatness and power of Sir Edward's music and Carleton's skill at conducting it. The rest was magnificent. The playful militancy (I could never tell which word applied more) of the Allegro, yielded with the fluttering brushstrokes of a summer breeze to the heart-filled yearning of the Adagio, and later the brilliant stroke of the "third theme" that entered near the end of that movement.

After elements of the march flashed in brilliant off-rhythms at the end of the symphony, I leaped to my feet with the rest of the audience. I like to think they were all as aroused as I was and that no one was acting as if the hall's attendants had installed springs in their seats, though I doubted it. Ritual is ritual. Or perhaps not. The orchestra and conductor were called back three times before it obliged calls for an encore with Elgar's *Fourth Pomp and Circumstance March*, complete with its clever tympani part that the LPO player executed with relish. More exuberant applause followed. This time Carleton responded in true European fashion by grabbing the hand of the concertmaster and pulling him to his feet. Time to go. Quickly now. The bus is leaving. After the applause subsided, I looked to my left and saw the back of Miss Sensitive heading toward the aisle to my left.

Violin concerto or no violin concerto, it was a grand concert, and I was in fine fettle as I made my way through the crowd—and it was a crowd, despite the intermission escapees. I wasn't surprised. Most of those who abandoned ship were seated on the floor in the expensive seats. Music lovers sit in the balconies.

I headed for a drinking fountain. There were three people in line, and since the crowd was still thick, it was a good time for a sip. The woman ahead of me finished imbibing, stood up, and turned around. She appeared to be scouring the crowd for an opening when her eyes caught mine.

It was Ms. Sensitive. Her face turned so red when she spotted me that I wondered if she *was* wearing rouge. (She wasn't.) Given how she looked at me, we could have been in a dark parking lot, with me wearing a black ski cap. She had no escape. The crowd was moving more slowly than before and had thickened enough to keep her frozen in position; at the same time, three people were pushing to get to the drinking fountain.

I am not the type to endure nervous silence for long. "Listen," I said to her, "I apologized several times back there. You didn't seem impressed, but please believe me. I'm really sorry I disturbed you."

The muscles around her mouth relaxed. She didn't smile, but she looked more pleasant than before. She blinked nervously and nodded. "Thank you." Her voice was just loud enough for me to hear, and it trembled slightly. "I guess it wasn't that bad," she added, just audibly enough to be picked up over the buzzing of the crowd. "But I really love that piece. . . ."

". . . and someone reading during it was just too much to take."

Her nod was almost imperceptible. "Yes. But really, I don't care what you do during concerts," she added, though the slight twist of her upper lip betrayed her disdain. "Please understand: my hearing is acute. I heard you turning those pages, and it was irritating."

My hearing is acute. She reminded me of an old acquaintance who claimed he had "super hearing." He played his stereo system so quietly that only a young dog could hear it and claimed it took him to nirvana. I found this hard to believe, but what drove me crazy was his insisting that only his opinion about how a system sounded was valid because only he possessed hearing capable of discriminating fine nuances. One night we got into an argument during which I insisted that it was impossible for one person to put his ears on someone else's head. *I have no way of telling how things sound to you, and you don't know how they sound to me.* He was having none of it. His ears were cultivated, mine were not, and that was the end of it. No one in his right mind keeps arguments like that going, so I made my escape, never to return. For the same reason, I made it my business to get away from Ms. Sensitive as soon as the crowd thinned. As it turned out, the old building's halls were designed for people who were on the average five inches less wide than they are now. Since I couldn't push through the crowd without turning myself into a fullback, we stood together like a couple with no place to go. When things loosened up, we shuffled along, still together, down the stairs to the first floor, out the door and into the cool night air. There was still traffic on the streets, and with many concert attendees milling about, the scene was quite lively.

What I did next, I cannot explain.

Ms. Sensitive and I were still linked as we reached the street, but there was no reason to remain side-by-side once we were out of the building. My car was parked in a garage around the corner to the left. In five minutes, I could be seated behind the wheel cursing the long lines leading to the exit. I looked at Miss Sensitive, prepared to say good-bye, and saw that she looked a little confused.

I asked if she was all right.

"Yes. But I'm new to this city and have lost my bearings."

"What are you looking for?"

"Where bus number 4 stops."

She didn't look the type who took the bus, but I pointed across the street to the right. "Just down from that corner."

She smiled for the first time since we met, and I could see she was rather pretty. Not beautiful, but pleasant looking in a plain sort of way. Her brown hair drooped over her forehead, just missing her left brow. Her uncovered lips were full but oddly inexpressive. She had dark eyes that should have smoldered but instead sat gloomily in her head, inarticulate, uninterested. I was puzzled. Where once she seemed haughty, she now seemed unsure and just a little forlorn.

"I'm headed that way," I said, referring to her bus stop. "I'll show you. It's a little tricky to find, and buses in this town don't stop unless you're standing right where you're supposed to be."

"I've seen that. Thank you."

When we reached the corner, I pointed across the street. "Do you see that red awning over there?"

She nodded.

"The stop is just this side of that awning."

She hesitated. "I see. Thank you." She still sounded unsure.

"The red one," I repeated forcing a smile.

"Oh, yes. I see it now."

The light for her to cross was red. There was yet another awkward silence.

As I said, I cannot explain it. Maybe I just didn't want to sit in my car waiting for cars to inch their way down the five floors in the parking garage to the exit booth. There was also the fact that I was hungry and would probably be sitting there chafing while my stomach rumbled in protest. "Listen," I spoke up awkwardly. "Do you really want to take the bus? You have no other way home?"

"I could take a cab," she replied. "I live near the university. It's not far. But the bus is fine. I've taken it several times."

She was right. It wasn't far. "Look. That's on my way. I'll give you a ride."

"Oh, no. I don't want you to do that. The bus is fine," she repeated.

I was about to insist, but the firmness around her mouth and the slight squint about her eyes confused me. I was not displeased at the thought of being rid of her. She was weird, but more than that, testy and taut, maybe even fragile, as if she would snap if pushed hard enough. People like her are mysteries best not solved, but for some reason, I couldn't just leave her there. It wasn't guilt over what happened during the concert, and I certainly didn't think we had bonded during the simple act of walking silently next to each other on the way out of the hall. Was it the vulnerability she exuded since losing her bearings in front of the auditorium? Or was it having to choose between nursing my hunger in a parking garage or satisfying its cravings at the only open restaurant within walking distance—a restaurant whose red awning signaled the bus stop—while she stood outside waiting for a bus?

I was doomed by hunger. I couldn't just walk with her to her stop and then go into the restaurant without inviting her to join me. It was just too awkward, even for strangers. Still, there was hope. She had said she was happy to take the bus. Perhaps she would refuse an invitation.

She didn't. Oh, she hesitated, but eventually, she accepted, with one contingency. "I can't afford to stay out late. If I join you, I will have to take the ride you offered. I'm sorry."

"No problem," I said, quietly regretting my earlier offer of transportation. Without it, this "date" might have been avoided. Now there was nothing left but to play out the drama.

We headed for Bailey's.

"You really didn't have to do this, you know," she said. By now, I was convinced she wasn't just saying this. She meant it. And somehow, it didn't sound that gracious.

"I know."

I sat back and studied her. It was the first time I could do so in a way that would commit her appearance to memory. The soft light in our booth near the back of the restaurant not only illuminated her features, it flattered them by adding color where there was none because of her pale skin and absence of makeup. She was about five inches shorter than I—around five-six. Her well-balanced, slim figure was enticing without calling attention to any particular part and without being overtly sexy. Her breasts were no larger than a B, and B described her overall in size and quality. Her face was attractive, though plain with flat cheeks. The brown hair fell straight and softly to her slim neck. Earlier, I thought her lips formed a permanent frown because of the way they dipped down at the corners. Now that they were straightened, she looked affable if not light-hearted. The few smiles she seemed capable of appeared in flashes when the corners would turn up. They seemed to be coaxed by the oddest things, and there was no way to tell what would catch her fancy. Her light tan, loose-fitting blouse was tucked neatly into a straight brown skirt—hardly formal dress for a concert, but tasteful. Neatness seemed to concern her, given how frequently she reached down to tuck in her blouse. The word that best described her, though, was tired. I wondered if she'd be more attractive if she didn't appear so fatigued. I believed her when she said she could not stay out late, but I couldn't help but wonder what was ailing her. Work? Drugs?

"My name's Graham Decker, by the way," I offered.

"Gabrielle Deschayes."

"French?"

"Swiss."

I nodded. "I took a trip to Switzerland a couple of years ago, but not to the French part. I wanted to go to Geneva but never got there. It's supposed to be a great international city."

She shrugged. "So they say. I've never been there, either."

"Really?"

"I'm from Zurich."

"Zurich?" I repeated. "That's in the German part of Switzerland."

"That's right."

"So how come the French name?"

My questions seemed to annoy her, but before I could be sure, a waitress approached. I'd never seen her before, which was odd because I was a semi-regular at Bailey's. She was in her fifties with tightly cropped grey hair that created the illusion of a haystack rising on top her head. In her heyday, she might have been a proponent of "big hair." Her fair skin suggested she might have been a blonde. I sensed she had known better times. Her name-tag suggested her name was May, but something told me that was not her real name.

"Your order?" she said, in a voice that sounded faintly like sulking. I didn't imagine her lasting long at Bailey's. Concertgoers don't like surly waitresses.

I felt pressured to order and kept it short. "Blueberry pie. Coffee. Black." I mentally pinched myself. I should have ordered for Gabrielle first. I looked uneasily across the table.

"The same for me," she said quietly. If she was irritated, it didn't show.

May nodded curtly and disappeared.

"My father's family was from Lausanne." Gabrielle replied to my earlier question as if May had never stood by our table. "That's in the French part. My grandfather was a banker there, but he was ambitious, and since the Swiss banking industry is headquartered in Zurich, he moved there. That is where my father was born, but he never cared much for the place. He, too, preferred Lausanne. Nevertheless, he followed in Grandfather's footsteps and entered banking, but unlike

Grandfather, who had made his peace with Zurich, Father took a job that was likely to transfer him to Lausanne. It might have, too, but he was offered a job in New York before anything from Lausanne was available, and for reasons I'm not entirely sure of even today, he took it. His last blow for Gallicism was to name me Gabrielle."

"Interesting," I replied. "I never think of Swiss people moving to the United States."

"Many do, actually," she replied. "Switzerland is beautiful, peaceful, never at war, wealthy, and clean. It can also be boring—for those reasons and because the Swiss are so insular."

"How come you never found out why he took the New York job?"

"He died before I could ask him. I was eight at the time, and he died two years after we arrived in New York." Living in the US since the age of eight explained the faintness of what I now realized was a German accent. "My mother said he came to the States because he had an urge for adventure, but I always found that hard to believe, given that he was so bent on moving to Lausanne. I never pressed her about it. It's not really important, and the subject of my father seems to be a painful one for her."

"I'm sorry."

"That's okay. My father was not a happy man. I don't think New York was what he wanted it to be, but then I don't think any place could be. Father was an incorrigible dreamer working in the most practical of professions. It was truly a mismatch. I have no doubt that he was daydreaming when he was crossing Sixth Avenue against the light and was struck by a taxi."

"Ouch."

"Yes, well . . ."

May arrived with our pie and coffee. As she spread them on the table, Gabrielle's eyes turned to the pictures of musicians and entertainers that lined the walls. "There is so much history in this place," she said in a rather dreamy fashion.

"Humph," mumbled May, apparently thinking my companion was addressing her. I suspect she hadn't even noticed those pictures.

"It reminds me of the Carnegie Deli in New York," Gabrielle went on.

At the mention of the Carnegie, May's expression lightened up. She had just placed my cup in front of me and grinned. It was a nice smile, warm, grandmotherly, even sexy. "I used to work at the Carnegie," she declared. "Several years ago. All kinds of famous people came there. Did you see that Woody Allen movie with all those scenes there? *Broadway Danny Rose?*"

"Yes, I did," I replied. "I missed it when it came out but saw it after I visited New York, went to a concert at Carnegie Hall, and did pretty much what I'm doing here at the Deli."

"When was that?"

"Last year."

May paused then shook her head. "I was gone by then." She stared at me, and I had the distinct impression that I had just been added to the menu. Suddenly, May seemed very attractive. Had it been that long since I'd had sex? She smiled. Her lips were fuller than I imagined possible. Her bust was buxom and just short of fat. Would she dare hit on me with Gabrielle sitting there? I was kind of hoping she would, killing two birds with one stone, but as quickly as she became sexy May, she reverted to mean May. "A good three years earlier, too bad," she added curtly. With that, she left the table as abruptly as she had arrived.

Gabrielle's gaze followed May's departing ample derriere for a moment, then turned back to me and lifted her eyebrows. "Does she always come on that way? This doesn't seem the place for it."

"I have no idea. She's new. I've never seen her before."

"Well you might soon again. I hope you like older women. I don't think she's going to take those three years seriously for long."

A randy shudder passed through me. I guess I hadn't misread May. I gave a passing thought to returning to Bailey's after dropping Gabrielle and glanced over to the front counter where May had retreated. She was busy cashing out another customer and passed not even a tiny glance in my direction.

"As I said," Gabrielle was saying, "I can't stay out too long."

"Yes. I know," I replied, not entirely concealing my irritation at her insinuation.

She tilted her head slightly toward the cash register. "I'd be careful if I were you," she said. "The question you should be asking yourself is did she work *at* the Carnegie Deli or did she *work* Carnegie Deli?"

"Aren't you presuming a few things?"

"Only one: if you come back here, she'll be waiting."

Uneasy silence. Neither of us had touched our pie. In near unison, we reached for our forks. It was as if we both realized that the sooner we finish them, the sooner we could get out of the restaurant and away from each other.

"I'm sorry," she said suddenly after taking a bite. "I was out of line. But that woman was so obvious."

Her words pricked the tension like a needle attacking a balloon. I laughed. "I guess she was. But like she said. Three years too late. There was a message in that."

She opened her eyes wide. "I certainly hope so."

I could have done without that comment. Did she think I was still pumping teenage hormones? I was beginning to feel sorry for her because I wasn't sure she was aware of when she was disagreeable. I picked up a piece of pie and returned to something safe. "What happened after your father died?"

"My mother and I moved to Boston."

"Why not back to Switzerland?"

She laughed, which in her case meant a condescending snicker spiked with a slight curl to her upper lip. "Mother? Return to Switzerland? Not likely."

"Is she another of the 'bored Swiss?'"

"Yes, though she never said so, outright."

"You people don't communicate much, do you?"

"It wasn't that. My mother loves Switzerland, but she can't live there. She's a big city girl. She adored New York, but as an alien with only a green card, she couldn't get a decent job that would support us in such an expensive city. We had a distant cousin in Boston. Through him, she got a job in the office of a surgeon. She did well, and was able to study nursing part time. Eventually, she became a nurse. She still is a nurse."

"In Boston?"

"Yes."

"What brings you here?"

"A residency at University Hospital."

I whistled in surprise. "You're a *Doctor*?"

"Yes."

I must say, there was nothing of the physician about her. I always thought of doctors as needing steady personalities, but Gabrielle Deschayes seemed flaky. I was noticing how she stared at me. Date books make a point out of keeping eye contact, but she didn't just make contact with my eyes, she glued herself to them.

"That explains why you can't stay out too late, I guess."

"Yes. I have rounds at 8:00 A.M."

I whistled. "We should get going then."

She looked at her watch. "Ten-thirty. We have a little time. As a doctor, I feel qualified to say that we shouldn't eat too fast." But she did dig into her pie in earnest.

I couldn't resist another question. "You said you liked Boston. What are you doing way out here? You're Europe. Big City East Coast. Not Midwest."

She nodded. "In fact, I'm not sure I made the right decision in coming here. But it's only for two years, and the residency at University Hospital is better than anything I might have gotten in Boston, which is a difficult market for medical students looking for good residencies. This is not the most exciting city, but it's a city, not a small town. It has museums and a symphony. Besides, I don't have much free time. A concert or two like tonight: that's about it. If you look at it that way, it matters little where I am, and I'm better off without distractions."

"So you think you'll go back to Boston when you're finished here?"

"Perhaps. Or I'll try some place like San Francisco. Los Angeles. Who knows?"

"Europe?"

Her eyes fluttered. She looked a bit misty all of a sudden. Almost as quickly, they cleared. It was as if she shook her head, though her gaze never left me. "That would be my first choice, but it's not a likely one. Medical degrees don't travel internationally that well. If I planned to practice in Europe, I should have gone to medical school there, but the program and grant I received in Boston were too attractive to pass up. So I made my choice. It's all right. I've been in this country a long time. I'm settled. Twenty years from now, I may wish I took on the extra work to move to Europe, but right now I'm tired of studying and am worn out." She flicked her hand through her hair in what I was betting was a trademark nervous habit. If so, it was an odd one, because her hair wasn't long enough to show much effect.

"So you're stuck here," I said.

"Yes." Her reply was more serious than my question, but what did I expect? She was a snob.

"Well, you should get back early."

"I can stay a little longer," she replied. "Eight in the morning is almost late for me. If I had to get up any earlier, I wouldn't have gone to the concert. Concerts inject so much life into me that I find it hard to sleep afterwards."

Next time, I would get firmer control over my better nature. I changed the subject. "Do you play an instrument?"

"Piano. Badly. I wish it wasn't so, but as hard as I practiced, I don't have the talent to be a fine pianist."

"Do you still play?"

"Oh, yes. I'll always play . . . and practice when I can, which isn't enough when I'm studying medicine. I almost quit because it's not in me to do something unless I do it extremely well. I thought of taking up a string instrument, which might have given me a chance to play in an orchestra, but it was too late, so I turned first to science and then medicine. But I'll always practice, read about music, and go to concerts." She gazed at me intently. "That's why it bothers me that you seemed so casual about music that you could read during a concert." Before I could react, she continued: "I don't want to seem harsh, but I'm trying to understand that. It would kill me to miss the playing even if it was a piece I wasn't fond of."

I shrugged. "I guess playing music never really gets out from under a player's skin even after giving it up as a life's work." It was a mean thing to say, but her preciousness was getting on my nerves.

"You're right." If my remark stung, she didn't show it. "But that's my lot." She took a deep breath as if to gather herself. She looked sad.

"I'm sorry. I shouldn't have said that."

"It was a fair observation. I haven't abandoned music. There will be time for it again. Meanwhile, tonight was such a treat. I'm sorry you didn't care for the Brahms. I find it exquisite, one of his finest pieces." She paused, perhaps wondering if she should continue. "The second movement especially. That exquisite oboe solo. I'm sorry you can't enjoy that moment as I do. It's so gorgeous. I wish I could explain."

"You don't have to." I briefly described my dislike of concertos. She seemed puzzled. "All concertos?"

"Mainly those from the nineteenth century. Those from the Classical era all sound more or less alike to me, but they're tasteful and well-balanced. By the twentieth century, composers writing concertos rediscovered the orchestra. But the nineteenth century concertos are like an otherwise well-proportioned person with a big gut—top and bottom, fine, but obese in the middle."

She laughed. Snickered, really, as if tolerating a clod. "Such a viewpoint!" she declared. "Why did you go to the concert, then?"

"For the Elgar."

"Of course," she interrupted with enthusiasm. Her eyes lit up. Music really did move her—in a way that medicine very likely did not. *Glad I learned that before letting her be my doctor.* "I'm so glad you like him, at least. Elgar is so difficult for some people. So many think he wrote nothing more than a graduation march. Others stop with *Enigma Variations* and never hear the two symphonies, *Dream of Gerontius,* and all those other wonderful pieces. Do you know what an odd man he was?" She hurried on to answer her question. "His wife was his muse. Alice, her name was. She was nine years older than he and plain, but he seemed unable to work without her support. He outlived her by fifteen years, but when she died, he essentially stopped composing and became a kind of landed gentleman. I wonder if that's all he ever really wanted to be, and might have been but for his talent and her pushing him." She continued on about Elgar. For some reason, I didn't stop her by telling her about my own Elgarian affinities. Not that she gave me much of a chance to. "You know, there is a marvelous biography about Elgar by Michael Kennedy," she went on. "You should read it. Kennedy is a wonderful writer. He's written biographies about other composers, too. Mahler, Strauss, even the conductor John Barbirolli. I've read them all." She seemed quite proud of herself.

I could have noted that as fine a writer as Kennedy is, he's not the primary biographer of any of those people, save perhaps Barbirolli. Since 1984, Elgar's major biographer has been Jerrold Northrop Moore. Mahler has several. With Strauss, there is Norman del Mar's three volume work and a few others in English.

"Funny you should talk about Elgar so much," I finally managed to get in. "I would have thought that Brahms appeals to you more."

"He does. It's odd that I've never read a biography of Brahms."

"You read a lot of biographies of composers, I take it."

"I do. They give me insight as to where their music came from."

"Do you really think a biography can describe the creative process?"

She shook her head. "No. But it can recreate a world, a time and place where a composer wrote his music. And it can tell me what was going on in the composer's life when he wrote a particular piece."

I don't know why, but I kept the discussion going. "What about Schoenberg, Berg . . . those guys? Do you like their music?"

"I like some of it. Early Schoenberg, before he turned to atonality and became 'Schoenberg,' you might say. I like Berg more. He's really a romantic who wrote with atonal tools. I don't care much for Webern except for his Opus 1."

"Early, huh? Before Webern became 'Webern'?"

"Exactly. But it's Schoenberg's disciples who really bother me. Schoenberg created a system of composing, but so many of his followers took the freedom of that system as a license to write anything they wanted without attending to what turns an etude into music."

She went on like that for the rest of our time in the coffee shop. I'm not quoting the rest because none of it was as interesting as her point about Schoenberg, though she did have a few ideas I was sure she thought were novel—Verdi's *Requiem* was his greatest opera, Wagner's music transcends his politics, Mahler was a link to twentieth century modernism and might have embraced it had he not died so early. None of those observations was original, but the one about Mahler wasn't bad.

"And of course, Haydn was a wonderful composer," she added, "but Mozart (with whom he's too often paired) was sublime." Her tone implied, "don't you think?"

I was growing tired of her recital of sensitivities to and knowledge of all that was music. At first, I thought she was just eager to impress me, but the more she went on, the more I was convinced that she was lecturing me for what I was pretty sure was "my own good." In a way, I was still paying for my conduct during the Brahms performance, not as penance so much as because my transgression made it clear that I needed enlightenment. There were things I could have said and wanted to say, but she never gave me a chance. Eventually, I stopped caring and was content to play the oaf.

It was time to go. Gabrielle was not a clod. She picked up immediately that the waitresses were starting to clean up. "I didn't realize it was so late," she gushed in surprise.

She was quite talkative on the way to the car. Always about music. I could have corrected her on a few things, but by now, her know-it-all chatter boxing was a shot of novocaine to my lips. Once we were in the car, she was much quieter. By the time she directed me around the last turn to her building, she seemed quite serious. If she had been drinking or using drugs, I'd have said she was crashing from a high, but more likely, her long hours had caught up with her. She seemed very tired.

As I pulled up to her building, I noticed a strange expectant glint in her eyes. She made no move to get out of the car. What was this? Was she expecting me to get out and open the door for her? That was crazy. It was not as if we were on a date. Maybe she was expecting me to make a move on her. I couldn't believe that, but she *was* lingering. Most men would have at least explored the possibilities, but I'd had enough of Gabrielle Deschayes for one night. Oh sure, I could have accommodated any sexual urges she might have had, but given the way I felt about her, that would have made me a cad. A lot of guys would have called me a sap. Well, I had been playing the oaf for the past few hours. I was comfortable with that, so I climbed out and walked over to her door. She had already opened it, so I took her hand and helped her to her feet. I looked into her eyes for a moment, wondering if my suspicion in the car was correct, but now I wasn't sure. Those eyes just looked dog tired. I suspected that her guard had dropped, and she was simply looking to get to her apartment and go to sleep. I released her hand and accompanied her to the front door of her building, told her I enjoyed talking with her, and said good night.

Her look of disbelief surprised me. Apparently, I was wrong about her wish to retire—at least to retire alone. As I returned to my car, I recalled a question about human nature that had long puzzled me. Women turn men down every day. We expect it. We may be disappointed, but few of us are so arrogant as to be incredulous when it happens. But let one of us back away from a woman's invitation, or in this case fail to make an advance that to this day I really thought she wanted but would never have accepted, not only are we insulting them, our manhood is called into question. I guess it's biology, but it never made sense to me.

ii

After an uneventful Sunday, it was back to work Monday, no harm done. The program for the weekend's concerts was one of the highlights of the season for me: Berlioz's *Corsair* followed by Beethoven's Third Piano Concerto (mercifully, no trombones), and Ralph Vaughan Williams's Fourth Symphony. That was a nice program for trombones, and it brings me to something that Gabrielle never gave me a chance to bring up until I dared not bother lest she chatter endlessly about orchestras, with her as the expert.

I was—and am—the Principal Trombonist of the local Philharmonic. The concert where I met Gabrielle Deschayes was a busman's holiday. As I have suggested, there was little she was telling me in Bailey's Coffee Shop that I did not know, and I might have said so had she given me a chance. No. That wasn't it. No conversation, regardless of how incessant, is a flowing river. There are always spaces, and there were open spaces in our talk. I just never tried filling one. You don't hold conversations with a monologue. Gabrielle loved hearing herself talk, pontificating, bestowing her knowledge upon the musically ignorant lout she took me for. Who was I to spoil her fun? Besides, it was the only night I was going to see her. Let her think herself superior to the mope who ruined the concert for her. A little penance was good for me. Beyond that, I must admit I took a little perverse pleasure in knowing how devastated and humiliated she would have felt had I told her who I was.

The Friday night concert went very well, especially given the rocky dress rehearsal. The scheduling of the program was ill-fated. Normally, when Music Director Jurgen Schmidt is away, and we play under guest conductors, Schmidt makes his return concert a relatively easy program so he can hear what kind of shape we're in. This time, he jumped into one of the more difficult concerts of the season. True, that should not have been a serious a problem for a professional orchestra, but for the last two weeks when we were supposed to be playing under Henri Levine, a pretty good French conductor with a bright future and an unfortunate interest in skiing that resulted in a broken leg, we were left to the incompetent mercies of some Italian opera conductor whose name I have mercifully forgotten. I'm sure his main qualification for the engagement was that he was available on short notice and worked cheap. He clearly didn't know the Aaron Copland Third Symphony that we played on his first weekend, for he hardly ever took his head out of the score, leaving us essentially on our own in a tough piece. That kind of experience can "make" an orchestra if the conductor's interpretation is good, and he can bring it across, but it can be exhausting if said maestro has no clue, which was the case with this guy. By the end of his first weekend, we were one tired group. After the second, we were a sloppy one, as well.

But we were also pros. We recovered quickly under Schmidt's steady hand. I didn't always like his direct style. I've called him a *Kapellmeister* more than once, but he was what the doctor ordered this time, and we jelled. Saturday should have been better than Friday, but it wasn't. Maybe it was because we were on total alert for problems on Friday and dropped our guard after things went so well. Whatever the case, there were a few ensemble slips in the Vaughan Williams, including one in the trombones that really upset me. Music is not supposed to be all about mistakes vs. perfection, but audiences have gotten swept up into that syndrome by the flawlessness of recordings (aided by edits) and the accent on technique in the conservatories. We say that as long as you make music, mistakes don't matter, but in the commercial world of orchestra playing, they do, especially when they start to add up, and more especially if the conductor is one of those guys who goes over every concert recording with a fine-toothed ear-piece. Schmidt was not one of those, however pedantic he may have been at times, but that doesn't mean I can't be tough on myself. I sat on the stage and stewed. When I realized that I was one of the last musicians left there, I felt foolish and got up to leave. I was in a rotten mood as I approached the green room, but given my track record, I expected—hoped, at least—to get over it by morning.

No sooner had I stepped into the green room, than I bumped into Jason Prout who was on his way out. He didn't have such a hot night, either. (Like slumps in baseball, when one player slips, it can spread.) The difference was Jason had probably shaken off his mistake—if he even remembered it. Trumpeters are an arrogant lot: they get over stuff quickly, and Jason had been in this business ten years longer than I, leaving me hopeful that even a trombonist can develop a thick skin after a while.

After packing up my horn, I was curious as to whether Jason had anything to say. We weren't close, but we sat next to each other on stage and were friendly enough.

I never found out because of the shouting.

"How dare you?!"

I didn't pay attention at first, partly because I was still paying attention to Jason, and partly because I didn't think the yelling was addressed at me. The voice sounded vaguely familiar, though.

"You heard me!"

Talk about *déjà vu*!

"Graham Decker, stop ignoring me! You bastard!"

It was her. Gabrielle . . . what was her last name? Deschayes. What was *she* doing here? Then I heard myself yelling almost those same words.

"You know damn well what I'm doing here," she snarled through tightly drawn lips.

The whole orchestra was now watching all this, and I'm sure they were as puzzled as I was. The only thing I had on them in terms of knowing what was going on was that I knew who the screaming woman was. Joy Greenwald, a violinist who was standing nearby, leaned toward me: "What's going on, Graham?"

"I have no idea."

"Don't you think you better find out before she slugs someone? A woman scorned, you know," she added winking viciously.

"Stop that."

She laughed. "Forget about me, Lover Boy. You better stop *her.*"

I looked back at Gabrielle. She was wearing a yellow sweater and brown skirt. Her brown hair was drawn back in a pony tail in a way that hardened her face and emphasized her fury. I never thought it possible for brown eyes to blaze, but hers were proving me wrong.

I thought someone might ask her to leave, but there was a force field around her that backed people off, leaving a swath wide enough for me to cross the room. Thoroughly embarrassed, I closed the gap as quickly as I could and confronted her. "Do you mind telling me what this is all about?" I demanded when I was close enough to speak softly.

"You know."

"No. I *don't* know. I haven't a clue."

"Then you're stupid."

"Okay. I'm stupid. Enlighten me."

"I shouldn't have to."

"Why not? You were so eager to educate me a week ago. And keep your voice down."

Her eyes lit up. "That's exactly my point."

"*What's* exactly your point?"

Her breathing, which had been rapid moments ago, was slowing down. I don't think she was less angry, but she seemed more in control of herself.

That was my chance. "Can we step outside and negotiate whatever it is we're negotiating without putting on a show for the entire orchestra?"

For the first time, she seemed aware that we were not alone in the room. Without replying, she turned and stormed toward the door. It was understood, of course, that I was to follow. Snickers, chuckles, and one outright laugh trailed our exit. In response, I turned and raised my eyebrows to the orchestra as if to assure them I knew not what this crazy woman wanted, and whatever it was, it was not what they thought. Judging from the grins all around, no one believed me.

The hall was almost empty when we left the orchestra room. "Not here," I grunted when she was about to stop. "Outside."

I led her to the musicians' exit at the back of the hall. We then walked far enough down the street so that other musicians leaving wouldn't hear us.

"Okay," I said. "What?"

"You know."

"No. I don't."

"You made a fool of me the other night. You can't see that?"

"No." I thought it best to play the village idiot.

"You let me go on without telling me you were a professional musician who played in an orchestra. Why?" She stepped back, hands on her hips in a classic stance of anger.

"I don't know."

"Yes you do."

She was beginning to irritate me again. "Well, if you're so insightful as to what I know and don't know, why don't you tell me?"

I expected her to shoot something back, but she hesitated and looked uncertain. "I don't know. I . . . I assume you do." All of a sudden, she looked sad. It was disconcerting how she could go from angry to vulnerable so quickly and unpredictably.

I took a deep breath. Until then, I hadn't noticed that we had been walking and were headed toward her bus stop—and Bailey's. For a second, I thought of asking her if she wanted to return there—I don't know, as some kind of a setting for a peace treaty—but there was no need for that. The explanation I owed her required only a few moments, and there was no point in putting it off. "There was a moment early on when I was going to tell you that I knew most of the stuff you were talking about, but I couldn't find a polite way to do it. I thought you were trying to impress me," I added foolishly

"You thought I was trying to *impress* you?" Her eyes narrowed and her face turned flush.

"Weren't you?"

"No. I was trying to . . . to . . ."

"Enlighten me?"

"Yes," she hissed angrily.

"Do you have a boy friend?" I asked without knowing where the words came from. It was an outrageous question.

"You have a lot of nerve to ask."

"You're right," I replied scrambling to save myself. "I'm sorry. I shouldn't have asked. I don't know why I did."

She stopped walking. "Nor do I."

We were silent.

"I don't," she said suddenly, looking straight ahead as if speaking to no one. "Why did you ask?"

By now, I knew the answer. I always did, of course. "I figured you didn't. People who make it their business to enlighten other people generally don't do well in the social department."

"You think that's why I'm unattached?"

"It could be."

"And of course working sixty-hour weeks has nothing to do with it."

"I'm sure it does. But it's not the only reason."

She turned sharply to face me. Her lips moved, but for a moment, no words came out. "You go straight to hell." The words shot from her mouth like bullets.

We were just across the street from her bus stop. The light was red, but she darted across, at the last moment dodging a car that was entering the intersection. It wasn't that close, but her action was reckless. Right after she hit the curb, the light changed, and I crossed behind her. "Are you nuts?" I shouted.

She shook her head like a dog climbing out of a stream. "Just pissed." The expression sounded strange coming from her.

"You asked. I was being honest."

"You needn't have bothered." We were silent for a moment. "Your garage is the other way," she said sharply.

I stood awkwardly without responding.

"I don't need a ride," she said.

"I didn't offer one."

"Good." She pointed to my hand. "And you'd better get your instrument."

"Jesus," I exclaimed, and headed back to the hall. After a couple of steps, I stopped and called to her. "Look. I'm sorry. If you must know, I thought you were trying to impress me, and it was a little overbearing. I could have said something, but after you had gone on a while, it would have been awkward. So I kept quiet. I never expected to see you again."

"You knew I went to concerts. Didn't you think I'd spot your name in the program?"

"Never crossed my mind."

Her bus was coming down the street. She could just make it to the stop at Bailey's. "I'm sorry for the scene I made," she said as she hurried off.

I shrugged. "We can always use some excitement in the green room."

"I'm sure you could," she shot back over her shoulder.

"You're not going to do it again, are you?" I called after her as she crossed the street.

If she answered, I didn't hear her. She just made the bus.

She didn't do it again.

iii

A common injury among bicyclists is a broken collar bone suffered in a fall. I was warned about that when I was in college, and it has remained with me because bicycling is one of my major hobbies. Ours is a good town for bikers, with lots of open space and hills. I ride a lot, not just for recreation but on errands. I enjoy it, and it's great exercise, but deep in my mind, that fear of falling or getting hit by a car was there. I continued to ride, though, and I was good. Not every rider falls and is injured, and there was no reason why I should be one of those who is.

But I was.

It never should have happened. I played a great concert the night before, complete with *Bolero*, which has one of the toughest trombone solos in the repertoire. I played it perfectly and musically both nights. I was going over it in my mind while I was riding down Downer's Boulevard, a tree-lined parkway with wide pavement and a bicycle lane.

It was when I was soaring to the high D-flats that I spotted a car parked illegally in one of the few bicycle lanes in the city. I glanced back in panic, saw the way was clear, and tried to turn into the car lanes, but I couldn't clear the left rear bumper of the parked vehicle. My front wheel bounced off it, throwing the bike into the car lane. Even so, it seemed like I was maintaining my balance when the wheels went out from under me. I fell to the right, missing the parked car with my helmeted head but landing hard on my right shoulder. The pain was immediate and excruciating, radiating across my collar bone, over the shoulder, to the rotator cuff. I couldn't move any of that part of my body. I almost blacked out, but somehow maintained enough control to lurch partially to my feet and stagger off the street before more cars came. The pain ebbed just enough for my head to clear. I had to get to a hospital but had no idea how to make the trip. Three cars rushed by. A fourth was moving more slowly. This one stopped, and the driver asked if I was all right. After I managed a few pained groans and a nod toward my shoulder, he threw my bike in his trunk and drove me to the emergency room door.

The pain grew worse as I stepped inside. I'd never been to an emergency ward, but I'd heard bad stories about them, including long waits, something I couldn't imagine enduring at that moment. Thankfully, if the stories were true, this hospital was different. The man who picked me up took charge of my situation and helped me with the admitting clerk. After he filled out the forms, I signed them left-handed (wondering if such a signature was even legal), and an attendant escorted me to a consulting room. Before my Good Samaritan left, he said he'd leave my bike with someone in the hospital. I think I thanked him. It's hard to remember through all that pain.

"The doctor will be in very soon," a nurse assured me. "I'd give you something for the pain, but if you can stand it, you're better off waiting. It makes it easier to diagnose you."

I said I'd try.

She proceeded to take my blood pressure. As she did so, I felt myself grow fainter. "You're in shock," I could hear her say. She shoved something under my nose; it felt like someone poured acid up there.

That was my introduction to smelling salts, and they jolted me back to consciousness very quickly.

The nurse didn't leave me, except to stick her head out the door and talk with an attendant. After nodding a few times, she returned. "You're to have X-rays," she informed me. She led me to an adjacent room, and instructed me to get on a table under the X-ray machine. An attendant came in, and together they gave me an agonizing tour of the subject of pain as they moved me this way and that, all the time with my shoulder touching the table while they shot photos from different angles. One thing I learned from the process was how much pain I could endure without blacking out. Several times I heard the attendant, a small man, no taller than five-six, complaining about how hard it was to get me posed correctly for the pictures. (I am just over six feet and nudge 200 pounds on most scales.) Finally, they were finished, and I was led back to the consulting room. "The doctor will look at the X-rays and be with you right after that," the small man informed me. I nodded. The pain was subsiding, though it was still intense.

A few minutes later, the nurse returned and told me the pictures didn't come out well. I had to go through the entire process again. This time no matter how painful it may be, I must remain as absolutely still as I could. That I found unbelievable. With all our technology, how come science still hasn't found a way to take a decent X-ray of a barely moving subject?

There is no need to detail the next fifteen minutes. With one exception, they repeated my first session, only the pain was slightly worse. The exception was that the attendant who moved me around the table was taller and stronger than the first one. She had no difficulty hauling me into the correct positions and scaring me into staying still.

When they finished, they didn't take me back to the consulting room right away, I suspect because they wanted to check the pictures first. When I finally was led back, I was sure that the pictures were good, and I need worry only about how much radiation I had just absorbed. I calmed myself with unconvincing assurances that jocks get this stuff done all the time, and they don't drop dead of radiation poisoning.

"Are you feeling all right?" the nurse asked when we returned. She handed me a glass of water and two pills. "Now I can give you these for the pain. Will you be able to get a ride home?"

I nodded.

"Good." She handed me the pills. "You will feel a little better in a few minutes, maybe even a little sleepy." She pointed to a button on the wall to my left. "If you need me, push that. The doctor will be in very soon."

I thanked her, and she left me with my thoughts. I had seriously injured my right shoulder or broken my collarbone. The right arm is the trombonist's slide arm. I had no doubt that I required surgery. I'd be out of the orchestra for how long? Three months? Six? A year? And not just out of the orchestra. I couldn't practice during that time. Not really. Maybe blow long tones, but that was it. I couldn't even play left-handed, since my right hand wouldn't be able to hold the horn. I shivered as a darker thought came to mind. Could I be through as a trombonist? The pain was rising again, contrary to what the nurse promised. I was thinking of pushing the button to call her when it receded. It wasn't gone, but it was tolerable, though my fears of what lie ahead were not. I glanced through the window at the back of a room. I could see the nurse but not the doctor. She glanced inside at me, perhaps expecting me to faint despite her unspoken assurances. That wasn't good.

"Graham Decker?" The woman's voice came from behind me through a door I hadn't noticed. I tried to concentrate, but the painkillers made it difficult. All I knew was that I wondered why they sent a different nurse, and I was not comforted by the possibilities.

"Yes."

"I have your X-rays."

She walked around me so that I could see her. I looked up. My entire body stiffened, bringing renewed pain to my shoulder. I couldn't believe what—make that who—was standing before me.

"Gabrielle?"

She didn't react. But it was Gabrielle Deschayes. She looked uneasy.

It occurred to my dim brain that formality might be what was called for: "Dr. Deschayes."

This time she replied: "Yes."

"What are you doing here?"

Her eyebrows lifted in surprise. "You don't think this is a proper place for a doctor? This is a hospital, yes? I'm a resident here. I am also your doctor, and that is not such a coincidence as you may think. I saw the patient list. Your name was on it, along with the nature of your injury. Since it's your right shoulder that's involved, and your right shoulder is your livelihood, I assigned myself because I'm the best qualified on duty to handle your case."

Her presentation was clinical, but I can't say that was unlike her. What bothered me was that she felt she had to explain my situation so thoroughly. That was ominous. Before I could say anything, she was pinning my X-rays onto a viewing screen. After they were secure, she pored over them with a magnifying glass for what seemed like hours.

"I thought you'd already examined those things," I remarked nervously, trying not to sound it, but only for a moment. "Jesus, how bad is it?" The way she was examining those pictures I had visions of a quatrofracture or whatever you'd call it, six hours of surgery, maybe even a prosthetic.

"A minute please," she said quietly.

She continued to pore over the X-rays. I cursed her lousy bedside manner. Why wouldn't she say something?

"I want to take one more look at something," she said suddenly, as if reading my thoughts. "I don't want to mislead you."

She turned away from the X-rays, walked behind me, and placed her hands carefully around my shoulder. What followed could be an introductory class in torture for interrogators. But only introductory because the pain-killer was kicking in.

She was Swiss, she told me. French Swiss. But she lived in Zurich. German Swiss. Then, just German. It was Mrs. Mengele working on my shoulder.

With the remnants of my not yet narcotized rationality, I could tell that she was being careful, but I couldn't help but wonder if she was injecting a zinger or two as she went about her examination.

After what seemed like the better part of a morning, but was really only a couple of minutes, she finished and stood before me, gazing down as if I were a lab rat. Her ministrations had accomplished one thing: my head was clearing.

"Can you get a ride home?" she asked without ceremony.

It was not what I expected, and I didn't reply right away. Then, "Yes. A friend can come for me."

"Good. You're not to drive. The nurse already gave you CoTylenol for the pain. That's a blend of Tylenol and Codeine, a narcotic. I'll give you a prescription for a little more plus another one for Motrin. Take one more CoTylenol this evening, then three tomorrow, eight hours apart—and then only if you need them. After that—or after you stop the CoTylenol—switch to the Motrin, which is not a narcotic. Take those three times a day, eight hours apart. And be sure you eat something each time you take one of these medications." She added a few more instructions, all of them precise, and concluded with: "I'll see you get a muffin from the cafeteria to eat before you leave. When you get home, try not to use your shoulder any more than you have to. Rest it completely for two days. On the third day you can use it for routine tasks, but I must insist that you don't practice your trombone."

At that, I was so shocked that I almost missed the rest of her instructions. How would I even think of practicing with my shoulder the way it was?

"You may not believe this," she went on, "but by the third day you very well may feel like practicing. But don't. Not for a week. Then if the pain is mostly gone, you can play. Even then, be careful. The pain may linger, in which case practice, but go easy until it's completely gone. That may take another week." She picked up the phone and spoke some Latin gibberish into the mouthpiece. When she hung up, she continued her instructions. "The nurse will bring your pills and your X-rays in a moment." She wrote something on a note pad and handed me the paper. "That's the name of an orthopedist. If you're feeling serious pain in one week or slight pain in two weeks, call him. Tell him you saw me in this hospital. He will give you an immediate appointment. If you have any doubts about your condition, see him. If you do see him, bring your X-rays. If you're feeling fine, you need not see him."

I couldn't believe what she was saying. Five minutes ago, I was planning a new career. Now she's telling me I may be playing in a week? I hoped she was a better doctor than a musicologist.

"I don't understand," I said haltingly. "How?"

"You bruised a nerve," she explained. "That can be extremely painful, but it's not serious. There is no sign of a break on your X-rays, and nothing in my examination indicates torn ligaments, though that is a remote possibility. If you have to see Dr. Leggett, the orthopedist, that will probably be the reason." She stared at me for a second, as if I were a display in a butcher shop. "You lift weights, don't you?"

"Three times a week, like clockwork. How did you know?"

"I could tell from the feel of your muscles. Weightlifting may have saved your shoulder. The muscle and circle of tendons around the ball joint that makes up your shoulder are strong; the solidity of the bone is excellent and extremely well formed. If you insist on bicycling on these roads, I suggest you not stop weightlifting."

I looked to the ground and breathed as much of a prayer as an agnostic is capable of. "Thank you." If only she was right.

"Again. No playing for a week," she repeated, as I got up to leave, my head still a little foggy. "Then you should be fine. Otherwise, call Dr. Leggett. I'm not an orthopedist. I may have missed something, but I don't think so. I've seen this before." She stepped back and nodded toward the door. As far as she was concerned, that was it. Another patient disposed of.

But I couldn't leave it that way. "Look. I want to thank you. I was really scared."

She smiled. It was a very pleasant smile. "I know you were."

"I feel like I should do something to thank you."

"There is no need. It's my job."

"I realize that, but still . . ."

"There is nothing you need do for me." Her voice hardened a little.

I thought quickly. "Maybe something small, then. We're playing the Brahms First Symphony next week. I'll leave you a ticket."

She shook her head quickly. Suddenly, she was very animated. "*You're* not playing anything," she reminded me.

"I meant the orchestra," I said, chastised.

She nodded, her expression quite serious. "Just checking." She hesitated for a second and seemed uncertain. "Okay. I'll be glad to accept the ticket. Thank you." She paused. "That way I can keep watch. God help you if I see you on the stage. It will make my last display seem quite muted."

"I have no doubt," I retorted, wishing I could pull back the words as soon as I let them out.

She blinked rapidly but did not reply.

"Tell you what," I said. "Since I'm not playing, I'll come with you. There's a concerto on the program. I forget which, but I'll behave— and no books."

More blinking. She looked down the hall. I could tell she was unsure and almost told her that it was a bad idea, that I'd leave a second ticket, and she could go with whomever she wished.

"All right," she replied suddenly. "I'll meet you in front of the hall."

"There's no need for that. I can pick you up."

'No. I'll meet you." Her jaw was set.

I extended my hand, and we shook briefly.

"Saturday night?" I asked.

She nodded.

She sent for an aide who helped me gather my prescriptions and call for a ride. It was a good thing she did, because I was getting drowsy. By the time Joel Stein, one of the horn players in the orchestra, dropped me off, I was nearly asleep. He led me to my bed. Just before I passed out, I was beginning to understand why people take recreational drugs.

When I awoke, my watch told me I had slept six hours. It was 9:00 P.M. I turned on the stereo for a while and listened comfortably to Ralph Vaughan Williams's soothing *Pastoral Symphony*. By midnight, the pain had returned, slowly at first, then with some force. I panicked for a second, before I realized that it was time for another pain pill. I hurried into the kitchen and took the pill quickly, remembering to eat a hastily prepared peanut butter sandwich as I did so. A half hour later the pill pushed the pain into the background, and my head felt narcotized. This time, before falling asleep, I realized something else that happens when people take narcotics. They do stupid things.

Back in the hospital, I had asked Dr. Gabrielle Deschayes for a date!

iv

We met outside the hall as she instructed. She said she'd be there exactly twenty minutes before the concert, which was supposed to start
at eight. Curiosity compelled me to arrive five minutes before that, and
sure enough, she was true to her word right to the minute—just like a
German train. Our tickets were complimentaries through the orchestra.
I had already secured them, so we avoided the lines at the "will call"
window.

She immediately asked about my shoulder.

"Fine," I replied. "I have to hand it to you. You called it almost to
the day. I really did have to resist the urge to practice on Thursday, and
it got steadily better after that. Tomorrow, I'll be up and running.
Meanwhile, I've been able to buzz the mouthpiece and play long tones
without moving the slide. That's kept me from going completely dead.
I'll be fine."

She seemed pleased as she followed me into the hall and up the
stairs to the balcony. Our seats were off to the left side about halfway
back. People in the know about these things thought these were very
good seats, and I agreed.

The program was light for brass, though the Brahms on the second
half had its challenges. The first half included Haydn's Symphony
Twenty-two and another violin concerto, this time the Sibelius, a composer I adore but for this one piece. Gabrielle asked if the Sibelius had
been consigned to my Concerto Hall of Hell—a direct quote, by the
way.

"It's the only major work by Sibelius I don't like," I told her.

"Because of all the pyrotechnics."

"Mostly."

"I understand. Sibelius was a violinist and wanted to write a concerto like Tchaikovsky's that he could play. Or am I being pretentious
in saying so?" She was dead-on serious as she said that.

"Not at all. Now that we have the ground rules as to where we
stand in the world, anything goes."

"I'm so glad," she said tersely.

Her tone jolted me. I wasn't anticipating any great evening with her, and certainly no romance, but I didn't expect her to act like a downed live wire stretching across the sidewalk, either. "Actually, it isn't just the pyrotechnics," I said, returning to the Sibelius. "It's that the piece is so atypical for him. Sibelius was a composer of atmosphere and mystery and the Finnish outdoors. His language was neither opulent nor excessive except for this concerto. The first twenty-four bars are sublime. After that, it's show time, as if the performer in him took over for the composer. Of course, it should come as no surprise that his Violin Concerto is popular with people who are otherwise not that fond of Sibelius."

I expected her to argue, but she merely nodded. "What are the trombone parts like?" she asked.

"Nothing much."

She glanced down at her program and absently flipped through the pages. She seemed uncertain. "Do you know the Haydn symphony?" she asked.

"This particular one, yes," I replied. The players were starting to drift onto the stage. "It's called the *Philosopher*, and it's very striking, with two English horns and two French horns."

She nodded. "I don't know it. Sounds interesting."

She seemed genuinely excited over the prospect of hearing it and in fact liked the piece a great deal. The dialogue between the two pairs of "horns," one a double reed, the other brass, was very striking.

Finally, the Sibelius. My injury would have saved me from this piece had I not come to the concert. I wasn't looking forward to it. Our orchestra doesn't carry an assistant principal trombone, and I was curious about who was going to sit in for me. Normally, I'd be on top of the situation, but only to be aware of what was going on. The personnel manager makes the decision with the principal unavailable. Sometimes second trombone Jason Whorley moves up, but Jason was a professional second trombonist in both skill and preference. Few people realize how important the second trombone is in the section. It's not a case of the first being the most important and the second the next most important. In many ways, the second trombone makes the section by balancing the two outer parts, blending different colors, grading dynamics, and holding the intonation together. It's a tough job, and not every trombonist is good at it, including yours truly. I'm more solo minded and used to leading, but Jason has the perfect team concept attitude for second trombone. He was really not comfortable on first, but as a professional, he was more than capable of playing the part. In the end, it didn't matter to the personnel manager, who knew only that he had to hire someone. First, Second. It made no difference to him.

All this I explained to a very interested Gabrielle as the orchestra added the necessary players for the Sibelius. "My goodness, I've never been aware of that," she admitted.

We were quiet for a moment. Things were still awkward between us. "Now there's something I've never seen," she exclaimed suddenly, a bit of wonder in her voice.

"What's that?"

"A woman playing trombone in an orchestra," she replied as Adele Stephenson took her place in my first trombone chair.

"Well, they're not as common as frogs after a rain in Georgia, but there are more of them every day."

"You sound like you don't approve," she remarked, picking up on the slight disdain I couldn't quite keep out of my voice.

"Oh, I don't mind," I countered, though clearly I did.

She picked that up, too.

I shrugged. "Okay. I guess I do."

"Why?"

"Because women don't have the strength for the instrument. It won't be that evident tonight because neither work is that large in scale. But if this were Bruckner, you'd notice that Adele doesn't really have the chops or the lungs for it."

"Are you saying this woman doesn't have the physical requirements, or all women don't?"

"I'm saying most women don't."

"Then you're a fool."

My back stiffened. I was in for it now.

"Have you forgotten that you're speaking to a physician?" she added. Until then, we were speaking softly, but her voice began to increase in volume. Normally, I wouldn't be concerned, because the concert hall usually has a dampening effect on people's conversation, but after what she pulled in our green room, I wasn't sure what to expect from Dr. Gabrielle Deschayes. "Do you think I don't know something about physiology?" Her voice was shaking, and her shoulders seemed to fold within herself. The woman was furious, but at least she seemed to be holding her volume down. Sort of. For the moment.

My God, what have I done? What kind of a scene is she going to make now?

Just then, I was saved. Violin soloist Vaclav Zhorin, a large Russian bear with a huge mop of dark curly hair and bulging shoulders, was making his way to the front of the stage, followed by Maestro Schmidt. Applause broke out. Zhorin was not that well known, but he was a rising star, and even if he weren't, the local Russian community had turned out in force. Gabrielle clapped with enthusiasm, but I could tell from the tightness around her mouth that Zhorin's appearance had not diffused all her anger. Normally, I would have looked forward to intermission because it would have meant that the Sibelius was over but not this time. As it turned out, Zhorin played the Sibelius very well in a way that allowed me to enjoy the piece a little. He didn't strut and preen like so many soloists do, flashing his bow like a sword while slashing notes all over the place. He treated the piece almost as chamber music, keeping at least one "eye" on the orchestra while bringing out the interplay between his part and what was going on behind him. It made a huge difference, one that led me to rethink the piece a bit, though I doubt it was what Sibelius wanted. As Dr. Deschayes pointed out, Sibelius wanted to write a virtuoso piece that he could perform, so I'm not so sure that he would have liked Zhorin's introspective approach. (A little research convinced me that he would not, but the joke was on the composer. The violin part was *too* virtuosic for his violin skills. Served him right.)

When the Sibelius was over, and we were still clapping, I leaned over and passed on my thoughts to Gabrielle, hoping my unexpectedly positive reception would lead her to forget my opinions on female trombonists.

"I wish this hall weren't sold out," she said as we prepared to leave for intermission.

"Why do you say that?"

"Because I really would like to find some other place to sit." She didn't forget.

"All right. I'm sorry. I shouldn't have said that about female trombonists."

She turned suddenly and stopping inching between the seats to the aisle, thereby halting the progress of five people behind her. "Why not? It's the way you feel, isn't it? Or were you just baiting me? I damn well hope not, because I don't like being made fun of. I should think you would know that by now."

"Oh no," I assured her stupidly. "I meant it."

"Good," she shot back.

At that moment the man standing directly behind her spoke up: "Do you think you could move, please? I've got a drink waiting for me at the bar."

Her head spun about as if on a swivel, and she glared at him. I took a sharp deep breath, certain I was going to have to intervene, but just as quickly, she turned back toward me, and gave me a shove toward the aisle, almost knocking me back into the seats. (So much for concern about my shoulder!) Barely maintaining my balance, I just made it to open space. She followed, but slowly. The man behind her was irritated, but he seemed intimidated and remained still until she stepped into the aisle. The second she did, he bolted like an animal released from a cage, clambered to the top of the stairs, and disappeared.

"I can't wait until he comes back," she muttered. "Nothing like listening to Brahms next to a drunk."

Oh boy, I couldn't help but thinking. Then again, maybe I should be grateful for the man's intervention. It might make her forget her crusade on behalf of female trombonists.

"Where did you get such crackpot ideas?" she challenged as we made our way to the exit.

No such luck. "All right. I'm behind the times." I had no doubt she was referring to my observations about female trombonists, not Sibelius. "As I said, there are more of them every day."

"And you don't like the competition."

"Who likes competition?"

"Are you afraid she may challenge you for your job?" she asked as we approached the common room with the bar and tables.

"She can't," I replied. "I have tenure."

"But if you didn't, she could."

"Maybe. But it's unlikely." I explained that if I didn't have tenure, the orchestra could dismiss me without cause and hire Adele, not that I thought Schmidt would do that.

Of course, I knew that wasn't her point.

"Okay, forget the business about tenure. Maybe she'll go against you if you audition for a better job. That could happen, couldn't it?"

"Yes, it could," I admitted.

"Some other women might, too."

"I suppose."

"And what would happen to your poor little ego if one of them beat you?"

I was getting pissed. "Do we really have to go on with this? I'm sorry I said what I did. It was out of line. Okay?"

"Fine."

I told her I didn't need a drink but would find a table.

She nodded. "But it would be better if you believed what you just said." In addition to her other stellar qualities, she had to have the last word.

Before I could reply, she was heading for the bar to order who knows what.

When she joined me, it was with a glass of what I assumed was white wine in her hand. "Riesling," she informed me. "I didn't know you could get a German wine here." She took a wary sip. "Of course, it isn't a very good German wine."

No doubt.

She took another sip. "But it will do."

Well, she could have her last word on German wines, but not about trombonists. "I won't lie," I said as if our conversation had known no break. "Women players make me uneasy. I'm not used to them. I'm sorry. But I really do think that the average woman lacks the lung strength and air capacity to play trombone when compared to the average man."

She shook her head. "Read the studies on air capacity," she replied.

She took another sip and set down her glass. Already, it was half-empty. "They're out there. Meanwhile, you'll have to take my word for it that women have enough lung strength to play the trombone. A few months ago," she went on, "I was in New York and went to a concert at Carnegie Hall. Actually, I went to three, and I forget which orchestra this particular person was in, but there was a male trumpet player who was positively obese. Now I'm telling you as a doctor that this man was in terrible shape, but there he was playing an instrument that I presume you will tell me requires a great deal of strength. Surely, you're not going to insist he was better qualified for his position than a skilled woman who weighed a healthy 130 pounds or so. You're a bicyclist. Supposedly, that means you have some interest in conditioning, so you know the answer."

I nodded, however reluctantly.

Mercifully, the muted chimes rang to call us back to our seats.

"Short intermission," she commented. "Good. My friend over there," she pointed to the man anxious to get around her to the bar earlier, "can't have gotten too inebriated."

We returned to our seats. The man from the bar actually got there first. I'm not sure how. Maybe he knew a short cut. Neither he nor Gabrielle acknowledged each other.

The second half started. The Brahms was very good, and Adele (okay I'm admitting it here) played the chorale beautifully. Almost as well as I would have. I couldn't resist noting same to Gabrielle, adding that the area I thought myself superior in was a matter of expression, not power. I must have enjoyed living dangerously, but she either took it in good spirits, or she saw no point in arguing with someone she was never going to see again.

The latter clearly was the case as I drove her home. She talked appreciatively about the concert and thanked me for taking her. She also assured me my arm would heal soon, and I'd be back in my first trombone chair by our next concert.

When we arrived at her building, I walked her to the front door.

"Would you like to come in?" she said.

Huh?

I couldn't immediately reply.

"Oh come on," she said, "We should have gone to that restaurant we went to last time. But I can make you some decaf here."

What was going on here? But Gabrielle was an intimidating person, never more so than at that moment, and I followed her upstairs. We didn't say much, and I had no idea what she had in mind. One thing that I was convinced of: Dr. Gabrielle Deschayes was at best eccentric and at worst, a nut. Of course, there are nuts and there are crackpots, though in my deepest core I was convinced she was little more than eccentric, if maybe a bit self-destructive.

Inside her apartment, she was serious, a bit stern, but efficiently friendly enough. With a brisk nod, she headed to her tiny kitchen to prepare the coffee, leaving me to look around. Her apartment was small but neatly kept with simple, tasteful furniture. On a shelf to the right were three rows of medical books. Below them were three more of music books. A door to the left probably led to the bedroom. On a desk next to the door was a practice piano keyboard. There was also a couch along the back wall behind a tiled coffee table, and two other chairs, one against the opposing walls to my right and left. I took a seat on the couch.

A few minutes later she reappeared from the kitchen, carrying a tray with two small cups of coffee, a creamer, and two slim pieces of some kind of cake. Her china was simple, and like her apartment, tasteful. And very European.

"Black, right?" she said.

I nodded, and she placed the tray on the coffee table in front of me. After pouring a little cream in her own cup, she took a seat across from me and demurely crossed her legs. As her skirt hem climbed toward her knee, revealing slim, shapely calves, I realized for the first time that they—and she, somehow—were very attractive.

"All right. Enough about female trombonists," she offered.

"Okay with me. I guess I was being stupid."

"Let's just say you'd find it hard to get into medical school." She reached for her knee and nervously scratched it. "So you actually liked the Sibelius," she said.

"Yes, I did."

"So did I, though I do admit that I missed the showboating. I will also concede that the piece doesn't fit Sibelius."

Grateful for at least one triumph, I awaited her next foray.

She smoothed out her skirt. "So what about the Brahms? Did you like it?"

"Yes. Schmidt is good with Brahms, though his approach is unusual. Despite that German name—he's American, anyway—he conducts Brahms like a Frenchman."

"Yes. He reminds me of Ernest Ansermet," she said, referring to a famous Swiss conductor and long-time head of *L'Orchestre de la Suisse Romande* of Geneva until his death in 1969. "Ansermet was wonderful in Debussy, Ravel, even Stravinsky, but he insisted on conducting Brahms and Beethoven, too, and he never was able to adapt his style to either. Schmidt was much better at that."

I wondered if she noticed how wide my eyes opened on that one. That little tidbit about Ansermet was not exactly common knowledge. "He did make one interesting Brahms recording," I observed.

"The *Requiem*." She really *was* up on this stuff.

"Yes. The *Requiem*." I gazed about her apartment.

"Are you looking for something?"

"Your record collection," I admitted. "What you just said is not common knowledge even among sophisticated concertgoers."

"I do have a lot of records, but most of them are in Boston at my mother's house. And I'm from Switzerland, so I should know something about Ansermet. My father liked him a great deal, and I picked up on that." She laughed. "You should have heard him go on about Honegger."

"He liked him, right?"

"Very much."

"So do I."

"Has your orchestra ever played any of his pieces?"

I reached for my coffee. "*Pacific 231*."

"The usual."

"Yes. Some American orchestras have played the Second and Third Symphonies, too."

She leaned over to place her cup on the tray in front of me. "A very odd work, the Third. You'd probably like playing it. There is a lot of trombone writing."

"There is, but a friend who played it with the Juilliard Orchestra told me that a lot of it is unison—three trombones on one part."

She looked surprised. "Really?" Then after thinking for a moment, "You know, it does sound that way. I never thought about it before." Seeing I had finished my coffee and cake, she reached for the tray. As she leaned over her blouse dropped slightly and I could see the top of her cleavage. "More?" she inquired.

I had this horrible impulse to reply by saying, "Yes, thank you," and reaching for her blouse, but quickly shook my head.

"Good," she responded. "As your doctor, I can tell you that even decaffeinated can keep you awake if you drink enough of it." She was speaking comfortably without any sarcasm. I don't think she was aware of any not-so-errant glances on my part, but I couldn't be sure.

"That cake is tempting, though. Did you make it?"

She laughed. "Of course not. There is a very good bakery a half block away. And that was the last of it, I'm afraid."

"Just as well."

"You know," she said after returning from the kitchen, "for all that business about the Third Symphony, it's the Fifth I really like." She was back to Honegger. "Especially that wonderful first movement with the chorale."

"I've heard it once," I acknowledged. "But I don't remember it very well."

"I'm sorry my records aren't here. I'd play it for you."

"This late? In an apartment building?"

"Most stereos have a volume control."

All of a sudden, I was overcome with a yawn which I tried mightily to stifle but failed.

"It is late," she agreed.

"Yes." It *was* late. As I struggled to my feet, I learned that I was more tired than I realized. "I should be going."

She moved toward the door, I thought to let me out. Instead, it was to block my way. "You don't have to go," she said. "But decide quickly if you want to stay. I can't stay up too late. I have to study in the morning."

"What?"

"Don't be naïve, Graham." She moved away, standing, facing the door to her bedroom. Almost in a trance, I turned around to follow the motion of her hips. It was more pronounced than in her usual walk, but still subtle. Not too subtle, though. Suddenly, her abrupt manner, which until that moment troubled me a great deal, troubled me no longer. Something more powerful replaced my irritation.

"Coming?" she asked quietly over her shoulder as she moved away. I took a single dazed step forward.

She stopped short of the bedroom door and placed her hand meaningfully on the knob. She seemed about to turn it, then hesitated. I couldn't see her face, but an apparent tension about her body indicated a slight uncertainty. She turned half around, her expression provocative, yet quizzical. "Listen. I know this is not the usual seduction procedure for you. But I don't have the time or energy for the customary *pas de deux* that goes on between the sexes in America. I have to work tomorrow—not as early as usual, thank God, but I'm a nervous wreck from all my hours at the hospital. My body can use some release. You're an attractive man, you're here, and you'll do. I'm sorry I can't put it any more romantically than that. I'm not skilled at propositioning."

I shrugged. "There are worse things than honesty." I stepped forward and placed my hands on her shoulders. She kissed me on the lips. We separated and stared at each other for a moment. Then she reached behind her and opened the door. I followed her into her bedroom. Then as if hit with a lightening bolt, my body jumped to life. I threw my arms around her, we kissed, ripped at each other's clothes, and fell as one body onto her bed.

Gabrielle didn't have to be at work until noon when she would be covering for another doctor. This left us time for a leisurely breakfast, more sex, some study for her while I read the newspaper, not much conversation, and more sex. One thing I can say is that I did perform a service to humanity. It was a very relaxed Dr. Deschayes who would meet with her patients that afternoon.

We left her building together, said our good-byes, and I stumbled into my car and drove off. There was something very formal and final about those good-byes.

We made no future plans to see each other.

2012

I was just putting some finishing touches to a manuscript when the door to my study opened. It was my son, Brad.

"Still working on that novel, Dad?" he asked.

I shook my head. "Not any more. It's finished."

"No kidding." He nodded and seemed impressed. "Are you going to find an agent now?"

"Nope." I got up from my desk. "I don't need an agent."

"How are you going to get it published, then? No one gets fiction published these days without an agent. Are you going to self-publish?"

"Who said anything about publishing?"

He looked chagrined. Brad was a pleasant, easygoing young man. He'd just graduated from college and was heading to medical school in the fall. He was very achievement-oriented for all his casual ways, and he couldn't imagine doing all the work I did without wanting to get the product published. "I hope you don't leap to your diagnoses like that," I admonished him with a smile. "Besides, it's not so easy to publish something like this. It's too short for a novel and too long for a short story."

He grinned back. "One of life's lessons and learned for free. I promise I won't make any quick diagnoses." He turned his gaze to the manuscript I'd just placed neatly at the side of my desk. "So are you just going to leave it in your drawer?"

"Oh no. In fact, I have an audience ready made."

"Really? Who?"

"You. Your sisters. Your mother."

"You wrote a book just for us?"

I saw no point in making the whole thing a mystery. All I was going to do was have the manuscript copied and bound. "Look." I handed him the early pages.

Brad read them quickly. His eyes opened wide in astonishment.

"You know your mother," I said. "She never told you how we got together. She has always been so embarrassed about it. And for years, I've gone along, as if the whole thing were a deep dark secret. Well it isn't. I've always wanted to write a book—something that doesn't have anything to do with playing the trombone. So I thought I'd write one just for the five of us.

Bradley's expression turned serious. "But then she'll know you told us."

I laughed. "So it goes. No patient can keep secrets from his doctor forever."

It was Brad's turn to laugh. He looked at the title page. "Cute," he commented. "The title. I take it, though, not the way you guys met."

"Heavens, no," I assured him. "Anything but. Perhaps you've noticed. Your mother is a very strange woman."

He nodded. "Quite so."

I handed the book out at a family supper that Sunday. The girls came with their husbands. Brad was single and still lived with us. Everyone was delighted to see it, and after supper, everyone but Gabrielle pored through the pages, pointing to this or that paragraph and asking questions all at once. My wife just leafed through the pages slowly, turning each of them as if they were delicate petals. Tears began trickling down her cheeks, and she made no effort to wipe them off. I put my arm around her shoulders. She leaned toward me, and I could feel her shudder. She was very quiet. Everyone in the room knew what was going on, but they gave this very strange woman, the mother of three of them, her privacy and continued chattering about the book.

ALICIA

I

She was blond, willowy and tall, clad in a summery white dress with a thin red belt about her waist. Her village of Canados was set in the Araman mountains in the bleak northern regions of the tiny country of Threnia. Her name was Alicia Auer. Today she was performing an act of rebellion, though it didn't appear she was doing anything more than sitting by herself on a mountain clearing two miles above her village nestled in the valley below.

It was a beautiful day. The sun hovered in the sky, lighting the valley with a golden hue that was rare so high in the mountains. The smell of late spring charged the air as if barely able to contain its eagerness for summer. Emerald Lake shown darkly to her right by the Outer Road that wound its way up from the village on the other side of the peaks to the south. The stream that poured into the lake gurgled cheerfully, while a soft wind wafted through the trees.

This was Alicia's favorite time of year. She should have been glorying in her surroundings, not trembling with defiance. She would have but for the tank parked below on East Street, casting a shadow over her village like that of a low-hanging thundercloud. It had rolled in at the head of a motorized column on a quiet Sunday morning, announced by a siren that jolted the townspeople out of their sleep. Some villagers thought the world was ending. They might have been convinced when an amplified voice ordered them to assemble at the clearing in the center of town in fifteen minutes. Everyone obeyed, sleepy-eyed and frightened, silently shuffling through the streets in robes and pajamas to meet the alien with the god-like voice. Many trembled. All comprehended his authority, yet their most vivid imaginings could not have suggested what met them at the square.

Parked at the western edge of the green was a huge olive-colored machine, atop of which stood a single man clad in green. Along the length of West Street, was a row of three hundred similarly attired men. Behind them was an array of vehicles, the likes of which the Canadosians had never seen. Its inorganic unity struck the people dumb; they could do little more than huddle together in the damp morning cold, trembling in their flimsy bed garments. When frightened children clung to the legs of their parents and began to cry, their anxious elders reached down quickly to shush them, lest the stone-faced aliens disapprove of sobbing children.

The man on the tank stepped forward. Speaking through a loudspeaker, he explained that he and his men were Balkhenians who came to Canados on their way to an invasion of southern Threnia. Canados was to be a rear line base of the invasion. As such it would be occupied indefinitely by Balkhenian troops. He would now outline the terms of occupation. The Canadosians could expect no problems if these terms were obeyed.

The Balkhenian command was now the official government of Canados. Any existing body had only liaison power. All village buildings were at the disposal of the occupiers, though whenever possible, homes would be left within the private domain of their residents. No communication by a villager outside Canados was permitted. No villager was to travel outside the village limits unless accompanied by a Balkhenian soldier. No large assemblage was allowed unless supervised by a soldier.

The officer covered the remaining rules in a few short minutes. When he finished, he gazed imperiously over the crowd, his eyes seeming to memorize the countenance of each of its members. He then dismissed the villagers with a sweep of his hand.

The frightened people shuffled off like robots, not daring to talk or even whisper among themselves. Once they were gone, and the square was empty save for the soldiers, the commander signaled his men with a second wave of his hand. The troops broke ranks like worker ants to set up the occupation. Their task was completed in a matter of hours.

The Canadosians offered no resistance: nothing had prepared them to react any other way. They had never seen Balkhenians, knew nothing about their country, and were in awe of their machines. And those loudspeakers! It wasn't so bad when one could see who was speaking, but the amplified voice of someone unseen was terrifying, especially at night. There was the matter of the strangers' clothing. Canadosians dressed simply but in a variety of colorful, attractive garments. The Balkhenians all wore a severely cut green garb that made a mass of them look like a small lake. Their discipline was frightening. Each one could be gathered on the square and made to march in strictly ordered groups to the cadence of a single leader. Even when they weren't formally assembled, they looked alike, acted alike, walked alike, and talked alike. Most impressive was how they had instantly materialized. The villagers would have been no more paralyzed had the Balkhenians dropped from the sky.

II

Until the Balkhenian invasion, Canados was virtually self sufficient. The Outer Road that connected her to southern Threnia was used only for tri-annual visits by delivery trucks that brought the villagers the few items they could not make themselves. In exchange, the Canadosians loaded craftworks and similar goods for the return trip south. These trucks were the sole link between Canados and the rest of Threnia. There was no postal service and no electronic communications other than a single telephone pole along the Outer Road midway between the village and the mountains. A dead wire dangled from its crosspiece, barely touching the ground. No one knew why it was built—only that it was a monument to a future that had never arrived.

No Canadosian had been to the outside world except for three "newcomers" and the town physician (who went for medical training), and no such travel was permitted. Two of the newcomers had arrived by accident, stumbling upon the village after being lost in the Aramans during winter storms. The third was a trucker who, after years of making deliveries, formed a bond with the villagers and decided to stay.

Each was accepted as a citizen after long deliberations at a village meeting. Upon their swearing in, the new citizens were required never to talk about their lives on the outside. All three learned trades and become loyal citizens; none broke his vow.

Alicia was the village enigma. Seized by frequent attacks of curiosity and wanderlust, she alone thought of life beyond the mountains. She knew not to ask questions around the native Canadosians, but the newcomers were another matter, and she approached each of them to learn of his life before Canados. Her queries were rebuffed with smiles and admonitions to be grateful she did not know what she wished to know. The truck driver, Rene Fahr, was the most forthcoming, but mainly, he described his old rundown neighborhood, his poor state of affairs, and how he had to drive a truck when he would have preferred the life of a merchant. "Here, I own my own store, and live with a dignity I never believed possible." His voice teemed with pride and said no more.

So Alicia turned to Canados's tiny, and largely unvisited, library. Its collection was small and uneven, delivered in random shipments by the truckers, but it housed several valuable items, and she devoured them all. She read the first volume of *War and Peace*, but could never obtain the second. She read some Dickens—*David Copperfield, Oliver Twist, Barnaby Rudge,* and *Dombey and Son*—and longed to read the other titles listed in the flyleaf of *Copperfield*, especially *Great Expectations* because its title paralleled her own feelings. Hugo's *Les Miserables* she found captivating and poignant; she wondered what else he had written, there being no flyleaf in the library's copy and no *H* volume in its encyclopedia. She knew a little of nineteenth century France, the revolution in America, and some Plato and Marx; she was as powerfully drawn to the *philosophes* of the Enlightenment as she was repelled by the inquisitors of the Middle Ages. She was especially grateful for the illustrations.

Alicia's curiosity and her studies at first made the Balkhenian occupation less dreadful for her than for her neighbors. She had read of armies and seen pictures of tanks. She knew the devastation they caused, but at least she understood what they were. Within her understanding burned the only potential for resistance to the occupation of Canados.

One day she voiced her feelings to Fahr in the hope that his experience might give her reason to anticipate the removal of the Balkhenian force. His response was disturbing. There was no way the villagers could drive the Balkhenians out of Canados, he told her. The southern Threnians had an army, as did their allies, so perhaps they would come to the village's aid, but, "If the Balkhenians can overcome a mountain barrier that had kept us free of their soldiers for centuries, they may have the power to overcome the alliance."

Alicia understood Fahr's implication too well. Seeing pictures of danger was not the same as experiencing it, and Alicia was eventually as frightened as the rest of the Canadosians. Even so, she did not give in totally to despair. Things may change, but some people soften the impact of change with imagination. For Alicia this meant dreaming of soldiers marching into Canados from the Threnian plain to drive the Balkhenians back over the mountains, after which things in Canados would be as they were. Sometimes she thought of herself as her village's deliverer, slipping out of the village under the cover of night, traveling south along the Outer Road, locating the Threnian army, and leading the soldiers back to her village, like Joan of Arc.

These illusions comforted her until her first contact with a Balkhenian soldier. She was walking down East Street toward the square where she encountered a group of soldiers talking among themselves. One stepped out to block her way, addressing her in heavily accented Threnian. She tried to walk around him without replying, but he grabbed her arm. With surprising strength Alicia freed herself, but the soldier reinforced his hold, squeezing her arm until she stopped struggling. He relaxed his grip, but in doing so underestimated her spirit. Alicia resumed battle. This time she broke away and almost escaped, but the soldier grabbed her shoulder with a force that nearly yanked her feet out from under her. She regained her balance with difficulty and confronted him, her face red and her breath pushing through her chest in quick hard gasps. The soldier's grey eyes were narrowed by a combination of lust and anger, but Alicia refused to back away. Instead, she aimed a blow at his face that he was barely able to duck. He raised his arm to retaliate when he was frozen—arm in mid-air—by the sound of a single "Halt!" barked in Balkhenian. Neither he nor Alicia moved a finger, until, as if on a signal, both turned at once toward the intruder. The soldier snapped to attention and stood without flinching while enduring what was clearly a rebuke. When the officer finished, the soldier saluted, pivoted smartly on his right heel and walked rigidly—and with ill-disguised shame—from the scene.

When the soldier was out of earshot, the officer turned to Alicia. He was older than the man he had just dispatched. The hair under his cap was grey, and wrinkles lined his face. His countenance was of a man who had lived a hardened life and had inflicted pain too often and not long ago enough. There was a hint of warmth in his light-colored eyes that had not been extinguished by campaigns, discipline and authority. His mouth was not as hard as those of his comrades. At one time he might even have been kind. He spoke to Alicia in a tone that was polite and guardedly amiable. "I regret the behavior of that soldier," he said in perfect, if slightly accented Threnian. "Please accept my promise that it won't happen again." He smiled, the first Balkhenian she had ever seen do so. She acknowledged his kindness by nodding awkwardly in return. "You are free to go," he said.

Alicia smiled weakly and thanked him. The officer bowed and took his leave. Alicia's knees shook. It wasn't just the physical harassment. Canadosian boys were boisterous occasionally, but this was different. She could not have resisted the Balkhenian soldier without his superior's intervention, and that was what troubled her. The officer's action was a sign of the restraint that had been the sole redeeming feature of the occupation, but how much longer would it last? Already a surliness had crept into the soldiers' manner. Womenless men occupying a defenseless village, men who could be sent into combat at any moment, were a volatile force, and she could not understand why their superiors denied them spoils when spoils were available. If the idea was to avoid antagonizing their subjects, the village had cause for worry, for the Balkhenian officers would learn soon enough that the villagers would never revolt.

Something more immediate also troubled her, something she couldn't immediately comprehend. The words of her rescuer. "You are free to go now," he had said. He seemed to mean them kindly, and she had been grateful to hear them, but that wasn't what was gnawing at her now.

Finally, the answer came to her.

That officer could just as easily have said, "You are not free to go now," and she could have done nothing about it.

Alicia looked cautiously about. A few soldiers were loitering in the street. One glanced toward her, but she averted her eyes and avoided contact. She thought she sensed the presence of someone behind her and whirled about, but no one was there. She was alone but for thoughts and emotions she had never known before. He said she was free to go, but she had never felt less free than she did at that moment.

III

The Balkhenians had begun their invasion in secrecy. As far as they knew, no one south of the Aramans was aware of their movements, and they wanted to keep it that way. Hence their ban on villagers leaving Canados without permission. Alicia was frightened, but it wasn't like her to submit completely. It was one thing for the customs of her village to keep her at home. It was another to be detained by outsiders. Though reason and lack of courage prevented her from acting on her dream of escaping to the south, her need to exercise a symbolic personal rebellion explains her presence in the mountain. Besides, she refused to believe that if caught her punishment would be severe. What threat could a village girl be to the powerful Balkhenians?

At first, it was a faint suspicion, an uncertain tug at her senses, but Alicia sensed she was not alone. She tried to dismiss her apprehension, but her tightened muscles refused to relax. She looked about but saw no one. Listening carefully, her ears picked up only the gurgling of the brook and the swishing of the breeze. Even so, she remained uneasy. Someone was nearby. She was sure of it. She stood up to examine her surroundings more closely but saw nothing. Her nerves told her she had rebelled enough, and it was time to start back while Fortune was still with her. With a sigh, she bent down to gather the articles she had brought with her, when she heard a *snap*, like a twig breaking from the direction of the road. Her heart jumped into her throat. Someone *was* about! A Balkhenian! It had to be! No other Canadosian would dare come up there.

Alicia was caught. Standing alone in the meadow, waiting for whomever it was to appear, she was more afraid than when she was accosted in the village. Gone was her frivolous attitude toward capture. Though her disobedience was nothing more than feistiness, she doubted the Balkhenians would admire that trait in their captives. Alicia had done no harm, but they might choose to make her an example of what happens when their wishes are defied. This thought struck terror into her heart, but it did not immobilize her, and she turned to run.

It was too late. She could manage no more than three steps before a single Threnian word—"Halt!"—shot through the air from behind her. She had no choice but to obey. Whoever was behind her had time to shoot if she tried for the cover of the surrounding trees. Overcome by despair, Alicia turned slowly about to confront a lone Balkhenian soldier standing across the meadow. A rifle cradled in his right arm was pointed directly at her stomach.

"Your name!" the soldier snapped in Threnian. It was a command, not a question.

Alicia fought to gather her courage. "Alicia Auer." Her voice was tightly drawn but not to the point of stammering.

"What are you doing here, Miss Auer?"

Staring directly into the soldier's eyes she replied, "Nothing." Her voice was still even. "Just sitting."

"You don't know this is forbidden?"

Her first thought was to claim she didn't, but the soldier's manner convinced her this would be poor policy. "Yes I know. But I'm not doing any harm just sitting here, am I?"

"It is forbidden for you to leave the village," he said in a voice made noticeably flat as a result of his trying to sound as stern as possible. "The colonel made that clear two weeks ago. You were given no discretion to disobey him."

"I'm sorry. I didn't think coming here was all that serious. I haven't really left the village, you know."

"As far as we're concerned, you have." The soldier stepped toward her. "You'll have to come back with me, Miss Auer. The colonel wants to see you."

So she was to be taken to the highest Balkhenian authority. She wasn't to be let off with a warning. They were going to make an example of her. And what would that mean? She wasn't sure, though she sensed it would be better if she could limit her Balkhenian contact to this young soldier. "You mean I can't just be taken back to the village and sent home?" she inquired, her words surprisingly calm. "I have to be questioned? Is that really necessary?"

"I'm afraid it is, Miss." The Balkhenian tugged sharply on his uniform tie. "My orders are to bring you back to the Colonel. Any questions you have can be taken up with him."

"Am I going to be tortured?" This query was uttered with the Canadosian ingenuousness that so mystified the soldier since he had arrived in the village, and he couldn't help but be disarmed. He smiled. He was young, no older than she, with dark features unlike those of his mostly fair comrades. His eyes were dark also, not evilly so, but deep and brooding. He looked like the soldier who accosted her in the square, but without the heavy gaze and the arrogant twist about the mouth.

The soldier answered her question with a shake of his head.

"Then what will he do to me?"

"Miss Auer, I really can't speculate. We don't torture civilians. You'll probably be let off with a warning." His tone, much lighter all of a sudden, indicated he might be taking the incident humorously after all. "This is your first offense, isn't it?"

"Oh yes. I've not come here since you arrived," she lied.

"Then you have little to fear, but you must still come back with me. Now."

Alicia remained still.

"*Now*, Miss Auer." He emphasized his words by thrusting the rifle in the direction in which he wished her to go. "It'll take a while to drive back, and the colonel is not a patient man."

"You didn't walk up here?" she inquired.

"No," he replied. "I came in a jeep."

"I didn't hear it."

"You wouldn't. The road's a long way down." He smiled again. Alicia observed that he was having a difficult time retaining his severity of countenance, suggesting he was more the boy he looked than the soldier he wished to appear. "I had quite a climb up here, and that was just from where I parked the jeep" he was saying. "You must be in good shape to hike up to this place all the way from the village."

She ignored his comment. "Sound carries well up here," she said. "I can't understand why I didn't hear your motor." She wanted to keep talking to him, hoping that extended conversation would break the soldier/civilian barrier between them.

He shook his head. "I parked a long way away, as I said." He gestured again with his rifle. "Now we must return, Miss Auer."

Her efforts had failed. Boy or not, he meant her to do as he asked. She started toward him, and the soldier stepped aside to let her pass. In single file, with the barrel of his rifle never more than a few yards from her back, they made their way down the treacherous path. At first they proceeded slowly, but soon, almost imperceptibly, Alicia quickened her pace. She had formed a plan. If her captor was unable to keep to the unfamiliar path, she might be able to slip away and make a run for it. She had no idea where she would go after escaping, but she was convinced he was lying about or was ignorant of the consequences of her capture, and that anything was preferable to being taken to his colonel.

"Slow down, Miss Auer!" His words cut into her thoughts. "Don't get too far ahead."

Reluctantly, she obeyed until the soldier again was only a few yards behind. At last, they arrived at the clearing where the Balkhenian had parked his jeep about fifty yards from the road. The soldier had followed a natural path through the woods to get there, though how he managed to locate such a hard-to-find place was a mystery. Alicia was delighted he had, for another plan took shape in her mind. By ignoring the Balkhenian rules of occupation, she had put not only herself in danger, but her family and friends as well, and the only way she could right things was to flee south in search of help. It was an outrageous idea. She had no idea if she could succeed, but the mere act of planning gave her courage.

When they reached the jeep, the soldier helped Alicia climb inside, stored his rifle out of reach of his passenger, and stepped in himself. Inch by inch, he guided the vehicle down the treacherous hillside. Its progress was excruciatingly slow, much to Alicia's satisfaction. Any quicker and it might be impossible to carry out her plan.

The idea was simple. Along the left side of the trail, they would pass a narrow pathway that led into one of the thickest parts of the forest. While the vehicle was easing past that point, she would leap out, cross the road and flee into the woods where, under the shelter of tree growth so thick that the sun could barely penetrate it, she should be safe from pursuit. Once dark descended she would make her way by moonlight down to the road and head south. What made the idea plausible was that she knew the woods, and the Balkhenian did not. Even if he anticipated her moves and took to the road in pursuit, she could parallel him and travel through the forest. Her only uncertainty was how far she would have to go, but the adventures of the two newcomers who stumbled through winter mountain storms before safely reaching Canados reassured her. Surely she could make the reverse trip during the mildness of spring.

Alicia prepared by fingering the door handle, testing it to learn which way to pull. She would have time for one, perhaps two tugs. Even if the handle didn't work she might still have a chance. The vehicle's door was slung low enough. Though five-feet eight, she could swing her legs over it and leap from the vehicle. She hoped it wouldn't come to that because the extra moments required for such a maneuver might give the soldier time to restrain her.

As they approached the path, Alicia's fingers tightened upon the handle. Experimentation convinced her that backward was the right direction to pull. She glanced aside at the soldier and noted with satisfaction that he was having too difficult a time controlling his bucking vehicle to watch his prisoner.

The junction was ten yards ahead, but the jeep was going so slowly that seconds crawled like hours. Doubts milled in Alicia's mind. Could she make it south by herself without supplies or survival skills? She didn't really know if Balkhenians treated violators harshly. What did she understand about military occupation? The Balkhenians had no quarrel with the Canadosians. Even if they did, what good would her escape do? Hadn't Fahr written off the Threnian army and the alliance as impotent? Maybe she should face the colonel, even plead for mercy if that was necessary. He might listen.

The plague of misgivings assailed the girl's spirits and drained the strength from her fingers, causing them to relax their hold on the door handle. She slumped back in her seat, trembling, weighted down by resignation, disgusted with herself and terribly afraid. She would go back with the soldier and take her chances. In the end, she was a true Canadosian: fearful.

At that moment, their vehicle hit a tremendous bump and lurched violently. The soldier struggled to keep it from turning over, but his first efforts seemed futile. As if suspended on an angled balance beam, the jeep rolled several yards on its two right wheels. Fortunately, its center of gravity was low enough to resist the impulse to keel over, and the soldier was able to regain control. When he did, the left wheels dropped to the earth with a resounding crash that seemed forceful enough to loosen every bolt. The emergency was over, and the jeep, now stabilized, groaned to a halt. For a moment he allowed himself to remain collapsed over the steering wheel before taking a deep breath that turned into an audible sigh of relief. Then, as if suddenly remembering something, he leaned back in his seat and turned his eyes to the right.

His prisoner was gone.

Alicia's grip on the door handle, though eased off, had not released. When the jeep leaped into the air, its thrust forced her hand to pull on the latch, forcing the door open. The severe rightward tilt of the vehicle did the rest, allowing her body to slide downward through the opening. She landed hard on the rocky ground and spun over twice before coming to a stop at the base of a tree. Thanks to the vehicle's slow speed, she was not injured and recovered quickly. Her first impulse was to yell, but she checked herself and searched the bank of trees for her escape path. When she spotted it a few yards up the road, she glanced at the jeep, which was still bouncing down the hill. Hesitating only an instant, she clambered up to the path and seconds later, turned and disappeared into the woods. Fate had intervened on the side of her plan.

Once into the cover of the thick flora, Alicia pressed ahead, heedless of the branches snapping at her face, until she heard the vehicle's motor stop. After that, she picked her way more gingerly until certain the soldier had, or could have, found the spot where she entered the woods. From then on, she moved only when she heard him move so that any sound she made would be covered by his. In that way she hoped to elude him until dark.

When the solder discovered Alicia had escaped, he cursed loudly, jumped out of his vehicle, and hurried back up the path in search of his erstwhile passenger. He failed to spot her, but when he arrived at a breech in the tree growth, he correctly identified it as her escape route. The thickness of the vegetation confronting him was daunting, but because of it, he knew she couldn't have gotten far. At the same time, he was aware of the lack of thrashing and crackling sounds that a human being would make running through woods. Clearly, his quarry was not going to lay down a trail of sounds for him to follow. He looked to the sky and saw that the day was turning dark. He cursed again, this time silently, as tiny droplets of sweat began to bead upon his forehead. Balkhenian Command looked negatively on failed missions, and he would have no acceptable excuse for this one. The first thing the colonel would ask was why he didn't tie his prisoner to her seat in the jeep. He couldn't say she didn't seem the type to try to escape, not after his training in dealing with civilians suspected of spying and his explicit orders to bring her back.

What was he to do? Stomping loudly through the woods in search of a quarry who knew the terrain better than he was playing into her hands. Perhaps a bluff, then. "Miss Auer!" he called out. "You've got to stop this foolishness. You may escape me, but I warn you: others will soon be up here to back me up. Already, they're probably wondering why I haven't returned; soon there'll be an entire patrol up here after you. You won't be able to elude all of us."

His words were greeted by silence. "Alicia, come out! It'll go a lot better for you if you let me bring you back. I'll say nothing about this, and you'll avoid serious trouble." He turned his ear to the woods once more with no result. "If more men have to come after you, if you make it difficult for us, you will be punished severely, I assure you." Once again, save for the chirps of the birds and crickets, the woods were quiet. Damn it, why *hadn't* he tied her to her seat? He checked his watch. The afternoon was passing quickly. Lieutenant Soyez wouldn't wait much longer before sending up reinforcements. Waves of panic swept through his bowels. The girl was not to be rousted by threats or cajolings. If he were to recapture her by himself, he would have to go in after her.

He stepped onto the cross path and pushed through the tree growth along the route of least resistance in the hope that the girl had done the same. All he could do was strike out randomly and hope to get close enough to his quarry to panic her into giving herself away. He felt like a beagle trying to flush a pheasant from the brush.

His progress was difficult. Unable to step quietly, his feet kicked up rocks and vegetation. The rifle across his back cracked into this and that tree, sometimes knocking him off balance as he lurched along. As he proceeded, he tried to pick up sounds not of his making, but his own racket was too loud. Occasionally, he would stop suddenly and listen, hoping to catch Alicia off guard, but the ploy was unsuccessful. If Alicia was moving about, she had the ability to anticipate his tactics and stop an instant before he did.

At long last, during one of his pauses he heard the sound of a twig cracking. Then another, not fifteen yards to his right. Was it an animal or the girl? He stopped to listen but hearing nothing more, started toward where he thought the noise originated. An instant later—before he had taken two steps—he was startled by a burst of thrashing just ahead. Long ears, and then the body of a large hare popped into view. The frightened animal stared at the soldier for a moment, then dropped his head, turned, and darted blink-quick into the foliage. Leaves and twigs flew about as the animal made his escape. Then all was again silent.

As time wore on, his certainty that Alicia didn't get far was replaced by the thought that she might have found a path and managed to cover a great distance after all. If so, there was no telling how far she had gone. The prospect of hearing the shouts and motors of an arriving patrol became increasingly likely, and he found himself listening for them as intently as he did for Alicia. He also began to rehearse the explanation for his failure.

Again he ceased his trampling and turned his ears to the forest, but as always, they picked up nothing but singing birds and chattering insects. He groaned.

He knew of one thing to do. The idea had been in the back of his mind from the start. He had hoped to avoid it, but his situation had become desperate. He unslung his rifle, a weapon capable of firing a long barrage of bullets in a continuous burst. He would lay down a spread of bullets in a semi-circular pattern about seven feet off the ground in the hope that the girl would be frightened into revealing herself. There was a chance she would be hit—a result that could be unfortunate for him because the colonel could not question a dead spy about possible comrades—but he saw no other way.

The soldier was decent enough to warn Alicia of his plan, but before he could open his mouth, he heard the dull roar of a motor, far away, down toward the village, faint at first, but growing steadily louder. He froze. It would take ten minutes for the jeep to negotiate the trail up the mountain—long enough for him to shout his warning, lay down a burst and, he hoped, recover his prisoner, but no more.

"Alicia! Do you hear that motor? That's another jeep, and it's coming up here. I told you they would come, and they are, just as I said. Now will you listen to me? You still have a chance. Come out now and you'll be all right." He paused for a breath. "If you don't, I'm going to fire blindly into the woods. Either a bullet will get you or that patrol will. One way or the other, you have no chance. Do you understand what I'm saying?"

There was an answering flurry of activity about twenty yards in front of him to the left. That was no small animal. He stared intently in the direction of the noise for several long seconds before spotting a white-clad figure darting between the trees. He plunged ahead in pursuit. The terrain and the branches that snapped at his face made it difficult to keep his quarry in sight, but he never took his eyes off where he thought she was. His efforts were rewarded, as he caught sight of her frequently. He was gaining with every step.

Suddenly, the figure disappeared. At first the soldier didn't realize what had happened, so intent was he on keeping his balance, but when he did, his head pounded in rage. He stumbled forward even more recklessly than before, once banging hard into a tree. The rough bark tore at his body, but he ignored the searing in his shoulder and the throbbing in his hip and charged toward where he had last seen the girl. No longer could he hear the roar of the jeep: the noise of his pursuit had drowned it out.

Suddenly, the soldier's right knee buckled sickeningly under him. His other leg scraped desperately for solid ground, but it too lost support, throwing him first forward, then downward. His head struck a glancing blow against a tree, and his body crumpled to the ground.

He lay stunned. Then he felt something move beneath his legs. His head cleared somewhat, and the damage inflicted on his body assaulted his senses. The pain, particularly the abrasion over his left temple, burned as if he had been branded with a hot iron. Again he felt movement under him. It was a violent lurch beneath his legs that shoved his lower body upward. He looked down and saw the slumped figure of Alicia beneath him. For a moment she was still and hunched over, but then her body jackknifed. Her head struck his chest with terrific force, throwing the already stunned young man up and back. He reached out to grab her, but his fingers caught only a wisp of the fleeing cloth of her dress, not enough to pull her back, and she broke away.

Alicia was no less wild than the hare. She had heard the soldier's warning and was almost panicked into revealing herself. Instead she regained her poise and was about to drop to the ground and lay prostrate under the expected barrage when she too picked up the sound of the approaching jeep. The soldier was not bluffing! Then again, why in the world should he have been? Wasn't it logical that his people would come up after him if he didn't return after a certain period of time? She thought of the horde of soldiers swarming about her village. How many of them were after her now? And what should she do? But that question was answered. The soldier already had suggested her fate if reinforcements were required to retrieve her. The only thing left was to flee deep into the woods.

She had then plunged ahead recklessly, unmindful of branches snapping at her face and vines tugging at her feet. When she tripped over an above-ground tree root and fell hard to the ground, her right fist was caught under her chest, causing an impact that drove the breath from her lungs. She lay immobile for several precious seconds before breath was pumped back into her lungs, and conscious sound returned to her ears. The thrashing soldier was almost upon her. She tried to regain her feet, but his onrushing legs crunched against her body, knocking her back to the ground. His heavy weight toppled over her as if he were a felled tree, pinning her. Should she try to squirm free or put her faith in a single powerful thrust? She took quick note of how the soldier's body lay over hers, judged the leverage to be favorable, and decided on the quick thrust. There was little room to add to her leverage: she had to go with what she had before the man on top of her recovered himself. Shoving her chest up against his weight and her hand behind her against the ground, she thrust upward. At first she felt no yielding, but at the last moment, the weight on top of her slid off to her right. She was still pinned, but now she had increased her leverage to the point where another thrust might do it. She took advantage of her increased maneuvering room to jackknife her knees under her chest. After a sharp deep breath she plunged her knees up and out. This time she was successful. Her strong legs had supplied just enough spring to throw the soldier's body off and allow her to escape the hand that grabbed futilely at the wisp of her dress.

Nevertheless, she knew she was lost. The sounds of the crashing behind her resumed and grew louder. How did he recover so quickly? She cursed her white dress which made her easier to spot in the woods. If only it were darker!—the dress and the daylight. She tripped and almost lost her balance again. A desperate grab of an overhanging branch saved her, but she had to hold onto it for several seconds before she could completely right herself. The delay was fatal. Before she regained her equilibrium, she saw her pursuer's dark shape looming through the brush. Immediately afterward, she spotted his face—now no longer youthful, but black with dirt and streaked with blood—staring at her from among the trees. Before she could let go of the branch, he was upon her. She twisted about and tried to break his grip around her waist, but he was too strong. She continued to struggle until the soldier flung his other arm around her shoulder and pulled her to the ground. Even then she didn't give in, but the soldier had her prostrate. He swung his legs about and dropped on top of her, pinning her body with a wrestling hold across her chest until she was paralyzed, her eyes screaming in pain, her mouth curled over her teeth, and her muscles drawn tighter than piano wire. It required every fiber of strength in the soldier's body to control her, but his weight atop her chest took its toll. Red in the face and gasping for air, Alicia gave up the fight.

The soldier held his position, not daring to move for fear she would take advantage of a change in leverage to throw him off. For a moment it was as if the trapped girl were master of the situation, but the roar of the now very nearby motor jolted him into action. He pushed himself off her chest, jerked himself to his feet, careful to yank his captive up at the same time.

The soldier stared at her a moment before mutely gesturing with his rifle for her to lead the way back to the clearing. She was bloodied about both knees and one arm, her face was coated with dirt, and her dress was torn about her shoulders and splotched with grime, blood, and twigs. Tears fell from her eyes, but her lips were bloodless and drawn, her jaw set, and her eyes were holes bored into her head. Wrinkles etched a scowl into her cheeks that aged her twenty years.

It took a few minutes for their eyes to adjust to the light when they reached the clearing, but when they did, Alicia and the soldier discovered they were not alone. Standing alongside a jeep across the glen, his hand thrown across the vehicle's right front fender as if it were a live mount, was a Balkhenian soldier. He was larger and older than Alicia's captor. His features were more barren and pale—suggesting granite rather than flesh and blood—and they were etched with the marks of battle. The young soldier recognized Sergeant Lothar Marco, one of the fiercest of Balkhenian warriors. A surge of desperation poured through the younger man's loins.

Marco studied the pair—posed silently before him like jack-lighted rabbits—through eyes resembling the narrow slits of a gun emplacement. His rifle, gripped in his hammy fist parallel to the ground, pointed midway between his prey. He spoke with the ominous roll of distant thunder: "Private Kahn. Where the hell have you been?"

The private was not sure how to respond at first. When he did, his words were etched with as much assurance as he could muster: "I realize I've been late in reporting, Sergeant," he said. "A moment ago I might have needed assistance, but I've got things under control now."

"A *moment* ago," snarled the sergeant. "You've been gone over an hour. That's a long time to bring back one female civilian."

"I know that, Sergeant." The soldier continued to speak guardedly. "I got lost coming up here. You can see how thick the woods are."

"What about her?"

The soldier looked puzzled. "What do you mean?"

"Look at her."

The soldier turned to obey. In the light of the clearing, the blood on Alicia's face and dress was redder and her cuts deeper than he had thought.

"What happened, Private?"

"S-she got away from me."

"She escaped!?"

"Into the woods. I chased her." He searched Marco's face for a clue as to how much he should disclose, but found none. "She played dead and hid for quite a few minutes before I was able to find her. But I did find her," he added hastily.

The darting of the sergeant's small grey eyes was the only affirmation that he was alive. The private tried to appear staunch, but it was difficult with shaking knees.

Alicia looked at neither the private nor the sergeant, but rather to the left toward the woods. She was conscious only of the pain in her knees and arm. She understood not a word of Balkhenian, but she had a good idea what they were saying.

The sergeant broke the silence: "You expect me to believe that? You're a Balkhenian soldier. Canadosian girls don't escape from Balkhenian soldiers."

"Yes, Sergeant."

"So what really happened, Private?"

The private repeated his story.

"All right, Private," the sergeant said when he had finished. "Have it your way. But you're lying."

"Then how else could she have gotten so messed up?" The private's voice rang from an unanticipated surge of bravery.

The sergeant's thin lips cracked evilly into a smile. "How else do you think? None of these sheep have the guts to do what you say she did."

"She does." The private's voice trembled as he spoke. "She's different."

"Crap!" The word dropped from Marco's mouth . . . like a lead ball, thought the young man; like a brick of ice, thought Alicia, though she knew not what the word meant. The big man took a few steps forward, stopping a few feet before the private and Alicia. "She didn't get messed up running. She got that way lying on the ground. Under you."

Kahn's mouth opened and closed, but no sounds came out.

Marco continued accusingly: "You dragged her into the woods, jumped on her, and screwed her." He pulled back his lips and showed his yellowed teeth, like grinning a jack o' lantern. He leered at Kahn, then Alicia.

Kahn regained his power of speech. "No! I didn't! That's crazy!"

The sergeant gestured threateningly. "Don't tell me what's crazy!" he shot back. "Look at yourself."

The private stood uncomprehending.

"Look at your clothes!!"

Kahn peered down. His uniform bore the results of his chase through the woods and his struggle on the ground with Alicia. It was especially dirty across the chest, and there was a rip in his jacket near the belt line. Blood had dripped—from his face or hers?—onto his right sleeve. He looked back up at the sergeant. "I chased her, like I told you. I had to run through thick tree growth. When I caught her, she resisted."

The sergeant ignored him, turned to Alicia, and in coarse Threnian, said, "You're a feisty bitch, aren't you. We'll soon tend to that." He licked his lips and turned back to the private. "You're dismissed, Kahn," he said, still in Threnian and almost offhandedly. "I'll bring the prisoner back myself."

Kahn started. In the Balkhenian army, having one's prisoner retrieved by someone else can have an unpleasant effect on one's service record and his standing with his comrades. The prospects were unpleasant enough to give Kahn the courage to protest. "You know I didn't . . . rape her," he said, also in Threnian, with unexpected courage.

A brief but knowing smirk flashed across Marco's thin lips. "You have your orders, Private." The smirk disappeared; the once steady voice became agitated. "Now get into your vehicle and get your ass out of here!"

"But the colonel . . ."

"Forget the colonel!" interrupted Marco with a sneer. "I'll cover you." His lips again cracked into his crooked grin.

"But . . ."

"But what!?" thundered the sergeant. He glanced at Alicia, still standing, now visibly frightened, under a tree. All of this and what followed was in Threnian. Clearly, the big Balkhenian soldier wanted her to understand what was going on. Indeed, the sergeant's lascivious glances in her direction had already clarified what the two men had been saying earlier in their own language. "You're not worried about your piece of ASS, are you!" the sergeant continued, laughing coarsely. "Well, let me assure you about that. Give you something to get hot about on your way back." He took a step toward Alicia. "I'm going to grab her, take her right over there," pointing to a flat area of the clearing, "throw her down, jump on top of her, and give her just as good a ramming as you did. No. Better. A sergeant has to be better than a private."

Kahn screwed up what courage he had left. "Sergeant, you know the orders on that. Besides, I didn't . . ."

"DISMISSED!" roared the sergeant, with a thrust of his hammy right hand.

When the private continued to hold his ground, Marco swung his rifle through the air like a machete until it pointed directly at the young man's chest. When he spoke again, it was in the former quiet granitic tone, devoid of emotion, empty of passion. "Kahn, right now you're in trouble," he said through clenched teeth. "But if you go back, you're clean. No officer's going to buck what I tell him."

Still, Kahn held his ground. "How do you know I won't tell them what you did? You know the rules about conduct toward civilians."

For just an instant, the sergeant stared at the young man with a tiny shred of respect. Not many Balkhenian privates would stand up to him that way. He would have to get to know this Kahn. He looked like such a boy. Maybe he was really a young man ready to be taken under the good sergeant's wing. It would be interesting to find out, assuming Kahn survived the next two minutes. "Those rules aren't for me," he hissed in reply to the young man's threat.

Kahn could feel the spirit go out of him like air from a stuck balloon. Marco's sway over the Balkhenian officer corps was legendary. There was the story of Marco's participation in the sack of a village in Carpio, a particularly grisly affair during which a segment of the population, caught by surprise, was wiped out, at least ten at the hands of Marco. Balkhenian intelligence had marked the village as the site of an arsenal, but Ordnance found only seven small-caliber rifles. When told the town had been destroyed and people killed for nothing, the coarsest of the invaders felt remorse—except for Marco who roared with laughter over the "lack of intelligence" of the intelligence people. When a lieutenant took him to task, Marco fiercely threatened to sack him like Troy. (The sergeant was well read in mythology.) The lieutenant backed down immediately. Other officers learned of this incident, but Marco was never reprimanded, a lack of action lost on no one in the Balkhenian army, Private Hans Kahn included.

"Don't go," the sergeant continued, "and I'll level you where you stand and turn your body over as a deserter." Marco laughed so hard that his sides shook; he had to press down with his hands to hold himself steady. "Now enough of this crap. You've got thirty seconds to get your butt into your vehicle and down that hill. I'm not telling you again."

Kahn was defeated. He feared for the poor Canadosian girl whom he had come to respect in an odd sort of way, but he had made what stand he was capable of and failed. He trekked across the clearing to the edge of the meadow, then stopped to glance back at Alicia, hoping she would look at him, but her eyes remained focused on the ground. She's the enemy, he thought. We're not supposed to concern ourselves with the comfort of the enemy. Then he disappeared from the glen.

Marco didn't wait for the sound of the motor starting before he advanced upon Alicia. Because of the idiot Colonel's ban on female plunder, which he observed for reasons he was not entirely sure of, he had been without a woman too long. Things would be put right now.

His attack was devastating. He tore at his prey's clothes so viciously that it was a miracle that most of the buttons were spared. When she was nude, his breath jabbed in strong powerful bursts, as he paused to revel in her nakedness. She was chilled and quivering, her face blank, her eyes full of surrender like those of a fawn whose neck lay in the jaws of a wolf. The two remained frozen for a moment, like sculpture, before his body burst into a second flurry of action, as he tore his own garments off. When he himself was undressed, he loomed over her like a gladiator, hairless and massive, before falling upon her. His thick right arm engulfed her body and crushed it to his chest. With his left he grabbed her hair and pulled it back hard, before his mouth crunched heavily upon her lips and teeth. He then drove her to the ground, piled on top, and ground his body over hers so fiercely that she could feel pebbles and twigs grating against her bare back. She thought she could imagine no worse pain than what she endured at that moment when she felt a burning between her legs. Its intensity increased past unbearable into numbness and finally, unconsciousness.

When Alicia came to, the sergeant's body was collapsed over her like a sack of wet meal. The burden of his weight was almost as painful as the burning between her legs. He was much heavier than the private. She wanted to squirm and throw him off, but dared not, for fear she would enrage him. She lay silent and still, taking shallow breaths so as not to increase the pressure against her chest and back. Finally, a voice rasped into her ear: "Maybe there will be another chance for us after you're interrogated," it hissed into her ear. "Think about it. I can help you. I can save your hide." His eyes met hers, though she tried to turn her head. They were not as hard as before. It was as if all their energy were spent, but there was no tenderness in them—only an emptiness commingled with intelligence. "You can come to me," he continued, his words oddly soft. "We can talk. And do this. I'll look out for you. It's your choice. None of those officers dare screw with Lothar Marco." The sergeant continued to lie still, breathing more easily.

Alicia did not respond. She was determined to turn off the spigot controlling the flow of thoughts entering her mind, but she could not do so entirely, and several wisps of deliberation trickled through.

Alicia was not a virgin before the sergeant's attack. She had slept with several boys, an act that was not frowned upon in Canados, which was as sexually free, within the confines of Western custom, as it was confining intellectually. She knew that after sex, the most aggressive men could be calm and tender until their loins were recharged, but the change in the sergeant's demeanor was startling. She felt herself holding her breath, daring not to imagine in what direction his attentions might lurch.

She had not long to wait. The sergeant's thick arms lifted his bulk from her, and he sprung to his feet. "No more time now," he said with exaggerated regret, "but there will be soon enough. It'll be good for you. I promise." He grinned. His voice turned hard. "Now get up."

Alicia obeyed with difficulty. At his signal she began to gather her clothes, making no effort to cover her nakedness. It was as if she were watching herself move about the clearing. Soon, she had picked up every garment but one shoe, but had put nothing on.

"You are beautiful," marveled the sergeant, "but you can't go down there in front of those animals like that. I won't have it. Get dressed."

Alicia ignored him, and leaned over to pick up her other shoe. Suddenly, while she was bent over, she sensed something in the area had changed. There was an eerie feeling about her—the same sensation she felt when the private had first appeared in the mountain clearing. She stood up and looked about. Expecting to see more Balkhenian soldiers, she spotted young Kahn standing alone at the opposite edge of the clearing.

The sergeant saw him at the same time. His normally pale skin burned with rage. "What the hell are you doing here, Private?"

Kahn replied without hesitating. "I thought about what you said, and I don't believe you." They were the words of a different Kahn from the one who had left the clearing moments ago. "You'll turn me in and say I was trying to desert. I'll get the firing squad. You won't leave me around to tell my story. Somebody might believe me and dare do something about it."

"So now that someone's you?" The sergeant nodded in mock disbelief toward the rifle Kahn held cradled in his arms.

"I'm going to bring you back and tell them what you did."

"Go ahead. You know what good that will do."

"Maybe, but it's the only chance I've got."

The sergeant glared through his gun slit eyes. "You're right, Kahn," he admitted after a deep, heavy breath. "It is your only chance." He grinned, knelt down to pick up a few pebbles, and haphazardly tossed them away. "Problem is, you got to get me to go back with you."

"I'll take you at gunpoint, if I have to."

The sergeant roared with laughter. "Let's see you try."

"Put your shirt on and let's go." Kahn injected every possible ounce of command into his voice.

The sergeant remained immobile.

"Sergeant! I mean it."

Marco moved not a muscle.

"Don't make me use this." A note of desperation crept into the young man's voice.

"Private, that's exactly what I will make you do," Marco replied. "There's a rite of passage you have to go through right now. And I'm Cerberus guarding the entrance to the cave."

Kahn did not entirely comprehend the sergeant's reference to the fierce, two-headed dog that oversaw the gate to the infernal regions, but he understood intent. Any thoughts that Marco's bravery was more legend than fact were dispelled by the way the sergeant advanced upon Kahn as he might an artillery emplacement. The private retreated until he was backed up against the surrounding circle of trees. He would have to shoot or flee. Kahn wanted to run, but the magnificence of his enemy, half-naked in his step-by-step charge, held him immobilized. In seconds, the sergeant was upon him, a towering fortress glistening with sweat. Wordlessly, Marco reached down and, with a motion he might use to pick up a pencil, grabbed Kahn's rifle and yanked it toward him.

The weapon went off a split second before the private's finger slipped from its hair trigger. Its explosion echoed throughout the hills, knocking the sergeant backward until he collapsed halfway across the clearing. A stream of blood oozed from his shoulder; his body twitched. The private froze in horror. He dared not approach the fallen warrior.

Then he heard the wounded man speaking through clenched teeth, partly in rage and very much in pain. They had been speaking in Threnian, but this was too personal for that, and the sergeant's words were in Balkhenian. "Kill me now, Kahn, or so help me, I'll kill you later.

My wound's not that serious," he added in spite of blood oozing from his shoulder, reddening his uniform. He paused for a painful breath, his grey eyes racked with pain and defiance. "It's what I would do to you." The words sounded as if he had wrenched them from his gut.

"Private Kahn!" The young man turned about, startled. It was Alicia's voice. "We must get away from here," she continued.

"What?"

"We have to get out of here," she repeated. She was suddenly very animated, as if the rifle shot had energized her. "You can't wait for the others, and you can't go back. Neither of us can. They'll kill you if you kill the sergeant, and if you don't, your life will be in his hands just as he said."

Kahn continued to stare at the girl. She was still undressed, but that wasn't the reason his eyes were fixed on her.

"Listen to her, Kahn." The sergeant was speaking Threnian again, through teeth clenched so hard it was a wonder any words came out. "She's right. You can't kill me. You'd better get in one of those jeeps and get out of here. They heard the shot down there. They'll be here soon." His words were delivered with increasing difficulty, but the sergeant was determined to finish. "Don't worry about me. We'll settle our score later. We're going to meet again, you and I." Marco struggled to sit up, then reached for his shirt which was lying nearby, and spread it over his shoulder like a bandage. The green cloth darkened as blood seeped through it. "Get your asses out of here! If you don't get away, they'll give you the firing squad. And," another fierce grunt of pain as the sergeant tugged on his makeshift dressing, "I won't have that. I'm going to deal with you myself." Marco flashed a grin that chilled Kahn's bones. "Colonel Blaunt will want you apprehended and brought back, and I'm the man who's going to track you down. You and the girl. When I do, you'd better be ready to fight like a man." The sergeant laughed, even managing to unclench his teeth. "She," blustered the sergeant, pointing at Alicia, "will be the real prize." He laughed one last time—an outburst that took its toll on his reserves. He fell back flat on the ground, exhausted.

Kahn shuddered. The *real* prize would be death, and it didn't matter to the sergeant whose.

The roar of the approaching vehicles became louder. "Hurry!" Alicia urged him. "They're coming."

"That's right," said the sergeant, his words produced with less difficulty, as if he were getting used to, even relishing, the pain. "They'll be here in a few minutes!"

Alicia was now dressed, her clothes badly ripped but serviceable. She bent over to pick up the sergeant's rifle. "We'll need this," she told Kahn who nodded dumbly.

"Check my jeep." It was the sergeant. "There are shells and a survival kit in the back. Pull the rotor out of the engine. That'll give them one less vehicle to chase you with." The sergeant managed to lift his shoulders off the ground as he spoke. "Get moving!"

Kahn couldn't take his eyes off the fallen Marco, who was a more frightening specter down and wounded, shouting advice, than he was standing and bellowing. The pain he must be in! The private shuddered.

A tug on the back of his shirt shook him from his stupor. It was Alicia. "We must get going!" she implored him.

Kahn turned and followed her across the clearing toward the jeeps. At the edge of the glen he looked back. The sergeant was now sitting up again. The fist of his healthy arm was clenched. Kahn wasn't sure he heard what the sergeant was yelling, but it sounded like, "Soon, Kahn. Soon!"

Alicia hissed loudly into his ear. "Hurry!"

Kahn did not tremble alone this time. Alicia's skin quivered as well, but it was a future horror Marco was promising, and her concern was the present one. She and Kahn removed the ammunition and supplies from the sergeant's vehicle and transferred them to the private's. Kahn made short work of disabling Marco's vehicle, before both of them climbed into his. "The road's this way," Alicia told him.

The fuel gauge read "Full." He started the engine. As soon as the engine sprung into life he swung about and headed south.

Tears fell from Alicia's eyes. They were for her fate and for what she envisioned might happen to her friends and neighbors—and to her village—whom she might never see again. Any dreams she had about returning a heroic leader of troops had been obliterated by her clash with Balkhenian power. She let the tears fall until her eyes were dry. She wasn't any less sad then; she simply had no more to give. She glanced over her shoulder as the jeep bounced along the rocky mountain road—there were no pursuers—then at her companion, then up at the sky. In ten minutes darkness would arrive to cover their flight.

THE ERRANT KNIGHT

It was Saturday, the final day of the Chicago Chess Championship. The summer sky was clear, the air cool and crisp. It was a day to be spent outdoors in pagan celebration. Only chess players and shut-ins would stay inside in such weather, and only chess players voluntarily. That was amply demonstrated when I entered the near-deserted lobby of the Palmer House, one of the most famous of Chicago's prestigious downtown hotels. The emptiness reflected my mood, not to mention my recent tournament record. It was no comfort that many of my losses were close, hard fought contests. I wanted to make a living as a chess player, and to do that, I had to be a Grandmaster. You don't get to be a Grandmaster by losing tournaments. So far, all I had to show for my last ten years of studying was a dead-end job in a warehouse, a crummy apartment, and no girlfriend. Worse, at twenty-nine, when most players are peaking, I was getting worse! I simply *had* to win a major tournament, and Chicago was as major as any of them.

Fortune was cooperating. With one game to go, I was tied for the lead with Frank Rostenkowski, so if I won my match, I would at least share first prize. I could win the whole thing if Rostenkowski lost or drew to the powerful Richard Morton. That wasn't such a long shot. Morton had a history of knocking off front-runners. My hopes should have been high, but I was uneasy. My palms were sweating even in the air conditioning as I crossed the lobby to the elevator.

I rode the elevator alone. When it halted, I stepped into a high-ceilinged chamber that recalled glamorous evenings when the proud and mighty pranced in top hats and white flowing gowns to the satin smooth brass of the bands that entertained the well-to-do who didn't know or care that a depression was going on in the streets below. The room retained the old walnut paneling and chandeliers whose rings of bulbs refused to bow to the clutter of tables and chairs that would be gone in a few hours. I could almost smell the fumes of brandy and hear the faint strains of band music and clinking glasses across the room. Perhaps ghosts were still dancing among the white Styrofoam coffee cups drunk from by men who pushed black and white figurines over checkered boards.

One of these men was seated alone near the east wall at Table One, staring blankly across the room. His name was Felix Cranmar, and he was the reason for the sweat on my palms. Cranmar was my opponent. Though rated below me in playing strength, he was a difficult rival to whom I lost more games than I can comfortably explain. His slow, plodding style upset me—I preferred a more wide-open game—but that was only part of the problem. I have beaten many cautious players. There was something else about him. He was spooky, an icy apparition. Creepy things happened in our games: I'd leave pieces hanging, make unwonted positional errors, miscalculate attacks— things that never happened against other players.

It's said there is no luck in chess. But there is psychology. Chess is a very intimate game. You contend not only with your opponent's mental skills, but also his personality and will. I was superior to Cranmar in ability. But of this mental thing, I wasn't so sure. I did not look forward to playing him in such an important game.

But there was nothing to be done. I shrugged my shoulders and looked up at the clock. 11:55 A.M. Five minutes to go.

Let him wait.

12:00 Noon. I walked to Table One and sat down. Cranmar acknowledged my presence with a slight lift of his head, waited for me to start the clock, and made his move. *Pawn to King Four.* The most common opening move in chess. And it struck me dumb. Felix Cranmar rarely played this move against anyone and never against me. *Pawn to King Four* generally leads to an open combative game, particularly against aggressive players like myself, who like to oppose it with the Sicilian Defense, an opening so sharp and treacherous that many players forbear "king pawn" openings altogether just to avoid facing it.

Cranmar was one of those players. I never got anything but *Pawn to*

Queen Four from him. What had gotten into him? Was he not feeling well? Maybe he hadn't the stomach for one of our long tough battles.

No. Whatever his shortcomings, Cranmar was no quitter. Besides, he'd had success against me.

Was he trying to take me by surprise? That would be something new. Cranmar was a creature of routine. Was he really so sure of himself against me that he thought he could afford to be reckless? In our previous games, he made things difficult by clogging up the board and steering the game into his favored trench warfare style. Was it possible that he did not know what lay behind his relative success against me? Or had he actually become cocky to the point where he thought he could venture onto my turf with a full-bore, open assault?

If so, he was asking for quite a lesson in strategic planning.

So why was that prickle of tension crawling over my skin?

I leaned back and studied him. Whatever had happened to his playing style, there was nothing unusual about his demeanor. As always, his spare body swayed back and forth in his chair like a marsh reed in the wind. His countenance seemed lifeless with its ashen complexion, the fishy grey eyes and small nose protruding over bloodless lips, the short curly hair, and the thick glasses with a chip of frame missing from their upper left corner. His rumpled pants and shirt blotched by a large coffee-stain along the front filled out the look. He could have been a scarecrow.

The Stare was in place, too. Most of the time Cranmar never lifted his eyes from the chessboard, as if fearful that one of his pieces would come to life and stroll across the board if he should ever look away. But sometimes he did look up, and when he did, he'd gaze directly at his opponent with a cold, lifeless, yet somehow insipid, Stare. My guess was that he did this when he thought he had an advantage. If so, he wasn't always right, but at times, his insolence could penetrate the invisible barrier that separated two chess players. When it did, his victim could either be intimidated or piqued enough to strike back, sometimes rashly. I know. It happened to me three times. Two of the games I lost; the other I barely pulled out.

Cranmar was Staring now, and with good reason. I had not made a single move, and already my mind was racing among thoughts beginning with "why" and "what." I wasn't planning strategy, I was . . .

Fortunately, the dull ticking of the chess clock broke through my daze. It made me shudder. It also returned me to the game.

Cranmar's surprise was not limited to one move. It continued to the point where he allowed me to use my favorite variation of the Sicilian, the Yugoslav, in which both kings are spirited to the opposite sides of the board, clearing the way for each side to attack the other's king without weakening the defenses around his own. Yugoslav games feature strong, sharp threats, and quick exchanges of material. It was like blasting away at each other with shotguns. If ever there was an opening that was not for Felix Cranmar, it was the Yugoslav Sicilian. He should have had no better luck using it against me than a turkey in a turkey shoot.

Yet, from the start Cranmar had me off balance. Employing a variety of subtle threats and clever retreats, he avoided the piece exchanges I needed to open attacking lanes. By the eighteenth move, the board was completely jammed up. My precious Yugoslav might as well have crossed several borders and become a blocked-up French. The price he paid to accomplish this feat was a slight disadvantage in space that he could afford to take on since I couldn't move my pieces freely enough to exploit it.

It wasn't that I feared losing the game. That slight spatial advantage should allow me to avoid that fate, but I could easily see the win I so desperately needed dissolving into a draw.

My body stiffened. "Not losing" simply wouldn't do.

Still, it was too early to give up. I had been slow to react to what was happening, but when I did, I bore down hard to inject some life into my pieces before they withered and died. The aura of concentration surrounding our table intensified. Neither of us left his seat, not even to stretch his legs or sneak a look at some of the other games. We had become inseparable, two parts of the same organism—each struggling for supremacy—from which nothing could be heard but the intermittent sound of hand striking clock: "Your move!" It was a challenge repeated over and over. Though life undoubtedly went on around us—people milling silently about, hands contemplatively stroking chins as they mulled over the games—we were oblivious to everything but the pieces before us.

I was distracted only once. At move twelve, just as I was about to push a pawn, Cranmar spilled the last of some coffee on the table, just missing the board. I was startled, and my sharp gasp indicated so. Cranmar looked up, muttered an apology, and cleaned up the mess with a tissue. His expression of regret surprised me. Usually, he welcomed the opportunity to break my concentration. It wasn't like him to apologize over such an incident. I wondered if he expected to win fair and square.

Was my position worse than I thought?

If that notion was disturbing, at least the coffee spill was the last of the distractions. But there seemed to be no end to my frustration. Cranmar had taken my favorite weapon and forged it into a sword of his own design. I played tentatively, my concentration plagued by the complexity of the position and the need to be alert for traps. Before each move, I struggled to find a combination that would break open the position. I considered several, only to pull back when I couldn't uncover a clear line of play. My head felt as if it were about to split open. I leaned back and took a slow, deep breath.

I had to get away from the table. With Cranmar on move and lost in thought, I slid my chair backward, lifted it slightly so it wouldn't scrape loudly across the floor, and stood up. The numbness that buzzed in my legs was startling, but it eased by the time I walked to the bulletin board. There, I shook my head sharply, trying to focus my eyes on the people scattered about the room. I stood in awe at the human mind's ability to concentrate on a single activity to the exclusion of all else. Outside there were millions of people doing a myriad of things, but for me there was only that room, the chess pieces, and whatever Cranmar and I might create with them. It was amazing. And frightening.

I turned to the scoreboard.

My God! It had happened! And so quickly! Morton and Rostenkowski had played to a draw! I scanned the rest of the standings to be sure my earlier assumptions were correct. No question. If I drew Cranmar, I would finish fourth. A loss could drop me as far as seventh, but if I beat him, the Chicago Chess Championship was mine! I looked for Rostenkowski, but he seemed nowhere about. Probably in the bar downstairs. That's where I'd be.

I gazed at Cranmar who was still hunched over the board. He'd had a lousy tournament and would finish no higher than the lower middle of the pack. Knocking off a front runner was the only meaningful goal he had left in the competition. Maybe that's why he was pressing me so hard.

I lumbered back to the table and looked down at my opponent. Still buried in thought, he gave no indication he knew I was there. I wondered if he realized I had been gone. Poor bastard. He was struggling over our game as if it actually meant something, but it was always like that for him. He was a grinder, not a thoroughbred. He entered every major tournament but rarely finished near the top. Now pushing forty—much too old to improve enough to make Grandmaster—he was still struggling and perhaps even dreaming. I wondered why he bothered.

But Cranmar's ill fortunes were not my concern. I wasn't too old to be a Grandmaster, but I soon would be if I didn't win a major tournament soon. Newfound determination surged through my veins. Get him! I implored myself. Get him now! Don't give him another inch! Not another square! Crush him once and for all!

Cranmar made his move. It was time to sit down and win this thing.

I leaned forward to study the new position, my eyes darting about, probing for a crack in the new enemy alignment. Up until then it seemed as if Cranmar had built an impenetrable emplacement. He believed it. I *had* believed it, but no more. Max Euwe once said that very few positions are so bad that there isn't a move to save the game. One simply must bear down and seek it out rationally. That's what I would do. Somewhere there was a loose brick in Cranmar's fortification, which, if pulled, would bring the entire structure crashing down.

The clock ticked precious minutes away as I pored over the position, but I held firm to my task. I hadn't found the "loose brick," but I *had* concluded that there was something wrong with Cranmar's position, regardless of how solid it appeared. True, his pieces were all developed, and his king was safely ensconced behind a shield of pawns, but something was out of synch. I wasn't going to give up until I found out what it was.

I leaned back, silently sucked in a breath, and dug in. I broke his position down to the elements: pawns well connected; one bishop exchanged, the other a bit hemmed in on the back rank. One rook was on the second rank, the other on the third, off to the side, ready to slide in front of its partner to double up on the file. An odd placement, but solid enough.

I turned to his queen. She was marginally well centered, but somewhat boxed in. I thought about jabbing at her to open things up, but rejected the idea as too speculative. It could force Cranmar into a mistake, but it might also drive his queen from a weak post to a more powerful one.

What about his remaining knight? (The other was exchanged for my bishop.) I had almost forgotten about that piece, and no wonder. There it was, squirreled off to the king-side of the board (away from the king which had castled queen-side) behind a phalanx of its own pawns. It too suffered from restricted mobility. Curious as to how it had arrived at such awkward circumstances, I traced the game backward from my score sheet. What I found did not please me. It seems the knight was driven to its predicament by mere token threats. Cranmar retreated it twice when he sniffed a hint of danger, overreacting each time. What terrible defense! It's one thing to recognize and anticipate threats. It's quite another to miscalculate their danger and react inappropriately.

How could I have failed to take advantage of those mistakes?

More unpleasant revelations came to light as I studied the score sheet. Indeed, I couldn't pull my eyes from it until the full saga of ineptitude and missed opportunities had paraded before me.

There! I could have advanced that pawn and gained territory, but I passively slid a rook over instead. What was I supporting with that rook? Nothing. What plans had I for it? None.

And there! I retreated my bishop when I should have left it where it was—bearing down on the white king position.

And there. I could have opened up the position for my heavy pieces by exchanging a center pawn, leaving a hole in the middle of the board. Instead I pushed a side pawn—in support of . . . what? Nothing I could see now.

Meanwhile, Cranmar had time to back up his own center pawn. If the exchange eventually occurred, the hole would be filled.

Thus did I learn how to deadlock a Yugoslav Sicilian.

I turned away from the mocking diary and concentrated on the board. Now things would be different, I promised myself. There was an opportunity before me, and that misplaced white knight was the key to finding it.

I began to analyze. There are three ways to exploit a poorly positioned piece on a cramped board. As a static target, cut off from its comrades, it may be vulnerable to direct assault. Or, emboldened by the knowledge that the piece will be unable to quickly break free to assist the defense, one can launch an attack on the other side of the board—in this case against the king. Or the weakness of the piece can be exploited more conservatively, as a positional negative.

I wanted the most active plan possible, so I began by considering a direct attack against the king. First I took note of the pawns in the shield around the monarch. One of them was advanced, leaving a key approach square undefended. That would be a formidable outpost if I could plant a piece there. I spent several minutes looking for a way to break a man through, but the position was too ambiguous. Even with Cranmar's knight unable to help, the jammed-up board rendered the weakness difficult to exploit.

What about capturing that knight? Not bloody likely. My rooks were blocked, and neither my own knight nor my bishop could get in position to attack it. Not unless I could break through this other pawn phalanx. But how?

I considered pushing pawns against the emplacement, but rejected that strategy. My pawns would be broken up like a ship on a reef. Attacking with my queen could be more decisive, but the position was so complex, I couldn't be sure she wouldn't be exposed to a counterattack that could force me to trade her for Cranmar's more passive lady. A four-man operation looked promising—bishop and knight as assault pieces with queen and rook in support—but this too could result in useless, and neutralizing, exchanges. And again. My rooks were blocked. There would be no immediate support for such an assault from them.

I thought of just charging in with the bishop and knight without rook support, possibly finishing with a piece sacrifice, but without rook support, both pieces would be shattered against the pawn phalanx.

This left the more conservative measures, which, in this position, would consign me to a draw. I wanted no part of a draw. I had to win this thing!

A shudder ran through my bowels. The chess pieces seemed to rise from the board and float in circles. I felt dizzy. I looked up hoping to focus on one or two stable human figures, but they, too, were whirling about. The room was a kaleidoscope. I closed my eyes and stared at the blackness. When I reopened them, it was with the fear that I would never be able to concentrate on the position again. I was relieved to find everything finally anchored, but now my lungs and heart were pounding furiously, almost out of control. It required a powerful effort to slow them down and return my attention to the battlefield.

I came to sense the presence of a crowd forming around us. I could feel the warmth of the bodies weighing upon me. (No doubt Rostenkowski was among them. Somewhere, over my shoulder, he was gritting his teeth, exerting his will, agonizing with Cranmar over every move.) The word had spread that a crisis had been reached in the room's top game. The buzzards were circling. None of this bothered me, though. My job was to bear down on the position, not to worry about spectators. Later, they could all take the game to the comforts of the skittles room, move the pieces back and forth, try this and that variation until they found the best one, and then declare the poor sap who had to figure it out over the board in an important game with a clock ticking beside him, blind and stupid. Then it would be their game. Now it was mine, and I had to "figure it out" before the clock ran out. I was not going to rush. I refused to believe I lacked the imagination to solve a position in which I so clearly had the advantage. I mentally moved pieces in every direction, testing captures and sacrifices, looking for weak squares or penetrable files. Asking, over and over: If this, what? If that, what?

And then I spotted something! My breath caught hard in my throat as if it had lost its way. Inhale? Exhale? I wasn't sure, and I had to look up and take a deep gulp of air to push my lungs back into their proper rhythm before I could go back and concentrate. It required only a second, but when my eyes returned to the board, the little quirk I had spotted in Cranmar's position was gone, its image lost, perhaps lodged in a deep fissure of my mind. I looked up; I looked down. I drilled into my skull and dug up other images I held beforehand, looking for clues that would trigger rediscovery. Pawns, knights, rooks. Diagonals. Holes. What *was* it I had seen? Had I seen anything? Had I just made it up? Was it all a mirage? I scoured the remotest regions of my brain, expending my last reserves of energy. Where, oh where had it gone?

The clock kept ticking.

And suddenly, in a flash, there it was. How could I have missed it? It was so obvious. On the enemy knight's immediate right was a pawn, backward and defended by the second rank rook. I noticed this pawn earlier but never considered attacking it because of the rook. Now I realized that the pawn's invulnerability to simple capture had blinded me to a far deeper truth about the piece. That pawn was anchoring the phalanx in front of the knight! I didn't have to capture it at all. I merely had to make it move one square forward. Do that, and the entire shield would collapse, exposing the knight to assault and inevitable capture.

For a moment, my entire organism seemed suspended in time while I searched for a plan to pry the pawn loose. This was something new. Something exciting, full of possibility. I scarcely dared to breathe. I looked. And looked. And looked.

And suddenly, I found it. Or at least I thought I did. A slide of one square by my bishop would allow it to bear down on the target pawn. But what then? I had seen that move earlier, when I thought of attacking the pawn. The same truth I found then was in place now. The pawn was guarded by the rook. I couldn't capture it.

Okay. I knew that already. I had abandoned that idea. But the question remained. If I couldn't capture it, why would Cranmar move it?

Answer. He wouldn't.

There was only one response, then. I would have to give up—in chess parlance, sacrifice—my more valuable bishop for that pawn. If I couldn't force it to move, I would simply have to take it off the board, and out of the phalanx, even if it cost me my bishop to do so. The bishop would be a minor loss compared to the resulting weakness in Cranmar's position. With the target pawn gone, the now undefended central pawn in the phalanx after an exchange would fall to my knight. That would give me two pawns for my bishop, a negligible material disadvantage, given that Cranmar's entire wing would be exposed to my troops. It would be a simple matter to push pawns against it. After that, my centrally placed queen and the one rook I could eventually free up would combine for a devastating attack.

So much for offensive analysis. Assuming Cranmar would see what I had planned after my bishop move (and we *always* presume the best from our opponents if we want to stay alive), what defense might he have? Cranmar could not just move the pawn out of the way. That would play into my hands. The central phalanx pawn would fall to my knight "for nothing," and my attack would proceed forthwith. He could push the central phalanx pawn, attacking this same knight, but that too would weaken the formation. I would just move my knight and force an exchange of knights with strong positional advantage to myself. He could try and bring one of his poorly positioned pieces over to meet my onslaught, but there was no time for that.

I knew it! His position was built on air.

But it was too soon to celebrate. Things had to check out first. I had to be certain my plan was foolproof and irrefutable.

Stage three had begun. Check for errors. Next assure myself that my combination would go as planned and that my anticipated attack was really there. Finally, search for any unusual defensive resources Cranmar might have available, such as a strong countermove or a sacrifice.

Everything checked out. Cranmar was doomed. I could see the subsequent attack almost automatically working itself out. I checked and rechecked innumerable other possibilities. Nothing . . . Nothing worked for him. Cranmar had several options, but they were all unsatisfactory.

Even so, I continued to study the position, looking for the slightest detail I might have missed. The clock ticked on incessantly, like a dripping faucet: "Too . . . much . . . time . . . too . . . much . . . time." It seemed to be getting louder, but I would not be rushed. There was no room for mistakes.

Eventually, I had to move. There were no flaws to my plan, and there is no passing in chess. My right hand, immobile for what had seemed hours, reached tentatively forward, drew back sharply, and slid ahead again like the tongue of a snake in slow motion. I was omnipotent; I held the entire fate of that moment in my fingers. Nothing could happen anywhere until I made my move. Everything, everyone was hanging, waiting for the gesture that would allow them to resume their lives. My power was awesome, radiating over people from the tips of my fingers.

Finally, I relented. With a slow intake of breath, I reached down and lifted my bishop. For a few seconds, I suspended the little figure over the board, twisting it between my fingers as if reluctant to let it go, before carefully settling it down upon its new home from where it would bear down on the target pawn. A push of the clock button and it was done.

Cranmar sat motionless, staring at the board. Not a muscle in his face moved. His eyelids refused to twitch; his thin lips could have been the edge of a ruler. Beside the board lay his right hand, frozen. The other was unseen, I assumed, in his lap. He was a study in granite and remained so, for what seemed eons. I had been in this position many times. Make a brilliant, but subtle, move with threatening consequences and wait an eternity for my opponent to discover its meaning and search painfully for a way out. The pain was not entirely one way, either. In chess there always lurks the unknown. Until Cranmar actually moved, a lump of anxiety would be lodged in my throat.

I prepared myself for a long siege.

But no! There was movement. The forefinger and thumb of Cranmar's right hand rubbed slowly together, a familiar quirk of his in tight spots as he was about to make a play. Their motion quickened perceptibly before his hand rose from the table. For a moment, it hovered over the board, motionless. Finally, he let it drop slowly atop . . . not any of the pieces I thought he might move, but the pawn that was in front of the square my bishop had just vacated! The pawn moved forward, driven by a slow flipping motion of Cranmar's wrist. Cranmar finished by reaching to press his clock button, after which, he settled back in his chair, his lips cracked into a thin smile.

Now it was my turn to be shocked. Why move *that* pawn? It did nothing to interfere with my plan. . . . A stab of fear shot through my belly. What was . . . Could Cranmar have failed to see? Was he blind? Why was he smiling? What kind of a fool would smile in such a situation? Unless he didn't know he was in it!

Suddenly the image of the chessboard and pieces in front of my eyes exploded into a thousand splinters. Alarm bells sounded in a deafening cacophony of ringing, clanging, dissonant clamor. Shouts echoed down the line: "Pawn loose! Pawn loose!" The lump of anxiety that was swelling in my throat turned savage and nearly choked me. Suddenly, horrifically, I knew.

The bishop I moved had been blockading that pawn! That was why I put it there—to keep that pawn from marching to my back rank and promoting himself to a queen. That threat was the one weakness of my position. As long as my bishop was in place, the pawn was frozen in his tracks, but in my desperation to launch a game breaking assault, I had forgotten him. Now he was three moves from my back rank with nothing to hinder his progress.

But, wait. Perhaps I was panicking for nothing. Wasn't my bishop perfectly safe on that square a moment before?

Of course! That's it. All he has to do is return and capture the brazen little bugger of a pawn.

The euphoria that flushed over me was generated by the sublime relief of one who had just escaped a terrible tragedy. My car, skidding on ice toward the guard rail, swings away at the last moment. Those pains in my chest? Nothing but indigestion. The fire down the street is in a garbage can, not my living room. The pawn that advanced so boldly was marching to its death.

I was just about to pick up my bishop and send it on its mission when my fingers froze. It was as if they could see where my eyes couldn't, and their assistance was required to inform my brain of the truth that inexplicably eluded my perception both before and immediately after I moved my bishop, a truth a beginner would have seen.

That enemy rook on the second rank. Nothing stood between it and the advanced pawn, and nothing would impede its progress to that square should my bishop capture the pawn. Before he abandoned his post, the bishop, in Nimzovich's words, was "under the shelter of the enemy Pawn itself." Now that shelter was no longer in place.

My mind scrambled. If I take the pawn with my bishop, can I re-capture the avenging rook?

No.

Can I bring pieces to bear on the pawn's square?

Yes, but Cranmar can match me, defender for attacker, defender for attacker.

The pawn was safe.

But I wasn't lost. The white pawn required three more advances before its promotion, and such progress through the heart of enemy territory was extremely difficult. Let my attack go forward, then, and leave it to Cranmar to find the way for his pawn through the thicket of my defenses.

I captured the original target pawn.

Without hesitation Cranmar pushed his passed pawn again, and in doing so, changed the structure of the board as if it were a kaleido-scope he had just flipped over. Now it was clear there was no denying the lust of the charging pawn. Suddenly, Cranmar's queen took on new life. As badly placed as she was, she was now able to add to the pawn's support. Worse. Even his bishop could throw his weight in. Nothing I could do would stop it. If I proceeded with my attack, I'd break up the phalanx, but the white pawn would turn into a queen—a far greater achievement—and my defeat would follow shortly. If I tried to capture the advancing pawn with a rook or queen, either piece would be lost at too great a sacrifice for me to carry on. From there, some players would crush me with a sharp blow or two. The more methodical Cranmar would grind me into dust, and it would take forever, like be-ing tortured by dripping water on one's forehead.

There is no point in going over the details. I'm not even sure I re-member them. Usually, after I play a tournament game, I go home with my score sheet and play the game over to learn from my and my op-ponent's mistakes, but I never replayed this game, and I never will.

All I know for sure is that I had committed the most heinous crime in all of chess: blundering. I was judged guilty and sentenced to defeat. It remained for me to choose the method of execution: resigna-tion or checkmate.

I recalled the words of a Grandmaster I once knew. "Defeat is something a great player must never consider possible and never accept. Losing is an accident and must be made to look that way. If you show you can be intimidated or disconcerted, they will never leave you alone. Be impervious. And imperious. Leave your vulnerabilities outside the tournament room. Never let them sense there are victims behind the thin frontisements of your eyes. If they do, they will press you harder. Remain unperturbed. Allow the corners of your mouth to lift, your eyebrows to arch quizzically. Never sigh or brush your hand across your lips. If you resign, do so quietly, with confidence, perhaps with a little smile. Be subtly arrogant, as if you derive pleasure from granting your victim a brief moment of life before you return some day to crush him. Accept his outstretched hand as you would that of a man condemned by the imminent charge of your best troops, encamped just behind you over the hill. He will fear you from the depths of his heart."

I coughed and cleared my throat before waving my hand slowly across the board. Staring coldly, I captured the second member of the phalanx with my bishop—almost as if I were now playing a game separate from Cranmar—leaving Cranmar's pawn to march on unscathed. The crowd gasped. I glanced up and saw the stunned look in their eyes give way to disgust. I knew what they were thinking. They wanted me to take the more threatening pawn and struggle on. They wanted Cranmar to earn his victory and Rostenkowski to sweat for his trophy. They wanted me to fight for fourth place.

The hell with what they wanted. The hell with that old Grandmaster.

Two moves later, Cranmar's pawn was on my second rank poised for the finish. I knew what I had to do then. . . . I could have done it two moves earlier . . . but I still clung to the notion that there was something constructive I could do. I remembered Euwe. I looked at the clock, then scanned the board. Counter threat? Sacrifice? Check his king? Take that pawn over there?

The clock ticked on. Time was running out. Why this last futile twitching? I knew my sentence, but I couldn't stop myself. I had to keep looking.

But there was nothing to be found—no last act of defiance. I hadn't the stomach for any more. The time had come. My left hand reached for my clock button and pushed it halfway down. The ticking stopped. My right hand hovered over my king for a brief moment before toppling the helpless piece onto its side.

It was all over.

Wordlessly, I accepted the fishy hand extended over the board and shook it weakly. I rose to my feet, all the while struggling to control the trembling in my knees. People stepped back to allow me to pass. A few of them shook their heads.

The rest is quickly told. Cranmar unctuously smiled up at the onlookers. "How clever I am," his expression boasted. Then someone leaned over the table—Rostenkowski, I think—and reset the pieces to where they were before my fateful bishop move. "How about this?" he said. People nodded, and Cranmar's smile faded. I was standing a few feet away, just outside the ring of the crowd, but I could see what was going on. Rostenkowski had found something I missed. What the hell could it have been? Anger flared in my chest and ripped through my body. I was seized by an urge to scream so loud that the plaster in the ceiling would crack. I turned to push my way out of the crowd before it overwhelmed me. Just as I reached the exit, I heard another voice: "You're right, Frank. He didn't have to do that. White was so weak at that point. What was Black thinking, giving up his blockade like that? It had White tied in knots." A short pause. Now I had to hear the rest. "That's it. Now Black has a nice attack against the king. Pretty." Then a few approving grunts.

So there was an attack against the king! Where? For an instant I had to fight off the urge to shove my way back through the crowd and see what Rostenkowski had demonstrated, but I couldn't face it.

Instead, I walked slowly toward the door. Nobody seemed to notice me. None of them heard my heart pounding in my chest or saw the tears in my eyes. When I reached the doorway, I was grateful to find no one there or in the hall, for by then, water was pouring down my cheeks. Hot needles jabbed into my brain. When I reached the stairs, three words—"blunder," "blind," and "failure"—"resounded within my skull as if trapped inside a bell tower. My feet pounded down the stairs in rhythm to my cursing: "Sonofabitch, sonofabitch,

sonofabitch, damn!"—the "damn" exploding each time I struck a landing. Several times, I barely avoided colliding into men with "Hi! I'm . . ." tags pinned on their lapels. Finally, I reached the second floor—the main lobby—there to search frantically for the stairs that led to the ground. My face was dripping wet. "Blunder! Blind! Failure!" was all I could hear. All the work, the hours of study, the tournament in hand—a winning position—but I couldn't find the key. How could anyone be so stupid!?

When I reached the stairs, I stopped at the edge and peered down as if about to jump from a cliff. When I took my first step, it was a tottering one, but I regained my balance and started again, more slowly, my legs still wobbly. About five steps from the bottom, I stumbled headlong into the arcade where my momentum carried me into a young woman who was crossing my path. When I collected myself, I tried to find the words to apologize. Surprisingly, she stood there waiting. She was smiling. I groped for words, but without success. Instead the images of chessmen danced mockingly before my eyes. Her smile faded from her lips. She hesitated a moment longer, stepped back, turned, and was gone. I wanted to follow, but she was already out of sight. There was nothing left but to exit the hotel, so I walked out into the street and plunged into the afternoon crowds that were moving up and down like a two-way cattle drive. Streams of honking cars and buses filled the road with dizzying confusion. The "El" tracks formed a huge iron bridge running overhead, down the middle of Wabash Avenue. A train, lurching and screeching with a deafening roar, passed above. The bright sunlight jarred my eyes, and the sharpness of the cool air stung my senses. I walked slowly down the sidewalk, my shoulders hunching forward, my hands in my pockets until I lost myself in the cacophony and the crowd of passersby. The city was engulfing me and had almost absorbed my pain when I felt a hand on my shoulder. "Paul! Wait up."

I turned around. It was Jenson, another tournament player. "Tough game," he commented as I reluctantly allowed him to pull alongside me.

I nodded.

"Well, you'll get another shot in the Cook County Tornado. Five weeks, right?"

I nodded again.

"You're due, you know."

"I know."

We walked on silently. Then he asked, "Want to go to the lakefront and play a few games?"

"Not really," I replied. "I've had enough."

"You sure?" Jenson persisted. "What else have you got to do?"

I paused. "Nothing," I admitted.

"Good. Let's play."

I turned to accompany him. At least this time I'd be outside.

AUNT JESSIE

I saw Aunt Jessie maybe three times in my life, and only once when I was old enough to remember. I was twelve. One reason was she lived with Uncle Hugh in Rochester, eighty miles away—a long distance in 1933. The other was that no one in my family liked Jessie very much.

For one thing, people in my family were extremely attractive, and Jessie was not. My father and four uncles looked like movie stars. My mother and Aunts Cora, Lucy, and Claire were blond, blond, blond, and brunette, in that order, and tall, tall, tall, and tall. They could have gone to modeling school if married women did such things sixty years ago.

Jessie was tall, too—taller than her husband—but she was homely, with mousy brown hair, a long pointed nose, a jaw like the prow of a ship, and thin lips. Her shoulders were edges, and her legs long and thin, although she never appeared ungainly. She wore drab clothes—a lot of brown and grey, as many people did during the Depression (but not my mother or my aunts). She had nice skin and a pleasant touch when she ran her fingers through my hair. Her best feature was her bright blue eyes which looked through you and understood you—as if they were more than just eyes. Her voice was kind of coarse, yet there was something about the way she talked that made her pleasant to listen to, like the radio.

The family didn't approve of my father's oldest brother Hugh marrying Jessie. Hugh was shy and kept to himself. Married a plain girl like Jessie real young because he couldn't find anything better, his mother said.

I saw Jessie last at our house, during a July Fourth family get-together. It was a clear summer day, but not real hot. It would be a couple more weeks before the real heat hit Syracuse.

Jessie looked tired when she stepped off the running board of the black Ford taxi that brought her and Hugh from the train station. She was in her early fifties from what my parents said, but she seemed older. "Michael, you look so tall!" she cried when I met her on the front porch. Her eyes lit up. For a moment I felt as if I were almost a man, even though I hadn't grown much the past year, and stood near the end of the line in gym class.

"Hello, Michael." This was Uncle Hugh. I waited for him to say more, but he stepped back, his eyes on Jessie, who bent over and planted a quick kiss on my forehead. I blushed.

"Don't be silly, Michael," admonished my aunt, noting my red face. She brushed her hand through my hair and led Hugh up the stairs, under the flag my father hung over the porch on the Fourth of July, and into the house.

Everyone gathered in the back yard. Jessie and Hugh sat in the shade near the edge of the yard. She was talking to him quietly, smiling. He listened intently and nodded. If no one else understood why Hugh married Jessie, *he* sure did. Two of my young cousins walked over to them, kind of shy, and said hello. Jessie looked down and smiled. She and Hugh were the only ones without kids. ("Poor Hugh," Cora once said, regarding this fact. Lucy shook her head.) Yet these kids seemed to like them. She grabbed each by the shoulders and whispered something in their ears. Both giggled. I hurried over to be in on the joke.

"I'll tell you," she promised, smoothing her long brown dress over her knees. "But you've got to keep it a secret between us kids." She wet her lips, which were real dry, but they stayed dry. Uncle Hugh jumped up for a pitcher of water. Jessie leaned over and told me a joke about a frog and a crocus, which I can no longer remember. I don't think it was real funny, but I couldn't help but smile. I think it was the way she told it.

Jessie had just finished her second glass of water when Mom called us to dinner. We sat around a long picnic table stacked with food. Jessie and Hugh sat at one end. Mother started Aunt Cora's potato salad; several other salads, including chicken and cole slaw, followed. There was sliced ham and bread, and one casserole from Aunt Lucy—she made a different one every year. This year it was turkey noodle.

"Roosevelt!" snorted Uncle Brad as soon as everyone had started eating. He was always complaining about the new President. "What's wrong with this country? Sure, we're in some trouble." Emphasis on "some." "But the man's a damned socialist!"

"Easy for you to say, Brad," my father replied. "Your bank's still in business. Things aren't so good for a lot of people."

"True," Lucy, Brad's wife, stuck in, "but have you ever wondered *why* Brad's bank is doing so well?"

"Because Brad is vice president?" This from Uncle Dave as he scooped some potato salad.

"I have been frugal with the bank's funds," Brad acknowledged. "You don't see me making loans to deadbeats. The whole country should be run that way."

"I really don't care for his wife." Aunt Cora, referring to Eleanor. Whenever the men talked about Roosevelt, the women chimed in about Eleanor. "She says too much. Too pushy. Not like Mrs. Hoover. You never saw her."

The others nodded.

"Hugh." Uncle Dave's address to his older brother turned the circle's collective head toward Jessie's husband. "How are you making out? Store still going?" Hugh and Jessie ran a music store. They did most of the work themselves. Ordering music and instruments, waiting on customers, Jessie giving singing lessons. Uncle Dave's question cut to the bone. But then Dave was a surgeon. Doing very well, too. People couldn't put off operations, even during a depression.

"Still going," replied Hugh.

"How have you managed?"

"Luck."

"How can people afford music in such hard times?" Claire wanted to know.

Hugh wasn't used to so many questions. His face turned red. I thought Jessie would speak up, but she just sat quietly next to him. She laid her hand softly on his arm. It seemed to energize him. He looked up at his family. I never realized until then how estranged he was from them. "How can they afford not to have music?" he said.

"But it's so expensive." I don't remember who said that or asked some of the other questions.

"We don't charge much," Hugh replied to one of them.

"Then how do you live?" I forget who asked that.

"We get by."

"You'll never get ahead that way." That was Brad.

"We'll never get ahead *any* way."

Jessie never said a word. She just sat there, beaming and holding onto Hugh's arm. At that moment, she looked prettier than all my aunts.

"But that's what's wrong with this country." That was Uncle Clyde. Clyde was doing well, too. He was an undertaker. People never stop dying. They even step it up some in bad times. Some folks joked that he and Uncle Dave were in business together, but that was unfair to Uncle Dave who was a good surgeon. "People are too willing to settle for little. No ambition. That's what got us into this mess. Nobody wants to work hard."

"I'd think running a music store is hard work," observed Dad.

"Hugh?" This was Lucy.

"I—I guess it is," Hugh said.

"The music store was your idea, wasn't it Jessie?" asked Cora.

Jessie eyes narrowed. "In a way," she replied. "I was a musician. Not a very good one, though. Which I discovered early enough not to subject people to my singing. A music store seemed the best thing for us."

"Jessie's a fine singer," protested her husband. "And she has terrific business sense."

"You mean, she found some fool bank to give you a loan," snickered Brad.

Jessie smiled at him. "Only it didn't turn out to be so foolish."

Brad looked like he just realized he had bitten into a tougher hide than he thought. Besides, everyone was tired of a subject nobody was interested in to begin with. Who knows how it got started? To tease Hugh, probably. Inside family stuff. Brad dug into second helpings of salad and ham. The other men followed suit.

Except Hugh. Jessie looked tired. I thought maybe the humidity was bothering her. It was often humid in Syracuse. She excused herself and repaired to her seats in the shade. Hugh followed her like a devoted retriever, and soon the gathering rose from the table. My mom and my three other aunts wandered to the far end of the yard, while some of the kids got to work with the final hand-churning of the sherbet. Later we'd eat it with Lucy's cherry pie. The men stood in a circle near the table. I remained nearby, not in the circle, but close enough to listen.

"So you're not about to put your money back into the market any time soon, Brad?"

"Not as long as Roosevelt is in office."

And off they went. I wasn't interested in the adult talk and didn't listen to much more. I do remember hearing Brad snort, "One term," and saw Dave nod.

Brad turned to Dad who stared at the ground, then nodded. He looked like a kid who was just bawled out. It was a long time before I found out that Dad had to watch himself around Brad because Brad was partially supporting us since Dad's job was cut back.

Eventually, Dad managed his escape and walked over to Jessie and Hugh. "Everything all right?" He smiled.

Jessie smiled back. "Of course."

"Why are you sitting so far away?"

"It's cooler here."

Dad nodded, though he knew that was not entirely the reason.

"You must come to Rochester," Jessie continued. She sounded serious. "You and Grace and Michael."

"We will," Dad promised.

"Gerald!" It was Clyde's booming voice. "Come here a minute. We need your opinion."

Dad looked down and smiled again, this time sadly. Jessie nodded.

The men were again at full steam about Roosevelt. Now I was getting curious, so I bravely marched into the conversation. "Uncle Brad," I inserted into a lull, "what's so bad about Roosevelt? Isn't he the President?"

Never before or since had I brought a group of adults to such a stupefied halt. Brad's jaw dropped as he looked down at me. Dad looked worried. He was about to put a hand on Brad's shoulder, when

Brad's stern, square-jawed expression broke into roaring laughter. "Out of the mouths of babes, eh boys?" he gasped, trying to catch his breath. "What kids don't say these days!" He turned back to me. "Why son, sure, he's the President. He's also an idiot!" He put on his best "loan disapproved" look and turned to my father. "What are you teaching this boy, Gerry?" Back to me: "How old are you, boy?"

I told him.

He vented an exaggerated sigh of relief. "Well, we got nine years to straighten you out." That was how long it would be before I could vote. Brad ran his hand roughly through my hair. It felt different than when Aunt Jessie did it. Just then, Aunt Claire joined us. She looked concerned.

"Nothing to worry about, Claire," Brad said gruffly. "Boy's young yet. And you know how soft Gerald and Grace are with him."

Claire took her turn running her hand through my hair. She didn't feel like Aunt Jessie, either. "Michael, don't you think you're a little young to be worrying about the President?"

Cora stepped in. "Don't blame the boy," she admonished. "It's all that talk about politics around the kids. My word, Brad. I'd think you'd know better."

Brad looked irritated, but Cora prevailed. Everyone broke up into smaller groups, where no man was allowed to get too far from a female. That stopped the talk about politics.

I drifted away from the men and back toward Aunt Jessie and Uncle Hugh, my feelings hurt by the way I was brushed off.

Jessie must have read my mind. "I heard all that nonsense they were telling you," Jessie said, as soon as I was close enough to hear her speak softly. "Don't you believe a word of it."

I looked at her quizzically.

"You're never too young to ask questions or to be interested in what is going on around you," she explained. "And nobody is too old or too busy to answer you. When they won't, something's wrong with *them,* not you." She smoothed her dress over her thin legs and smiled.

"Is it true what they say about the President?"

She shook her head. "President Roosevelt is a great man."

"Why?"

"Because he feels for people like you and me, and your Uncle Hugh. But don't just take my word for it, Michael. Decide for yourself. Just because you're young, doesn't mean you can't learn things for yourself." She put her lean hands with their long fingers on my shoulders and squeezed. It should have hurt, but it didn't, and it wasn't because she wasn't squeezing hard. "And don't you be afraid of people like your uncles. You're a good boy, Michael. Don't sell yourself short. And don't let anyone else, either." She sounded sad, as if she feared I'd never take her advice. "Set your principles and stand up for them. Just like your Uncle Hugh did." With that, her hand shot to her mouth, as if to put the words back where they came from. She turned to look at her husband, unsure of herself for the only time that day.

Uncle Hugh put his arm around his wife and pulled her close to him. "She meant, how I went off to marry her when my brothers and parents said I shouldn't," he explained.

"Should you have?" I asked with the naive boldness of a child.

"Absolutely." It was the most assertive word I ever heard him utter.

"Michael!" It was Mom. "Why aren't you playing with your cousins?" They must have finished the sherbet.

"I'm talking to Aunt Jessie and Uncle Hugh."

"But James wants to know why you won't play with him." Mom sounded concerned.

I looked pleadingly at Jessie.

"Go ahead, Michael," Jessie said. "We'll talk later."

I went to join James.

I never talked to Aunt Jessie again.

But she did to me. It was late afternoon. We had just finished gathering around our new radio. Everyone was milling about on the front porch, saying their goodbyes, when beautiful, twelve year old Beatrice Poindexter walked by the house with a boy whose name I forget. My heart sank when I saw her with him, because I had a crush on Beatrice. They were just passing my walk when the boy shouted at me: "Hey, Shorty Roberts." "Shorty" was a nickname for me that was catching on around school. Then something even more disastrous: "Hey, *Shorty!*" It was Beatrice, her delightful blond hair waving in the breeze.

I could feel my face turn red as I watched Beatrice and her friend skip off laughing and yelling, "Shorty! Shorty!"

I turned around, hoping no one saw or heard. No such luck. No one said anything, but everyone looked at me with pity.

At that moment, Aunt Jessie stepped forward, with Hugh clinging to her arm. "I think our cab is coming down the street," she announced.

A cab was approaching.

She stood beside me and tousled my hair affectionately. Everyone else was still shaking their heads. "Good bye, all." She waved cheerily. "We had a wonderful time." She and Hugh proceeded down the stairs. When they reached the bottom, Jessie turned around and looked at me. It was the last time I would look into her bright blue eyes. "And by the way," she said to me loudly enough for everyone to hear. "My husband—your Uncle Hugh—is short. And I love him dearly. As somebody much more worthy than that little scamp will love you." She turned her gaze to her in-laws on the porch. "And is Hugh ever *romantic!*" she added. She ran her tongue over her lips.

When she did that, the jaws of each of the adults dropped as if a lever connected to all of them was pulled. Except for Hugh who put his arm around Jessie and pulled her close. Both laughed gaily as they headed down the walk—Hugh with a swagger I had never seen before.

My heart sang as I watched their cab sputter down the flag-lined street and disappear. I looked forward to the day I could visit Rochester and see Aunt Jessie and Uncle Hugh alone.

That day never came. Jessie was ill that afternoon. Had been for some time, though I never knew until she died six months later. Uncle Hugh followed the next year. Heart attack, my father said. Broken heart is what I always thought.

Jessie wrote me twice before she died. They were short notes, encouraging me to work hard, be myself, and not worry about things. But like the dumb kid she refused to believe I was, I never got around to writing back. After she died, I grew up and forgot her. I had become my family's good boy.

For a while.

The service is over, and the funeral chapel is empty except for me and Esther. I am sitting in a front pew, staring at her beautiful face as she lies at rest. There is so much I want to tell her. I always had something to tell her. We had few secrets, Esther and I, so there are no regrets on that score. But that is scant comfort now. Tomorrow, our three children will leave for their homes around the country, and I will be alone for the first time in forty-eight years. Nobody can or ever will fill the void Esther has left.

I was twenty-three when I married Esther. World War II had just ended, and I had been home for two months when I met her at a symphony concert. She was a plain woman, quiet, but extremely intelligent. We talked during intermission, and I fell for her as if someone had pulled a rug out from under me. I wasn't sure why. I'd hear men talk about what they found physically attractive in women, and I saw none of those things in Esther, who was very homely. Yet I loved her like mad. My mother said I was crazy when I told her I was marrying Esther. My uncles thought the idea preposterous and said so, two of them within Esther's earshot. I was another Hugh, they said. Esther never gave them a thought, and neither did I. I was no longer my family's good boy.

There are voices around me. I barely hear them. It had been sixty years since memories of Aunt Jessie had flooded over me. Now they have returned, singing:

> *Esther was Aunt Jessie's gift to you.*
> *Now she is gone,*
> *Her legacy is that which Jessie left to Hugh:*
> *A broken heart,*
> *Whose ache in his soul he did not one day rue.*
> *Now you shall know that ache as well.*
> *Treasure it, as did Hugh.*